Aberdeenshire Libraries
www.aberdeenshire.gov.uk/libraries
Renewals Hotline 01224 661511
Downloads available from
www.aberdeenshirelibraries.lib.overdrive.com

0 8 JAN 20

D0334407

2 1 MAY 2016

2 9 JUN 2016

HEADQUARTERS

0 1 SEP 2016
2 7 MAR 2018

ABERDEENSHIRE LIBRARIES

1942205

when

mr

dog

bites

brian conaghan

BLOOMSBURY

LONDON · NEW DELHI · NEW YORK · SYDNEY

FT
Pbk

Bloomsbury Publishing, London, New Delhi, New York and Sydney

First published in Great Britain in January 2014 by Bloomsbury Publishing Plc
50 Bedford Square, London WC1B 3DP

Text copyright © Brian Conaghan 2014

The moral right of the author has been asserted

All rights reserved
No part of this publication may be reproduced or
transmitted by any means, electronic, mechanical, photocopying
or otherwise, without the prior permission of the publisher

A CIP catalogue record for this book is available from the British Library

Young adult hardback ISBN 978 1 4088 4253 9

1 3 5 7 9 10 8 6 4 2

Young adult export paperback ISBN 978 1 4088 5158 6

1 3 5 7 9 10 8 6 4 2

Adult hardback ISBN 978 1 4088 3833 4

1 3 5 7 9 10 8 6 4 2

Adult export paperback ISBN 978 1 4088 3834 1

1 3 5 7 9 10 8 6 4 2

Typeset by Hewer Text UK Ltd, Edinburgh
Printed and bound in Great Britain by CPI Group (UK) Ltd, Croydon CR0 4YY

www.bloomsbury.com

For Norrie

1
Lists

When I found out, the first thing I did was type *100 things to do before you die* into Google.

The internet is, like, wow! How do those Google people make their thingy whizz about the world in mega-swoosh style before sending ME, Dylan Mint, all this big-eye info? No one could answer that question – I know this for a fact because I've Googled it myself, six times, and there is nada on it. Nothing that I understand anyway. Frustrating or what?

But here's the thing, which is capital letters FRUSTRAT-ING: I was super disappointed with the info Google swooshed me because there were too many things on the list that I didn't want to do.

Ever.

Who wants to *write the story of your life?*

Or *ride a camel in the desert?*

Or *go to the shops in your pyjamas?*

I mean, who wants to do *that?*

Not me, that's who.

The three most bonkers things on the list were:

1. *Skydive naked with a video camera strapped to your head.*
2. *Dive into a swimming pool full of beans.*
3. *Have sex with your boyfriend or girlfriend on a train.*

All of them meant taking your clobber off and there was No Way, José I'd take my kit off so everyone could gawk at my willy. Number three was the one I really didn't get: surely a bed would be a comfier place to do the dirty. *And* there would be millions of people on a train – going to work or going on a shopping spree – so it wouldn't be a private moment.

I think whoever made up the list didn't have the foggiest idea about cacking it. The info Google sent me was too Dire Straits so I used my initiative and decided to do my own list. Special just to me. Not 100 things though – that was far too many and there was no way on this earth I'd get through them all. Not in my state – are you mental? No, I'd settle for 3: the magic number *and* my number on the Drumhill Special School football team. For boys. (The team, not the school.)

Oh shizenhowzen!

I lied. Not a biggie but a lie is a lie is a lie.

*

When I found out, the *real* first thing I did was cling to Mum and wipe her tears from my face. She left my cheek all salty and yuckety. I've never understood why mums do that. Amir told me that his mum does that too when people shout 'Paki' or 'nig-nog' at them in the street. But Paki and nig-nog are opposites so there's No Way, José Amir and his mum can be both. I told him that, so I did. I also told him people who scream evil words like that have some brain-cell malnutrition and will probably end up living off benefits or working in the garden section of B&Q or collecting trolleys at Lidl.

Amir is my best bud. He knows all about me. I know all about him too. He goes to Drumhill for his mental problems, which are too many to mention, but let's just say he does a lot of staring into blank spaces and making bonkers noises. He also has a wee bit of a stut-stut-stutter. He's a nut-nut-nutter though, in a good way. We have a secret pact not to call each other any of those evil names other people call us. Especially the ones we hate. The ones that make our throats have lumps in them the size of a gobstopper. We sort of look after each other because that's what best buds do, isn't it? We're each other's homeboy even though Amir's real home is, like, on the other side of the world. But even if he had to go back there we would still be best buds because we have a telepathic brain thing going on.

We haven't had any man chat about who will be his new best bud when I'm away. Some things we don't chat about. Whose mum cries the most? We do talk about that. It used to be his.

Oh shizenhowzen again!

*

When I found out, one of the first real things I did was feel for my wee stone and rub it through my thumb and fingers. It's more like a green piece of glass really. But it's dead smooth and sooooooooooo green that from a distance people might think it's a precious emerald gem. But people never get to lay their peepers on my green stone because it always stays in my left pocket. To me it *is* a precious emerald gem. Green is sort of like my best bud number two. I know it doesn't chat but it keeps me safe and soothes the old napper when things get hairy canary. But Amir is my best *human* bud.

I thought I might let Amir do some of the things on my list.

2
School

When Back To School Day came on 12th August I knew it would be a mighty problemo for me. A paradox even, which is a bit like a contradiction. When I was having one of my *normal* days during the school holidays, Mum said things like, 'Dylan, go out and play for a while. You're getting under my feet.' This drove me round the Oliver Twist because I was sixteen years old now and everyone knows that sixteen-year-old geezers don't *play* – we hang out or chillax. Also, and this is also a capital letter ALSO, if I really was 'under Mum's feet' that would make me a carpet, floorboards or some sticky linoleum. So Mum's down a point for that one. But the morning of my return to school Mum lost some major pointage for seriously twist-ing my melon, man.

'Just what have you done with yourself over these past seven weeks, Dylan?' she said.

I stared at her like a true teenage rebel rooster, not really knowing how to respond.

'Eh?' she said. 'Eh?' Ah, I got it! It was an actual question.

'Well . . . I . . .'

'That's right. Nothing.'

Not true! I did mountains of brain-gym exercises, and on *Championship Manager* I got Albion Rovers all the way to the Champions League final, which took flippin' donkey's weeks to do. We lost 3–1 to Hertha Berlin. We had a mare in that final.

'You've not done a thing, Dylan.'

'I've –'

'Sat up in that room most of the time. You've hardly been over the door.'

'Not exactly correct, Mum.'

'You'll become obese sitting in front of a computer day in, day out.'

'No I won't.'

'Yes you will.'

'Don't think so.'

'You will, Dylan.'

'WON'T.' I didn't mean to shout, but I don't enjoy the feeling I have in my tummy when I'm made out to be an eejit. What Mum didn't know was that I had a Strictly No

Munching Policy when sitting at my keyboard so the obese thingy was a fat red duck. Then I put my chin down on my chest and whispered to myself, 'I won't become obese.'

'And you know who they'll blame. Eh?'

'Who?'

'Me, that's who, and your father . . . if he was here.'

'Who's *they*?'

'Your teachers for a start. The folk at the clinic and the neighbours.'

'Mum, I'm eight stone. I have to do the crucifix position when I'm walking over drains.'

Mum looked up at the ceiling. 'Jesus! And now blasphemy.'

Blah-blah blasphemy. Mum lobbed in big mad words when she was losing the argument and wanted to teach me the lesson that *old people know the score*. But I knew what that word meant.

'Mum, I'm not going to become obese.'

'That's what Tim Thompson's mum thought.'

'Tim Thompson's not obese.'

'No? You tell that to his trousers.' Tee-hee-hee. Mum cracked a funny. I love when Mum goes all stand-up.

'He's just got a bit of a pudgy belly.'

Tim Thompson, aka Doughnut. Not because he shoves doughnuts in his gobby gob, but because his pouch looks like a massive round sugar-plum doughnut. Doughnut is the most horriblest person at Drumhill: he's one of the baddies who love using the words nig-nog, Paki, mongo and spazzie. This was another paradox (I think) because here I was doing a mad defending job on him when, really, I couldn't stand him. If Doughnut went to school in America he'd be known as the school dork or douche bag. At Drumhill he was just Doughnut the dick.

'Well, all I'm saying, Dylan, is that I don't want you sat up in that room all the time. It's not good for you. It's not healthy.'

'It's not as if I'm hurting anyone.'

'You're fading away.'

'Make up your mind! One minute I'm Blubber Boy and the next I'm Sammy the Stick.' Sometimes mums are real-deal barmy; no wonder someone invented the padded cell.

'I mean your mind is fading away, Dylan. Oh, you know what I mean.'

'Look, Mum, I wish I could stay here all day and do some chatting, but I have to boost or I'm going to be late.'

'So why are you still standing here talking? You don't want to be late on your first day back. Good God in Heaven, I don't know!'

I made a grab for my brand-new bag.

Grey rucker.

No name.

No logo.

Jaggy diggy-in straps.

Stiff zip.

Rough as an old tattie sack.

A killer on the back.

Everyone would know it was out of Matalan, Primark or some other nasty cheapo shop. Mum didn't tell me where it came from. I didn't ask.

See, I was one of those cats who began a new school year decked head to toe in new gear. I never understood why though, because I liked the last set of clothes I had. I think it was just to show that we weren't really *really* poor and didn't have leather carpets or empty kitchen cupboards. But it was bottom-of-the-barrel cheapo clobber whichever way you looked at it. My new clothes told me that we were a teeny-weeny bit poor. Not as poor as the mega-poor kids though, the ones with a pong off them, the borderline mingers – they've got zilch. Their pot to piss in has a hole in it. They never have new bags or shirts or shoes or anything. It's a sin. I feel heart sorry for them.

Mum helped me put the bag on my back.

'Have you written to Dad lately?' I said.

Mum said nada.

'Mum?'

'I heard you, Dylan.'

'Dad needs his letters, you know.'

'I'll do it tonight.'

'Maybe we can do one together?'

'We'll see,' Mum said, which I knew meant *No bleedin' chance*. 'Right, young man. You're going to be late.'

'I'm not.'

'Try to be good, OK, Dylan?'

'*Sì, signora.*' That's Italian. Mum likes hearing me speak new languages.

'Right, come here.' She reached out her arms, a move I'd seen tons of times before. I knew what was coming. I was used to it. 'Look at you – you're so handsome.' Mum's 'so' sounded more like 'Sooooooooooooooooooooooooooo'.

SMACK-A-ROONY!

Flush on the face. Hitting lips, nose and chin at the same time. Dis-gust-ing or what?

Salt.

Salt.

Salt.

I can't wait until I'm too old for Mum's slobbers. But thinking things like that made me sad in the dumps, and I'm not allowed to be sad in the dumps. So I didn't think about it. Dad had told me that I was the man of the house now, and in my mind men of the house aren't supposed to be sad; they're meant to be like Hercules or Samson (before he got his hair chopped).

'Try to be good, Dylan,' Mum said again.

'I always do.'

'Love you,' Mum shouted after me.

I tucked my ear into my head and went *Mmmmmmmmmm-mmmm* in my mind, pretending not to hear her. Then the door shut and I knew that in two minutes she'd be Bambi blubbering. But I tried not to think of that, which is Hard Rock Cafe so I tried to see if I could get *all* my fingers to touch Green at the same time without touching each other. That took my mind off it and made me think of sugar and spice and all things nice.

I couldn't fit all my fingers on Green though.

Bloody pinkie fingers!

Why do we need them?

3
Letter

Dec

Hi Champ

Youll probibly wake up and wondur were Ive gone
two. Thats the thing about being in the army, you
have to be ready to go at the drop of a hat and
as my troop are part of a secret mishon this
time we couldnt tell a sinnir when and were we
were going. I hope you undurstand this kiddo. I cant
say two much about our mishon or the opirations
were going to do as it is far two dangerus. Not
for me but for YOU!!! But the crappy thing is
that they wont tell us wen were two get home.
Im hoping in the nixt year. Supose it depends on
how many arabs and suicide bommers we get. So
your the man of the house now wich means youv

got to keep it safe and look after your mum, dont let her burst your arse two much. Keep working hard at that school of yours and dont let anyone take the piss. Remember what I told you, always look out for number one. Mum said shed send letturs on to me if you want to write. So if you do give the letturs to Mum coz she's the only one who knows the address here at base camp, this is for securety reesons.

See you soon.

Love Dad

4

Babe

Would you Adam and Eve it?

That's cockney rhyming slang, which is strange coming from me, as I'm not cockney. It didn't actually leave my mouth in words; I just thought it. But I thought it in cockney because we don't really have Glaswegian rhyming slang for the word *believe*. I don't think many people at my school know anything about cockney rhyming slang. If they did, they'd be using it constantly, which they don't, and all the thick kids would be saying the word *cockney* all the time and laughing their tits off because it has the word *cock* in it. It's my slang and no one else's.

Would you Adam and Eve it? On the way to school I eyeballed Doughnut with some of his cronies. It was the first time I'd seen him since the end of last year. I didn't miss him.

His belly jelly wobbled; he had extra blubber on him. Maybe Mum was right. He'd probably been inhaling ice cream and lard over the summer. She's some super-sleuth cookie, my mum. He didn't clock me. I kept a safe distance, all ninja-like. I tailed him, eyeballing his every move. Eavesdropping his every laugh, his nasty comments about anyone and everyone. About my best bud, Amir. Amir says that Doughnut is just like a hole that's looking for a doughnut. Amir should be on the stage.

Doughnut's comments about Amir started the rumblings. SMALL VOLCANO ALERT!

It starts with Mr Right Eye and quickly moves to Mr Jaw, then the red-hot lava flows and Mr Head shakes at super-rapid speed.

Whoosh!

Whoosh!

Whoosh!

Mr Head is dizzy Miss Lizzy. That's the worst bit.

Mr Sweaty arrives with Mr Pong and Mr Panic.

Mr and Mrs Eyes start to pee themselves.

Mr Throat doesn't miss the boat.

Here he comes: Mr Bloody Twitch.

This is how life's a bitch for Dylan Mint.

Not far behind is Mr Tic. Can't stand that prick.

It's the docs who like to call them tics.

I prefer volcanoes myself, because they're like mega eruptions in my head.

The main reason I've no street cred.

I don't suppress it – the docs with the big brains told me not to. 'Always allow it to escape, Dylan, always allow it to escape,' one bright spark doc said.

I want to shout out.

I want to scream.

I want to bellow, holler and yell.

Soooooo badly it hurts like Hell.

Dylan, *don't* shout out, scream, bellow, holler or yell!

Don't bawl, 'DOUGHNUT, YOU UGLY FAT WANK-BUCKET FUCK-HEAD SOCK-FACE BELLEND.'

Don't shout that!

Whatever you do, don't shout that.

The last thing I wanted was for Doughnut to march right over and rattle the ears off me, maybe even plonk his head on the bridge of my nose. I wanted my nose to be in one piece so I did the opposite of what the super brains have told me. I suppressed the volcano. I kept it in. Instead I brought Mr Growl on as my substitution. Mr Growl is not Mr Dog's little brother though. He's more like a gentle bear. Or a car engine that's on its last wheels. I was terrified for a split second that Mr Dog was going to be released. But he wasn't. A phew moment.

Bloody Nora. It meant I had to walk the long way to school. Away from Doughnut and his chums. I had to find a spot on my own, rub Green like a speed polisher and get it all out.

Mount Etna or even Edinburgh Castle, which is also a volcano – not many people know that fact . . . I guess you need to have some sort of brainpower to know stuff like that. I'd been OK that morning and my anxiety about returning to school was getting better; I was only teensy-weensy anxious. Now I had balmy clammy hands and I kept swallowing saliva. But it was OK. I would be OK.

Mum also said I was the man of the house while Dad was away being a hero and I had to start acting like a proper grown-up. I'd been doing some of that over the summer. Mainly in my room. It made me feel different to this time last year. More confident. Ready to take part in some of those conversations that terrified me last year. Ready to take no shit. It made me feel much better, knowing I was a man. Even though I was a sixteen-year-old man. I had biceps and triceps. I felt better, better, better. Eye of the Tiger better.

Would you Adam and Eve it again? Michelle Malloy was in the distance. A new bag slung over her shoulder. A Converse one. She was soooooooooooo sex on legs. It was unbelievable how sex on legs she was. She oozed sex on legs, even though one leg was longer than the other. She wore one shoe bigger than the other. I think she got them specially made by a special big-shoe-wee-shoe-maker because I'd never seen them in the shops. I couldn't give a Friar Tuck, as this dame was nothing but sex on wonky donkey legs.

I wanted to run up and say, 'Hiya, Michelle. How was your summer, babe?' But I was afraid it might come out as: 'YOU'RE A SLUT NEW-BAG WHORE PEG-LEG, MICHELLE MALLOY.' With this in mind I kept a super-secure distance for both our safety. Apart from mangled legs, Michelle Malloy had ODD, which means Oppositional Defiant Disorder, which really meant she was a mad-hatter cheeky mare of a chick who always kicked off at the teachers or pupils and called them pure mad sweary names. Another good reason for keeping my distance. She *was* ODD all right. But sex on wonky donkey legs ODD.

Wowee zowee plus twelve! She had new Adidas high-tops on. *Wizard of Oz* red ones. How cool was that? Bought for the first day back, no doubt. I dug her black tights and wee black skirt combo too. Michelle Malloy knew her onions when it came to clobber. I bet she'd have given that Gok Wan a run for his loolaa. She looked like one of those girls off E4.

I peered down at my new trainers.

Half shoe, half trainer.

Plastic numbers.

No logo.

No stripes.

No name.

Mum to blame.

No swoosh.

No class.

Pure vile.

Shite style.

Painful to the eye.

Painful to the smile.

I looked like I had a club foot with these concrete clumpers on. I'd best be careful in case someone tried to tee off with me. That was what they said about Michelle Malloy. If you called her Pitching Wedge she'd boot you a cracking sore one with her big shoe.

Michelle Malloy walked dead, dead, dead slow but I cased her until she disappeared into the school building, just under the battered sign that said *Drumhill School*. I took a huge deep breath and went the same way. Check me out saying things like *dig* and *sex on legs* and *E4*. Mr Confident. Amir would kill himself laughing when he heard me saying this stuff. He got a lift to school because his oldies believed that all those people who think Asians are in the wrong country will do something disgusting to him on the special bus the school laid on, which meant I always walked to school on my tod. I walked because there was no danger of me getting on that bus. Dad was embarrassed by the bus. I knew this because he always said I would be a *pure redneck* if I took it. The only time my neck was red was when I got burnt to a cinder when we went to Torremolinos, which is in Spain, on a fun-packed family holiday.

Oh, sweet Mary Jane! If I'd reached out I could've stroked Michelle Malloy's hair I was so close to her. She'd probably have punched me full force in the throat or something if I'd dared try, but this was the first day back. A new year. What happened last year stayed last year. We were all more adult people now so what harm could a good old-fashioned 'Hi, Chello. I'm diggin' the new high-tops' do?

She stopped suddenly.

Schweppes!

I was beside her.

She looked at me.

I looked at her.

My eyes wide like I'd seen a ghost.

Hers slitty like she wanted to eat a ghost's spleen.

Holy squeak bum!

'Hi, Michelle. How –'

'Don't even bother, Mint.'

'OK. BIG SHITE SHOE.'

I bolted and went in search of Amir.

I sensed that this year at school was going to be different.

5

Buds

When I first realised I wasn't able to talk too well, it felt as though I'd just swallowed an eight ball (not the drug), and as if my windpipe would explode if I tried to say anything.

I twiddled Green around in my hands so much that I covered it all over with snot. I didn't snotter up Green on purpose. After all the gobbing and shouting – lots of SHOUTING – I stiffed up my top lip and thought about my best bud Amir. I thought to myself, *What's that looper going to do for a best bud now?* Then I had to stop thinking about that because my windpipe problems were returning.

It was happy days when I spied Amir in the distance. We didn't do any of that *did you have a good holiday?* mince. No, we just went straight into best bud mode.

'Guess who I clocked?'

'Don't care.' Amir says things like this when he really does care.

'Course you do.'

'I don't.'

'You do.'

'Don't.'

'I'll give you a clue.'

'Don't want a clue, Dylan.' Amir says this when he really does want a clue.

'She's the –'

'Not listening . . . Not listening,' he said, while cupping his hands over his ears, like a bomb had just gone off in the school. Or in the war. 'Not listening.' Then he squealed, high-pitched, like a cat being gang-raped by some dingoes, which are crazy Australian dogs that trick you into thinking they're house dogs before eating all the children they see. Amir does this loads, but I just ignore him and then he stops.

'You *are* listening.'

'OK, I am listening, but I'm not interested.'

'Come on, you are interested.'

'No I'm not.' Then he made another one of his sounds. He's got a load of them floating around in his noggin. This sound was like when vets have their whole arm up a cow's bum. No thanks to being a cow!

'Stop being weird, Amir,' I said.

He stopped the sound in a flash. '*You*'re fucking weird.'

'Amir, best buds don't swear at each other.'

'So don't call me weird then.'

'I'm just trying to tell you who I saw coming into school.'

'I'll probably hate them.'

I forgot to say that Amir hated school. Not the building – the people inside it. In normal schools everyone is super excited to see each other after the holidays. All the new clothes, exotic holiday stories and sun tans. Not in our school though. It's a pain in the bahookie meeting your classmates again. Seven weeks of being normal and doing groovy stuff is shot to shit as soon as you lay eyes on the rest of the school. Drumhill is like the scene from the bar in *Star Wars*: mentalists cutting about, talking bonkerinos to each other or themselves. Amir went to Pakistan for six and a half weeks so I was super psyched to see him again. Even if he was acting all weird.

'You won't hate this person,' I said.

'I hate everyone.'

'Including me?'

He looked at me and kind of shrugged. Then his head jerked. 'Well, not everyone, I suppose.'

'You suppose?'

'OK, I don't hate you, Dylan. Happy now?'

I didn't say anything. Instead I tried to tuck my ears inside themselves, counted to seventeen über rapido and twiddled Green in my pocket. I'm not sure if I was happy then. When

I got to number fifteen I saw his face change, like he remembered all of a sudden.

'Best buds, Dylan.' He nudged me.

I wanted to call him all those names that others call him, but I am NOT a racist bampot. The force was strong, however. I clenched my teeth and squeezed my eyes closed. Amir has seen this face a bunch of times before. He nudged me on the shoulder.

'Best buds, Dylan.' I guess it takes time to readjust after a summer in Pakistan.

'You won't hate them.'

'It better not be Doughnut.'

'It's not.'

'I hate that fat banana.'

'It's not Doughnut, Amir.'

'If he says anything to me this year, I promise I'm going to . . .'

'Michelle Malloy.' The very mention of her name stopped Amir in his train tracks. He blinked hard.

'Michelle Malloy?' Amir said.

'All of her,' I said.

'What was she doing?'

'Walking.'

'Walking?' Amir said, all confused voice.

'Walking.' I nodded.

'Properly?'

'In the Michelle Malloy way, but with better footwear.'

'Wow!'

'You know what I mean.'

'Wow! Two times. Wow! Wow!'

'She's changed her style as well,' I told him.

'Really?'

'Big time. She looks like some cool chiquita now.'

'Three wows in a row. Wow! Wow! Wow!' Amir sounded like a scared puppy. No wonder he went to this school. 'What was the kitten wearing?'

'Adidas high-tops and a wee black skirt. A sexy number.' Amir did a *mmmmm* in his head. I could tell.

'Did she say anything to you?'

'It's Michelle Malloy we're talking about here, Amir.' I didn't say anything about our nano-conversation earlier.

'I forgot she thinks you're a knob nuzzler.'

'No she doesn't.'

'That's what sh-sh-she said.'

'That was last year, which doesn't count.'

'So you're not a kn-kn-knob nuzzler any more?'

'What? No, Amir, I am not a knob nuzzler, nor have I ever been a nuzzler of knobs.'

'Well, you better tell her that then.'

'This is a new year for Michelle Malloy and me.'

'No chance,' Amir said.

'What do you mean, no chance?'

'What I said: no ch-ch-chance.'

'Every chance. This is a new me we're talking about this year.'

'She's all cool with her new image and woman smell, and look at you,' Amir said.

'What about me?'

'Those trainers for a start.'

'What about them?'

'They're like something my dad would wear.'

What we were doing was called banter. We did this all the time. Some of the time anyway. Some people call it taking the piss.

'Your dad wears sandals. He wouldn't even know how to do up the laces.'

'At least my dad is –'

'You're a dick.'

'You're a dick.'

'No, you're a dick.'

'You're a dick.'

'You're Dick Turpin.'

'You're Dick Whittington.'

I was glad the bell rang because I couldn't think of any more famous Dicks. Our best bud banter made both of us feel better about being back in school.

6
Lies

77 Blair Road

ML5 1QE

12th August

Dear Dad

Sorry I haven't written since May – it was the school holidays and I was really busy hanging and stuff. Then I had to get new clothes for going back to school, which took forever. I guess as I've grown up I've become fussier about what I wear to school. The new gear isn't worth talking about though so I won't mention it. Let's just say I'm having a fashion crisis. That guy from the telly, Gok Wan – do you know him? – well, he tells you to wear one thing and before you can say 'skinny hipsters' the whole town is wearing the same clobber. I prefer to have my own style and be different from everyone else. But it's hard to be different when you're a wee bit poor. Well, I *am* different, I suppose, so that's one consolation. I was thinking of accessorising more. That's one of Gok's words.

You could say that my life has been hectic lately and that's why it has taken me ages to write. I know you are probably going to tell me to slow down and be careful and take care of myself and look out for number one, but I am. Promise. Mum nags me about all that stuff too. She misses you loads. She cries sometimes. So do I. Not cry loads, but miss you. When do you think they will allow you to come home? Maybe they will say that you can come for a little visit. That would be good, wouldn't it? Anyway, I have to go cause I've masses of homework to do for tomorrow.

Bye-de-bye
Dylan Mint xxx

I licked the envelope and gave Mum the letter to post.
I told a lie to Dad.
I didn't have masses of homework.

7

Pen

Drumhill School wasn't my favourite place in the world but I did quite like the English class. Learning new words was mega. My top five new words last year in descending (a new word from two years ago) order were:

5. Paradox
4. Discombobulate
3. Degenerative
2. Circumspect
1. Proselytise

It was top-notch when you got to use them in a spoken sentence, but the paradox (ya beauty!) was that most people around here wouldn't have a clue what big cool words meant so I was better off talking the hind arms off a brick wall. Except for Michelle Malloy, maybe, because that dame had a quality brain behind all that cheeky bastard syndrome.

The first 'assessment task' in Mrs Seed's English class was to write about our school holidays. What we got up to and all that jazz. She called them 'assessment tasks' but we knew, or at least Amir and I did, that they weren't anything important. Mrs Seed only pulled out the old 'assessment task' gun when she couldn't be arsed to actually teach; sometimes when she'd had that extra glass of wine the night before. And when she said 'assessment task' she did that thing all teachers enjoy doing: that annoying little inverted commas sign with their two fingers, like they're flicking V signs. As if we needed to be reminded that we were in a school full of spazzies. Another reason Mrs Seed played her teacher game was because she was afraid that we were all going to go Billy Bonkers in her class. Although on the first day back Jake McAuley actually took the 'assessment task' way too seriously. I knew this because he constantly clawed his nose, rolled it, flattened it and munched on it. He did that when he got Mad Max nervous. Jake's breath was rank rotten.

I did two things.

Firstly, I did Mrs Seed's task. I wrote some drivel about travelling around Europe with Mum and Dad and going to all these groovy places and seeing all these cute chicks cutting about in their sizzling summer get-up. I wrote about how

Dad bought me my first glass of beer at a bar in Rome, because young people can legally have glasses of beer in Italy. Then I wrote that Dad and me got half cut, which is when you're not fully blotto but maybe only thirty-six per cent steamboats. Basically a whole page of pork pies.

Mega words I used:

inebriated

renaissance

culturally

risotto.

I ripped that assessment task's arse out and left it without a name.

Secondly, I wrote *Cool Things To Do Before I Cack It* in the back of my jotter using my new pen, which was actually four different coloured pens cleverly stuffed into a non-transparent plastic tube. Red, green, black and blue. It was utterly wild and I loved it. This pen would've had the *Dragons' Den* mob fighting like scabby dogs to get their greedy mitts on it. It could have made them gazillions back in the day. This gem pen had sooooooooooooooo many possibilities. I then underlined my heading using my new ruler. Twice. In different colours: black and red. I wrote the next line in green.

Number one: have real sexual intercourse with a girl. (Preferably Michelle Malloy and definitely not on a train or any other mode of transport. If possible, the intercoursing will be at her house.)

What a knockout tiny wish! And I used the grown-up phrase for *shag* too. I put my hands behind my head and leant back on my chair, like Tony Soprano does when he's feeling A-OK. My mind played pictures of me doing the real deal with Michelle Malloy. Then the sound came a-blasting and it was Michelle Malloy doing sexy talk like what the girls do on the internet. Jeepers creepers, some of the things they say.

Double jeepers creepers! I scanned the class to see if anyone could tell that I was thinking about mucky stuff. Well, they could have – who knows, it could have been one of their things: thought-reading. Maybe someone in my class could have been the next Derren Brown. It might happen. But anyone who I thought could have been the new Derren Brown was 'head down, thumbs up'. That was what Mrs Seed told us to do when it was time for some 'reflection on our school work' or our 'mental milieu'. Like tiny tots we put our heads on the desk with our thumbs sticking up. Wee antennae. Apparently it helps concentration and relaxation. Mrs Seed had some seriously loopy ideas. Sometimes she treated us like a mad shower of window-lickers. This is a phrase I hate. In fact, we all hated it because it was what we were collectively known as by the lads who went to the 'normal schools' in our area. They said *windy-lickers* though, which sounded worse and dead threatening when it came out of their mouths. But I could use it in this case because I wasn't saying it out loud.

Michelle Malloy didn't have her head down, thumbs up. No, siree. That's how ODD works sometimes; she just did the opposite of what everyone else was doing. Most of the teachers kept schtum because they wanted an easy life. She was gazing out of the window, flying high somewhere in a dream all of her own making. Looking all smashing and lovely.

Her legs dangled under the desk. I thought about those legs wrapped around my back, like a knot, as if we were doing the bare-arse boxing.

Then I wondered if she would be able to manage a manoeuvre like that.

Then I thought about the people who go to the 'normal schools' in our area and whether or not they thought about us lot at Drumhill; if we thought about the same things that they thought about, like sex, drugs, rock, rolls, internet porn and Facebook.

Probably.

Then I wondered if Michelle Malloy was gazing out of the window thinking of intercoursing it dirty style with me.

Probably not.

Then I wondered if my willy was the right size to do the deed.

Probably not.

Then I wondered if Michelle Malloy ever thought about me in the same way I thought about her.

Probably not.

I was dead to her.

Number two (in blue): *fight Heaven and earth, tooth and nail, dungeons and dragons for my mate Amir to stop getting called names about the colour of his skin. Stop people slagging him all the time because he smells like a big pot of curry. And help him find a new best bud.*

Number two was cheating a bit because I'd written three things to do instead of one. So I did a head down, thumbs up for a minute before changing it to:

*Number two: make Amir a happy chappy again instead of a miserable c***!*

Never, ever, ever would I call him this word to his face, but he was. I scanned the class again. The bold Amir was staring straight at me.

Serial-killer eyes.

He was doing that thing where he pretended to have a big willy in his mouth and it was pushing his cheek in and out. I put one eyebrow up as if to say, *You are a maddy laddie and need help immediately.* Amir's jokes were weird sometimes.

They made him seem like a real bona-fide windy-licker. But that was part of his condition; he was on this mad circle called the Autism Spectrum, which stopped him understanding people's feelings or personal boundaries. He'd never touched me in my basement place or anything like that, but he would do barmy things like pretend to have a giant willy in his mouth or make out that he was licking the lady place through his fingers.

After I wrote number three, in red, I did another head down, thumbs up, making a cave for myself by wrapping my arms around my head. My cave was so secure that I could hear myself breathing. In and out. Deep breaths in, long breaths out. The docs told me to do this when I got stressed or anxious or so annoyed that I wanted to pummel someone's nose into a strawberry. Or when I had the urge to say something totally mad-hatter to someone. They called it 'inappropriate' at the clinic. My arms were so tight that my head could hardly move, which was goody-two-shoes as it meant that it wouldn't be twitching all over the place. Like Elvis's hips.

I lifted my head and looked at number three for such a long, long, long, long time it made my eyes go all blurry. Maybe it would have been easier to write *Run around town in women's underwear* or *Smash all the windows in my school* rather than what I had written. At least I could give number one a fair go. Number two, the Amir thing, would be trickie dickie but number three – that would be a toughie as I had no control over huge decisions that governments made. I'd try though. Like a mad mofo I'd try. Peace out, bro!

Number three: get Dad back from the war before . . . you-know-what . . . happens.

8

Doctor

The last time I went to the doc was for my big head scan. They had to give me a special pill so I'd be statue still when I went into the scanner tunnel. It was a bit like being on the slowest escalator in the world. After that nothing much happened. I was lying in there thinking scans were dead boring and I didn't even feel a thing. I couldn't hear the camera clicking for the pics. Mum was there when I escalated out. She told me what to expect because she'd had one of her own, but I wasn't allowed to go to her scan because hers was a scan for lady things and I'm not a lady and I didn't really want to see Mum with just her pants on anyway.

Last time the waiting room was empty. This time it was full of women who looked as if they were having the most miserablest day ever. It was as if they were waiting for their name to be called to enter the Bad Fire. I was staring straight ahead trying NOT to tick, twitch, jerk or shout like I'd done last time. My concentration was Grand Chess Master and I didn't really notice Mum chewing at my lug.

'Dylan . . . Dylan . . . *Dylan*,' Mum sort of angry-whispered.

This made some of the death faces look at me, which then made me twitch three times, clear my throat with a massive roar and punch myself twice on my right thigh. Ouch!

'Sorry, love, but I wanted to give you this.' Mum handed me a brown bag. 'I forgot to give it to you earlier.'

'What is it?' I said with my confused-dot-com face. It wasn't Christmas, birthday or Fantastic A Grade At School Day, so why the presents, eh?

'Open it.'

I opened it.

'Aw,' I said loudly, and had to stop. I didn't want people gawping at me and thinking I was straitjacket material.

But I really wanted to lick Mum's face, give her five hug specials, roll around on the floor and scream, 'YOU'RE THE BEST MUM IN THE WORLD. AND FOR BUYING ME THIS PRESENT I'LL LOVE YOU FOREVER AND MAKE US A SPECIAL "PIMP MY SOUP" DISH TONIGHT AS A WAY OF SAYING THANK YOU FOR BUYING ME THE *499 FOOTIE FACTS TO AMAZE YOUR MATES!* BOOK.'

'How did you know I wanted this, Mum?'

'I'm your mother, Dylan. Mums know everything.' Whoever

invented mums should win the Nobel Prize for Fun. 'You've been so brilliant about things recently. Dad, school, your scan and all that stuff. So I thought you deserved a little present.'

'Thanks a gazillion, Mum.'

'And sometimes, Dylan, things get worse before they get better so it's always important to be brilliant and brave.'

'I agree, Mrs Mint.'

'So promise me that you'll always be brilliant and brave about things.' Mum put her hand on my left thigh and squeezed with about ten per cent of her power. 'Promise me, sweetheart.'

'What?'

'That you'll be brilliant and brave about things.'

'Promise.'

Mum had sparkle eyes. I thought she might even get some wet on my jeans if her eyes started to leak. She liked it when I promised things.

499 Footie Facts To Amaze Your Mates! A-MAYONNAISE-ING!

'Can I read my book when we go in?' I asked.

'Only if the doctor isn't talking to you.' Mum squeezed four of my fingers. 'We'll need to be there for each other today, Dylan. OK?'

'OK.'

It was a different doc this time. He sat Mum down on the chair next to him and put me in the corner and didn't look at me. This is what grown-ups do when they feel uncomfortable about something. He muttered to Mum and she whispered back. She flicked a glance across at me and I drilled my eyes into my book. No Way, José would they catch me looking at them.

FACT 318:
ZINEDINE ZIDANE WAS NEVER CAUGHT OFFSIDE IN HIS ENTIRE CAREER.

'I know this isn't what you expected to hear,' the doc said in his soft voice.

Mum's chest heaved in and out. 'Are you sure?'

'I'm afraid we are, Mrs Mint.'

'One hundred per cent?'

'Yes.'

'Would a second opinion help?'

'The scans are pretty conclusive.'

Mum put her hand up and covered her peepers. She gulped for breath as if she'd just swum a marathon. I looked at her because I wanted to be brave and brilliant and be there for her, but she wouldn't look at me. She wiped the water away from her face. I groaned because I wanted her to look at my eyes. I wanted Mum to wipe away the water from my face too.

'When?' Mum said.

That's when I wanted to throw the chair through the

window so some air could enter the room. Then we wouldn't all have been sitting there gulping.

'We'll monitor things closely but I think it's safest to assume no later than the beginning of March.'

'Oh, God! That's sooner than we discussed,' Mum wailed.

All her body shuddered and I didn't know what to do. I didn't know if I should hug special her or put my head on her lap or stroke her hair, like she does to me when I'm in the horrors. I wanted to know what was wrong. I flicked another page.

FACT 209:
ABERDEEN WERE THE FIRST CLUB TO INTRODUCE DUGOUTS.

'I don't know what to say, Mrs Mint. I really don't,' the doc said.

Mum looked at me for the first time. I love my mum's beautiful eyes, but these red puppy ones were like a butter knife in my heart.

'We have people you can speak to, if you think that would help?'

'It wouldn't help.'

'All I'm saying is that you don't need to go through this alone.'

Mum sniffed as if she'd been chopping a gazillion onions. The doc gave her a hankie from the box on his table and she tried to blow all the tears out of her nose. I wanted to be in the waiting room again. I wanted to be with the people gawking at me. I wanted Mum to give all her crying to me so she wouldn't feel so bad. I WANTED TO KNOW WHAT WAS WRONG.

FACT 6:
THE SCOTTISH CUP TIE BETWEEN FALKIRK AND INVERNESS THISTLE IN 1979 WAS POSTPONED NO FEWER THAN 29 TIMES BECAUSE OF BAD WEATHER.

When I peeked up from *499 Footie Facts To Amaze Your Mates!* Mum's head was wagging like a dog's tail and her body was Shake, Rattle and Rolling. Even though I had my hooter and peepers in my book I still had my floppy ears out there. I knew that the doc and Mum weren't looking at me, which meant they didn't want me to know the full meat and potatoes, which meant:

1. This was an adult conversation, meaning . . .
2. I had to watch my Ps and Qs, meaning . . .
3. I had to be seen and not heard.

I still listened because this doc couldn't pull the wool over my ears.
    'I don't think I can cope with telling him . . .'
    TELLING WHO?

'. . . I understand, Mrs Mint . . .'

'. . . Not with the way he is,' Mum whispered to the brainy doc.

THE WAY WHO IS?

'Would your husband be able to help with that?'

'God, no! No, it has to come from me.'

HELLO!

HELLO!

I'M DYLAN MINT, NOT DYLAN MINT THE DEAF MUTE.

'There's absolutely no doubt at all?'

'None.'

'OK . . .'

'I'm sure once you've had some time to think, you'll feel clearer about things. Then you can prepare yourself and Dylan for . . . what's going to happen.'

Mum closed her eyes and did some heavy sniffing. I grunted, snorted, rapido blinked and squeezed my fists. I could feel my back and bum-crack getting Sweaty Betty because I sensed the words coming.

'FUCKER DOC.'

'Dylan!' Mum said.

'Sorry,' I said.

'It's OK, young man. How's your book?' the doc said.

'LIAR WANK . . . Sorry . . . It's good,' I said, and put my hooter back in it.

'I'm so sorry that this is so incontrovertible, Mrs Mint.'

FACT 77:
THE HIGHEST ATTENDANCE FOR A EUROPEAN CLUB COMPETITION MATCH WAS AT CELTIC V LEEDS UNITED IN THE EUROPEAN CUP SEMI-FINAL IN 1970 AT HAMPDEN PARK, GLASGOW. OFFICIAL ATTENDANCE: 136,505.

'I'm just trying to get my head around telling him. I mean, how do you break that news?'

'Well, you don't have to tell him right away, but there will come a point when you can't hide what's happening.'

'I know.'

'And come March life as he knows it will come to an abrupt end. You need to prepare him for the inevitable.'

FACT 499:
DAVID BECKHAM HAS TWO MIDDLE NAMES: ROBERT AND JOSEPH.

Since it was scorching outside I thought about our holiday in Torremolinos, when the sun was so blooming Hell blistering it made the bits between my legs burn like fried eggs. Dad said I was cutting about like John Wayne, which made me laugh out loud. I never knew who this John Wayne fellow was, but I thought it could have been someone who worked with Dad. Maybe this John Wayne character was a Private or a Corporal or a Special Ops dude. If so, I was dead happy to be Dad's version of John Wayne. Dad was a massive joke man.

Something rattled in my head. Why did the doc say that in March '*life as he knows it will come to an abrupt end?*' Then I understood why Mum was at the same thing she was when her and Dad used to shout at each other: breaking point. I was there now. She also said she was 'totally scunnered' but she never told me what 'totally scunnered' actually meant. My brain cells told me that it meant totally effing peed off.

With my quick rapido thinking powers I cracked it. When the doc said, 'prepare him for the inevitable', I didn't need to be the Bourne Identity or Mr T.J. Hooker to figure out what the bloody Hell was going on. I hadn't reached the point of being totally scunnered but I surely would have if I hadn't been ace at figuring things out.

'AAAAAARRRRRGGGGGG' happened.

Then 'WWWWWWHHHHHHAAAAAA' followed.

The doc and Mum did some sitting and staring. They didn't even reach a hand out to show me that everything was A-OK. They didn't smile as if to say, 'Don't worry, Dylan, everything's A-OK. You're in safe hands with us.' I suppose Mum was used to me being the way I was so she let me get on with it.

'FUCKING BASTARD. SPECCY WANK.'

My blurt was directed straight at the doc. But, and it's a capital letter BUT, the doc was a Pakistani, which made the rant ten times worse. Or maybe he was an Indian? Or perhaps a Bangladeshi? He was definitely one of those things. I couldn't really tell which though. All those evil things that Amir has to listen to because his skin is not chalk white came bolting out of my mouth and blootered the doc full force in the face. Tears waterfalled from my eyes and flooded my cheeks, not because I was calling the doc these racist thingies, but because I knew that I was hurting my best bud Amir and best buds never ever hurt each other. Ever. Unless one of them tampers with the other's gf or bf – only then is it OK. Then everything started to go blurry because I couldn't see through the water in my peepers. I was like a Fiat Uno in the rain with its wipers gubbed.

At the same time that I was turning into a racist I said in my head,

> Please don't let Mr Dog get out,
> ## please don't let Mr Dog get out
> over and over again.

And guess what happened?
Mr Dog came out.

It was what Mr Comeford, our PE teacher, called Sod's Law. He put his hands on his hips, looked up to the sky and said, 'Sod's bloody Law' every time we went outside to play football and it started raining or when we were stuck inside the gym doing roly-polies and the sun was splitting the trees . . . and the roly-polies were splitting my head. Wee Tam Coyle, who also had Tourette's, used to bark and growl like a boy (or dog) possessed. He'd growl so much that spit would be dangling off his two front teeth. Amir was terrified that Wee Tam Coyle would pounce on him and chew his face off or something mad like that. Amir was sure that Wee Tam Coyle had been brought up by a pack of wolves sometime in the past. But I told Amir to knock it off because I knew what was going through Wee Tam Coyle's head while he was doing his dog–wolf growl. The school eventually got rid of Wee Tam Coyle cause his level of Tourette's was too bonkers for them; the teachers just didn't have a clue how to deal with him. So they booted him into touch.

I started barking and growling at the doc and Mum. There was no spit dripping from my teeth or anything yuck like that, but the last thing I remember was putting my hands up as if I had these giant paws, like the daft lion in *The Wizard of* Oz. That had never happened before. And when I was doing the barking it got so bad that it began to make my head

thump
hump
bump.

It was as if someone had put a balloon in there and blown it up. I thought it was going to pop. Honestly, I did.

And then darkness.

*

'It's OK, darling. It's OK.'

When I opened my eyes, Mum was standing at the side of the bed.

'You OK, sweetheart?'

Negative. I groaned.

'You had one of your turns. Nothing to worry about. It was just a little one.'

She smiled and I could see her teeth. When I saw Mum's teeth smile I knew that she was telling porkies. It was all in the eyes. There was No Way, José that this was 'just a little one'. I was lying on this weird bed that had a huge toilet roll as an under-sheet. I didn't say anything, but closed my eyes and counted to ten. The rule was that when I got to ten I had to return to one again and so on. I learnt this at school. It seemed to work for me. In total I counted to about 2,047. Until, abracadabra! I was back at home.

*

'Mum?'

'Yes, love.'

'What's happening in March?'

'March?'

'Yes.' Mum's brain spun, I could tell.

'St Patrick's Day. You like that.'

'No, I mean, what big thing is happening?'

'Well, we don't have a holiday to go on or anything like that. Do you have a school trip?'

'Don't think so.'

'It might be the start of springtime that you're thinking of.'

'No.'

'And I know you like spring.'

'Do I?'

'Yes, Dylan, you like spring.'

I had to think about this for a second.

'Suppose I do.'

'So maybe that's why March is on your mind.'

'No, there is definitely a special thing happening in March.' I was quizzing Mum in the way people do when they're playing the I-know-that-you-know-that-I-know-that-you-know game. This, however, was what's called a stalemate.

'Well, I'm stumped,' she said. Her voice changed from lovey dovey to *it's time to put a sock in it*. 'Now, do you want your favourite?'

'Is Dad coming home in March?'

'Jesus, Dylan!' When Mum Uses Our Lord's Name In Vain it's time to put socks *and* trainers in it. 'Look, do you want soup or not?' Her totally scunnered voice. When my eyes did their traffic-light blinking, Mum went to Voice Level One, which was like a whisper. Voice Level One was supposed to calm me down. 'I'll put some tomato sauce in it, just the way you like it.'

'Okey-dokey,' I said. When Mum was in the kitchen stirring my soup, I shouted at her in a Level Three voice, 'Maybe I'll write to Dad to see if he knows what's happening in March. Maybe he'll have some good news for us.'

The Voice Levels at school only go to four, but if I had some voice-recording equipment with me on the couch I'm sure Mum's level would have been about Level Seventeen when she came in from the kitchen.

'Can you stop fucking talking about this, Dylan? Can't you see I'm at the end of my tether here? Jesus Christ! I don't need this shit right now.' Then the phone rang and Mum said, 'Saved by the bloody bell.'

When I went into the kitchen to check on my soup, Mum was in the hall talking on the phone in hush voice. An adult voice. She turned her back on me as though she didn't want me to see her, but I could tell that her peepers were raw red. I stirred the soup two times clockwise and three times anticlockwise, but something had pressed my curious brain button so I turned the soup off and did the glass-to-ear-to-door thing that kiddie spies do.

'...Hmm...Hmm...I don't know how to even approach this...Hmm...See, that's the thing, isn't it?...Hmm...I should've told him about this situation long before now...Hmm...I wish I'd done that...'

The glass slipped from my ear, but I caught it in my hand. It was hard not to headbang the door ten or twenty-six times.

'...I know. I know...He's always been my little baby, my little Dylan...Hmm...Hmm...It's not fair to land this on him now...I'm terrified for him...' Then the tears again and again and again.

I couldn't remember her hanging up the phone. I screamed. The sound hurt my ears. Then everything became black.

One.

Two.

Three.

Four.

Five.

Six.

Seven.

Eight.

'Dylan?'

Nine.

Ten.

One.

Two.

'Dylan?'

Three.

Four.

'Dylan?'

Five.

'Dylan, I'm sorry.'

Six.

'I didn't mean to shout.'

Seven.

'I love you.'

Eight.

'It's been a crazy week.'

Nine.

'I'm sorry, Dylan.'

Ten.

'Mum loves you.'

One.

'Open your eyes.'

Two.

'Open your eyes, love.'

Three.

'Your soup's ready.'

Four.

'Mum's sorry, Dylan.'

Five.

'Mum loves you more than anything else.'

Six.

'More than anyone else.'

Seven.

'Come on, sweetheart.'

Eight.

'Your soup will get cold.'

Nine.

'Open your eyes, Dylan.'

Ten.

'That's better, isn't it?'

'Yes.'

'Sorry for shouting, love. Everything OK?'

'Everything's A-OK.'

'OK, I'll bring in your soup.'

'Thanks.'

I sat up and waited for Mum to bring me my chicken soup and tomato sauce.

9
Plans

When I was a pup, like, super wee, I thought that after you cacked it you simply jumped on a bus and travelled up to Heaven, munched on a huge ice cream with a gigantic cherry on top and chilled out with the other cackees. Everyone would be sitting on big fluffy white clouds singing songs, telling funnies and just enjoying the day. If you wanted to, you could play football, watch films, muck about on video games, have a hairdo or cut your toenails. It would be up to you to choose. Everything would be whiter than snowflakes. A magic place.

But now that I was more grown up every time I thought of the land of the cacked I didn't see white stuff any more; everything now was much darker, the cackees were sweaty, dirty and some had cuts on their faces. Nobody was having fun; instead everyone was digging, shovelling or hacking at something. The sound too was brutal – it was like being in the shittiest disco in the afterworld. That place terrified me. When I thought of it, I had to tuck *both* ears into my head, which was hard, so my technique was to lie on my left side with one ear pressed hard to the mattress and use a pillow to force down the right ear. When I did this, all the disco noise flew away and in came the white clouds again.

In that first week back at school I found it hard to clamp close my gob. I didn't have that oh-I-so-need-to-get-this-off-my-chest-or-I'll-end-up-setting-myself-on-fire desire, but I really wanted to have a man to man with my bff, my Phone-a-Friend.

Amir didn't Adam and Eve me at first. In fact he was downright RudeTube about it.

'Don't ta-ta-talk poo piss, Dylan.'

'I'm no joking, Amir. Honestly I'm no.'

'Yes you are.'

'I'm not.'

'You bl-bl-bloody are and if you keep going on about it I'll be forced to speak to Miss Flynn and tell her you're off your rocker.'

Miss Flynn was the counsellor at Drumhill; you only went to see her if you had been super duper mad loopy, or if you wanted to slit your wrists, or slice open your arms or thighs, or wanted to rape someone, or someone wanted to rape you, or if a dirty old man showed you his willy on the internet.

Even though we all had her mobile number (only to be used in school hours . . . not for fun texts) in case we needed to speak to her in a super hurry, I hardly ever went to see Miss Flynn. It was weird that we didn't go to see her more often, because we thought she was the real deal Sssseeexxx on Lllleeegggsss. And she wore red lipstick.

'Well, I'll just tell her that you made the whole thing up and I haven't a Jimmy Choo what you're blabbing on about and then she'll think you're off *your* rocker and she'll phone your mum and dad and then your dad will play human pinball with you when you get home.'

Amir said nothing. He scrunched up his face. He does this when I've done him like a smelly kipper. Amir has that dead-famous Greek guy's heel, which is threatening him with his dad. I hated doing it but sometimes it had to be whipped out of the bag. I only did it on special occasions, which this was. A very special occasion.

'This isn't easy for me, Amir. I'm telling you because you're my best bud and at times like this a man needs a best bud . . . Are you still my best bud, Amir?'

There was, like, this four-hour-long pause. Amir put his finger in his ear and shuffled it around a bit.

'Of course I am, you stupid bloody idiot.'

'Coolio Daddio,' I said.

'Spunkalicious.' When Amir said this, I knew the band was back together.

'So, as I was saying, this new doc was going on about all this mad stuff.'

'Mine does that all the time. I haven't the foggiest idea what he's saying half the time.'

'Tell me about it, Amir.'

'The problem is, neither do Mum or Dad.'

'Ditto, amigo, ditto.'

'So what did you do?'

'Thankfully I was there to break it all down in my napper.'

'I'll say.'

'It was all mad shit though.'

'Like what?'

'He said, "I think what's best now is for you to prepare yourself and Dylan for what's going to happen."'

'Really? He said that?'

'Yes.'

'So . . . erm . . . what *is* going to happen then?'

'What do you think?'

Amir's toe stubbed the ground.

'Get this. He also said, "You need to keep your spirits up and prepare for life afterwards."'

Amir let it swirl around his head like a school of steaming fishes. 'Holy Moly, Dylan, that does sound bad.'

'You bet your bottom dollar it sounds bad.'

'I'm trying to.' Sometimes talking to Amir was like asking

a foreign person on holiday in Spain if they liked watching Scottish football.

'Do you know what *in . . . contro . . . ver . . . tible* means?'

'I think so.' Not on your nelly did he know what this meant.

'The doc said that too.'

'W-w-wow!'

'I think he was maybe saying we should get a car when the illness gets worse.'

'Makes sense.'

'Like for the days I can't walk.'

'Yeah, a car would be the best bet sure enough.' Amir looked at the ground and booted a few stones. Then he whooped in a really high-pitched voice. 'WHOOP!'

'But it's OK, Amir, cause it's not happening until March.'

'March?'

'The doc said, "It's safest to assume no later than the beginning of March."'

'Great balls of fire. WHOOP!'

'I know.'

'That sounds mad, Dylan.'

'Bottom dollar, Amir, bottom bloody dollar.'

'So what's wrong then?' Amir said AGAIN, all confused dot com.

'Well, I don't know exactamundo because the doc was ultra-confusing.'

'Oh . . . OK.'

'All I do know is that I'm going to cack it. But Mum doesn't want to talk about it and I'm not allowed to ask questions.'

'I don't know what to say.'

'Nothing you can say, Amir. Sometimes best buds don't have to say anything. They have this sick sense between them.'

'Sixth.'

'What?'

'Sixth sense.'

'Same difference.'

'Not really, because –'

'Whatever, Amir . . . Maybe I should be sad.'

'That wouldn't do any good.'

'But I am sad,' I said. Then it was my turn to look at the ground and rattle some stones across the yard. My face twitched a couple of times.

'Me too. I'm sadder than the saddest guy in the saddest town in the world, but it's no good being all Dot-Cotton-faced about it, Dylan. It's going to happen so we have to live with it. WHOOP!'

'Suppose,' I muttered, and scuffed a stone away.

'That's funny,' Amir said, but I don't think he meant hold-on-to-your-belly funny. He scuffed away some stones too and smacked his lips together.

'What's funny?'

'Me saying *we have to live with it.*'

'So?'

'So *live with it*. It's funny.'

Then I got the joke. Amir was always making jokes that took ages to understand, which meant they weren't funny any more. Not that most of them were funny in the first place. I think it's his not-understanding-boundaries thing.

'I see what you've done there. I think that's called irony, Amir.'

'I know, I meant it.'

'See?'

'What?'

'How easy it is to forget about what's going to happen and have a great big laugh?'

'Suppose,' Amir said. He was acting all gloomy-two-shoes, as though he was the one about to big style cop it.

'But remember: you should never ever laugh at dying people, Amir.'

'It's not fair,' Amir said, tut-tut-tutting as he said it.

'What's the matter now?'

'Who-who-who's going to be my new best bud?'

'Don't worry about that, we'll sort something out.' I was a pubic hair away from telling Amir about my *Cool Things To Do Before I Cack It* idea. *Number two: make Amir a happy chappy again instead of a miserable c***!* That one was for me to worry about.

'B-b-but you're my only bud, Dylan.'

'Not true. There's . . .' And then I couldn't think of anyone, so I said a dafty thing, '. . . Miss Flynn.'

Amir swore like a pished sailor in his napper. I could tell he wanted to belt out rubbish things to me, but he didn't cause I was going to be seeing the Grim Reaper soon and he didn't want to be Insensitive Boy.

'No one else likes me,' he said.

I twiddled Green in my pocket through my Sweaty Betty fingers.

'I know.'

'Nobody wants to hang about with a Paki.'

'I know.'

'Especially a spazzie Paki who goes to a spazzie school and can't sp-sp-speak pro-pro-properly.'

'It's shite, isn't it?'

'What am I going to do? WHOOP!'

'Honestly, Amir, don't worry. We'll sort something out.'

'WHOOP!'

'And you're not a spazzie.'

'I-I-I am.'

'You're a wee bit autistic.'

'So. WHOOP!'

'There's a difference.'

'No there's not. I'm a spazzie Paki.'

'You're not a spazzie, Amir.'

'WHOOP! What am I then?'

'I don't know.' I hated these types of questions, especially when I didn't know the stinking answers, like that numbers puzzle on *Countdown*. A real head-wrecker, that.

'Eh? What am I?'

'Erm . . . Maybe you're a bit retarded. But not mad retarded, just a wee bit, and sometimes you have a wee stutter, but only when you're sad inside.'

'You're some best fu-fu-fucking bud, you.'

'You asked.' This was just one example of people being weird but *not* wonderful.

'I know, but it was an historical question,' Amir said.

Then he lost me. We kicked stones around for a while in silence, which was Daddy Cool because the one thing that's different between best buds and stupid acquaintances is that it's fine and dandy to boot stones around in silence with your best bud, but with acquaintances you have to think of rubbish things to say all the time in case they think you're dead boring, or a mongo. My new shoes were all scuffed and scuzzy as well. I didn't care though because I was happy as a pig in piss that two best buds were kicking some stones around in silence. That's what life's all about.

Silence.

Kicking.

Silence.

Kicking.

More silence.

More kicking.

Even more silence.

Then some more kicking.

I wanted to hug Amir, not in a sword-fencing-our-willies huggy way, but just, well, just because.

The silence went on for yonks and yonks, making me a bit uncomfortable. Occasionally I glanced at Amir but his eyes were always on the stones, doing his mad staring thing. When we had booted all the stones away we made noises with our mouths, like puffing out air and tick-tocking with our tongues. Then I had enough of Amir being my mad weirdo pal.

'Do you want to hear about my plan?'

'What plan?'

'I made a plan. A list of stuff I want to do before . . . you know . . . before.'

'Yeah, yeah, yeah . . . before you . . . eh . . . before you . . . eh . . . yeah, what's the plan to do stuff?'

'Do you want to hear it?'

'Defo. What kind of stuff?'

'Mad stuff. Shit stuff. Mad shit stuff.'

'Like what?'

'Well, think of the maddest shit that I could do before . . . you-know-what happens?'

Amir went into Thinking Incredibly Hard Mode. His eyes got mega wide when he was in Thinking Incredibly Hard Mode.

'Got it!'

'What?'

'You could do a sk-sk-skydive from, like, the highest height you could ever imagine.'

'Really?'

'Yes, like, from miles and miles way up there.'

We both looked up to the grey clouds.

'That is high.'

'That would be pure animal.'

'You think?'

'It would be as mad as anything.'

'Really?'

'Mad as, man.'

I looked at him and shook my head because I was the brain of this operation.

'Don't be a twit twat, Amir.'

'What?'

'Well, first of all, how the Hell am I going to get up there?'

'In a plane.'

'I don't have a plane.'

'A helicopter then.'

'Rubbish. How else?'

'I du-du-dunno.'

'Exactly. It's a crap idea.'

'Well, you tell me a better one then.'

'I will, and it's a stonker.'

'So what is it?'

'I am going to get it on with Michelle Malloy.'

'Michelle Malloy?'

'Michelle Malloy.'

'Get off with her?'

'*Get it on* with her.'

'Michelle Malloy?'

'Are you deaf, Amir?'

'So you're telling me that you're going to get off with Michelle Malloy?'

'No, I'm not going to GET OFF with Michelle Malloy, I'm going to GET IT ON with her.'

'What's the difference?' Amir asked.

So I did that dirty thing of placing my right index finger through a tiny hole I'd made between the index finger and thumb of my left hand. I put the index finger in and out eight times. Amir's eyes got really wide again.

'NO WAY.'

'Way.'

Amir looked around to see if anyone was listening to us. 'You mean you're going to sh-sh-shag Michelle Malloy?' Amir whispered the word *shag*. Mum did the same when she didn't want me to hear the word she was saying. The funny thing was, the word sounded louder when she whispered it. Sometimes she even spelt out words because she thought I wouldn't understand them, but what Mum didn't know was that spelling was one of my strong points at school. Mrs Seed made me Spelling Master on the first week back at school. I even spelt the word *discombobulate* correctly.

'You, Dylan Mint, are going to shag Michelle Malloy?'

'Hard as.'

'But-but-but can she actually do it?'

'What do you mean, can she actually do it?'

'Well, with her club foot and all?'

'It doesn't affect her punanny, Amir.'

'Jeezo, Dylan.'

'I know.'

'I mean, Jeezo.'

'Mad shit, isn't it?'

'Does she know? I mean, is she OK about it?'

'No.'

'No?'

'No, but she will be.'

Amir was searching for more stones to boot around. He couldn't find any so he twiddled his ears. 'But Michelle Malloy thinks you're a mad freak.'

'No she doesn't.'

'She does.'

'She just doesn't know me yet, that's all.'

'But how are you going to make her want to shag you?'

'Can you stop whispering the word *shag*?'

'Shhhh, Dylan. Blooming heck.'

'What age are you, Amir?'

'I'm sixteen and two months.'

'Exactly.'

'Exactly what?'

'We are at the age when we should be shagging girls.'

'I dunno about that, Dylan.'

'Well, I do, and I am saying I'm at the age for shagging.'

'Really?'

'I'm like a tomato.'

'A tomato?'

'Ripe.'

'Wow! Dylan! That's pure head-mong stuff. How are you going to do it?'

'There are ways.'

'Seriously?'

'Loads of ways.'

'Is it not really dangerous?'

'Dead easy.'

'So when are you going to rape her then?'

'What?'

'When are you –'

'Are you serious?'

'Erm –'

'What kind of person do you think I am, Amir?'

'I j-j-just thought –'

'Well, if you're going to think, use your noggin first.'

'You said it.'

'Said what?'

'Rape.'

'RIPE, I said. RIPE! Not bloody rape!'

'Oh.'

'What kind of nutter do you think I am?'

'I just –'

'You want me to go down for a five to ten stretch in the jail or something?'

'Of course I don't want you to go to the jail.'

'Well then.'

'OK then.'

'So then.'

'Well then.'

'That's sorted then.'

'Well, then it's sorted then.'

'Just don't act like a pure zube when I'm telling you things.'

'OK, Dylan.'

Then Amir laughed, but he was trying super hard to stop himself from laughing in case I socked him a stonker across the face. Or I gave him a Glasgow Kiss or a Mars bar down his cheek or a swift kick to the balls. But he didn't need to worry because there's no way on earth I'd have laid a finger on Amir, or anyone, not even Doughnut – although when Doughnut called me Dildo instead of Dylan I wanted to crack his head open with a big giant concrete slab. Mum told me to wiggle my fingers and count to ten in my head when that happened. I rubbed Green in my palm and thought of how many grains of sand there are on Largs Beach. That was where we went with the school last summer for our annual day trip; it was pissing down and we had to watch the waves crashing on to the shore from inside the bus. It was crap. Lisa Degnan shat herself as well and the whole bus smelt like a baby's nappy. I started counting the grains and breathing out of my mouth.

'Why are you laughing, Amir?'

'Because of the jail thing.'

'And?'

'There's no need for you to go to jail, because you will never see out your five to ten stretch.' What Amir said blasted me in the face. 'Because, you know . . . you'll be . . . you know . . .'

Then I knew. We knew. And my face and insides felt all sad.

'Oh, Dylan, I'm sorry . . . I didn't . . .'

'It's no probs, Amir. We're just having some banter, that's all.'

'Well, if it's banter you're after, think about this . . .'

'What?'

'You might get Michelle Malloy up the duff and leave behind a wee baby Mint.' Snap! Crackle! And Pop! Amir was right. I'd never thought about baby Mints.

'What if I put a sleeping bag on it?'

Amir looked confused.

'A Johnny-bag.'

'Oh.'

'I'd be OK then, wouldn't I?'

'Erm . . . I . . . erm, suppose so, but you'd have to flush it down the toilet to wash away the evidence.'

'Right.' I tried to act as if I knew what the Hell's fire I was talking about. The problem was I hadn't really seen any Johnny-bags in the flesh, unless you count water balloons and the skanky ones left in the park. And the ones I saw on the internet looked like rolled-up nipples. I'd be terrified to buy one. Maybe Amir could be an incredible bud and buy them for me. Or steal them from his dad. Wow! That would be something. I never considered Johnny-bags.

Then we kicked some tiny stones around because all the big ones had already been booted away. There was this weird silence between us, which made me want to slap my forehead twelve times in a row.

'I'm going to make my move at the Halloween disco,' I said.

'With Michelle?'

'Yeah.'

'But Halloween's ages away. We're still in August.'

'That gives me plenty of time to put my master plan into action.'

'Phew. That's OK then, isn't it?' Amir said. 'Are you going to tell Michelle what's wrong with you as well?'

'No chance.'

'It might be easier to . . . you know . . . have it off with her.'

'How?'

'She might have some super sympathy for you.'

'I don't want her super sympathy.'

'But then you could get one of those . . . what-do-you-call-its?'

'A pity pump?' I said. I knew what Amir was getting at but I couldn't think of the exact phrase that was on the tip of his tongue.

'That's it. A pity pump.' That wasn't it though.

'No need. Once she hears the Dylan Mint patter, her knickers will fall down like Mad Skittle's do.'

Amir laughed loudly. Skittle's real name was Philip Doyle and he was in our class. He had a leg disease thing, which made his bones all squishy like plasticine. 'You'd better not say that to Skittle's face.'

'Spaz-ball!'

'I would never say anything ba-ba-bad to Skittle,' Amir spurted. 'Never to his fa-fa-face.'

Sometimes Amir got a wee bit ruffled when bits and bobs flew out. Miss Flynn told me to 'always stay positive' when they came out unexpectedly. I didn't know what this meant, however. Dad used to say that Miss Flynn was 'getting money for old rope'. Imagine paying someone for old rope when you could just go to B&Q and buy new rope. Freaky deaky.

When we walked home I felt as if I should put my arm around Amir to remind him that things would be A-OK between us and to make him understand that we would be best buds for life. I saw the lads in the film *Stand By Me* do the same thing and that was brilliant. Mum said I was crying during it, but I wasn't. I only had a lump in my throat . . . the size of an eggcup.

'By the way, don't say anything, Amir.'

'About what?'

'About you-know-what.'

'The de-de-dead thing . . . March?'

'Yes, and don't call it *the dead thing*.'

'What should I call it?'

'You could call it *the holiday* or *the trip* or *the thing* or *the journey* or *the elephant*. Call it anything as long as you don't say the word *dead*.'

'Okey-dokey, captain.'

'Mum's the word, OK?'

'Mum's the word,' Amir said.

We half punched, half pushed each other on the arm to put a stamp on it and then continued to walk.

'What are you going as for the Halloween disco?' I asked him.

'Don't know. What about you?'

'Don't know.'

Amir rolled his eyes because he had his thinking hat on. And when this happened it was Strap Me In Time!

'I know what you could dress up as,' he said.

'What?'

'A Johnny-bag!'

That guy was

fun

fun

funny.

10
War Zone

77 Blair Road

ML5 1QE

15th September

Dear Dad

Mum told me all about the ban on letters being sent out from your war zone area. That's Billy Bonkers! She said that the war zone you're in is mad dangerous and that if they find out where the letters are posted from it could be a major life threat to you and your ultra-brave buddy comrades. But she told me you two sometimes speak on the phone, although this is usually during my school time, which is a major super pain in the bumbaleery because it would be good to have a wee chat with you on the old blower now and again. This could be why she cries loads. Because she misses you like a crazy woman when she hears your voice. So do I, even though I don't get to hear your voice that often.

I think it was December last year – just before you got the call from the big bosses – that I last heard your voice. I remember you creaked into my room and said, 'Dylan, wake up. I've brought some chips in. Come on! Wake up and come down for the chips I've bought.' But by the time I got downstairs you had gone on a snooze cruise. It was dead funny seeing you face down on a bag of chips. Sorry for laughing, Dad, but it was a real YouTube moment. I bet it would have got bagillions of views as well. But when the chips are down (that's a joke!) and I want to hear your voice, I just look at the letter you sent me. Thanks for that. Maybe I'll put it in a frame on my wall.

I guess she's told you all about my situation? This also makes her cry loads, I think. Sometimes I spot her curled up on the sofa with her hands around a mug of tea, sobbing and sniffing away. And it's not too *Eastenders*, even though it's really sad at the moment. Maybe I shouldn't be saying all this stuff about Mum but, since you are her One True Love and One And Only, you have a right to know. And since I am your flesh and blood I have a duty to tell you. Anyway the big day is in March so it would be amazing if you could be here. Mum said that there is a brilliant chance that you could be home way before that time anyway. She told me that it all depends on the level of madness in your war zone. Fingers and toes crossed!

Remember when you used to say *a-mayonnaise-ing* instead of *amazing*? I liked that. I'm going to start saying it from now on. I made up a new word of my own but you can use it if you want. The word is *shizenhowzen*, which you say instead of saying *holy shit*!

Amir and me are playing for the school football team next week. You remember Amir, right? He's my best bud. Some people call him a Paki, which makes both of us as angry as a couple of mofos. He's not very good at football, which is a shame. His favourite game is cricket, which is a mega shame because it's mental boring and I don't fully understand the rules. I don't think anyone does it at Drumhill anyway, apart from Amir, so he's stuffed if he wants to play a game. He can't exactly bowl and bat to himself, can he? It would be a howl to see that though. The thing is, the football team was short of players so we had no choice but to ask Amir. If he's rubbish we'll just chuck him in goal. I'll let you know how it goes.

I have a ton of pipeline things to do before March. Like school stuff mainly. I still want to pass all my exams. (Maybe they will let me do them early.) I also want to make sure that Mum's A-OK and full of beans again. But there are some other 'personal' things I need to do. I will tell you more about them nearer the time.

Now, since Mum's gone to her boot-camp class, I'm going to play some computer games. She says I shouldn't be playing them because it can make the old brain get even more wonkier. It doesn't. It just makes me blink more than normal, that's all. Anyway, please don't tell her I was playing computer games. Just imagine if you were here — you could be her boot-camp instructor and she wouldn't have to go out twice a week for three hours a pop. I'm going to whisper this bit, but I can't really see the difference in her weight! Please don't tell her I said that. Please. Please. Please. But if you were here you could just shout instructions at her in the back garden and I'm sure that the weight would fall off her in no time. That would be funny to see. I could bring you a beer for your trouble and Mum a piece of celery in between exercises.

OK, Señor Mint. I am off to master level four of *Halo 2* before Mum gets back from fat camp (I can't believe I said that). Speak to you soon, amigo. (I do Spanish in school now.)

Dylan Mint xxx

11
Chores

When I heard the front door opening I nearly cacked a brick. Mum would go jumbo bananas at me for playing computer games all night. She'd be *Herbie Goes Bananas* at me for not doing these bleeding house chores:

- Homework (but the house wouldn't fall down if I didn't do my homework, so I didn't understand the reason why this was in the House Chores part of Mum's brain)
- Separate my socks from their little balls (cause 'our washing machine doesn't bloody separate socks')
- Pick up the orange pips that were scattered over my bedroom floor after they pop pop popped out of my fingers (brill game to play when I'm feeling anxious and annoyed with myself or the world)

- Dust the window sill and tops of the radiators (my top tip is to do this with a stinky sock then that means the sock will get washed and I've killed two rabbits with the one stone!)
- Change my sheets and pillowcases (Mum said I had to do this once a week now that I was a big teenager. She didn't know that I knew what she meant, but I didn't want to tell her that I wasn't that type of teenager cause I tried to avoid redneck conversations)

These sheets hadn't been changed for two months. I didn't like sleeping on new bed sheets. The front door slammed as if a ten-ton axe had battered it. I heard Mum chugging up the stairs. A heavy footstep on each stair.

Boom!

Boom!

Boom!

My heart was doing laps of my body and I went into tic-tastic mode. I hadn't done any chores; I hadn't even managed to get on to level five. The brick was coming fast.

Then another door crashed shut. Mum's bedroom. Banging's not good for me and my haywire potential.

'BASTARD DOOR! SLAM FUCKING DOOR! BITCH SLAMMED FUCKING DOOR! FAT FUCKING DOOR BITCH! BIG DOOR ARSE BITCH!'

Shut the beep up, Dylan, the man in my head shouted. *Shh-hhhhhh, for the love of God.*

I flung my face deep into my pillow so that the sound was muffled, but it was hard to breathe. I had to make a Great Escape from the voice. It must have been a tough boot camp. I licked Green.

'Go to sleep, Dylan,' she shouted across the landing.

I stayed quiet as the quietest mouse in a wee quiet town. I played statues with myself.

'Did you hear me?' Mum shouted.

I was like a master POW.

'Dylan, I know you can hear me.'

I was the David statue from the Italian Renaissance, which was what we were doing in our history class. But David isn't really real because he's got a big giant muscular body and a wee tiny willy. The class was really boring though. Maybe I'd show my teacher my stiff David moves.

'Dylan, answer me.'

I didn't.

'Dylan, stop playing games. I know you're there.'

I stopped being stiff David and shook my head from side to side and blinked as fast as possible for forty-three seconds. A new improved record: one hundred and sixteen blinks. My head hurt.

'Dylan, I know you were playing computer games.'

Shit, bum, bugger, arse. How did she know?

'But it's OK, son, it's OK. I don't mind.' Her voice sounded all blubbering woman again. It was much softer. My favourite. Like velvet and chocolate in a blender. Tender to make me feel safe and snug.

'You mean it?' I said.

'What?' There was a big giant pause. 'I can't hear you.'

'YOU MEAN IT?'

'Mean what?'

'THAT IT WAS OK TO PLAY COMPUTER GAMES?'

'Yes, it's OK.'

'Ta.'

'What?'

'TA.'

'Did you do your chores?'

'YES ... NO ... YES ... NO ... NO ... NO ... NO ... YES ... FUCK CHORES.'

'Dylan, did you or didn't you do your chores?'

'NO.' I put my ear towards Mum's room and listened for the silence but all I could hear was Mum saying things under her breath, like wee rats having a good old-fashioned chinwag. 'EVERYTHING OK, MUM?'

'Everything's OK, Dylan. Go to sleep now.'

Sleep was miles away.

'How was boot camp?'

'What?'

'HOW WAS BOOT CAMP?'

81

'Boot camp?'

'YES.'

'It was the same as it always is.'

'TOUGH?'

'Yes, Dylan, boot camp was tough. Very tough.'

'IS THAT WHY YOU'RE TIRED AND ANGRY?'

'Yes, Dylan, boot camp makes me tired and bloody angry.' Actually, she said, 'BLOODY ANGRY' with lots of '!!!!!!!' at the end.

'I'M SORRY FOR NO DOING MY CHORES.'

'You can do them tomorrow.'

'Okey-dokey.'

'What?'

'OKEY-DOKEY.'

'Right. Night then.'

'I didn't have time because I was writing a letter to Dad.'

'What?'

'I DIDN'T HAVE TIME BECAUSE I WAS WRITING A LETTER TO DAD.'

'Go to sleep, Dylan.'

'IT TOOK ME AGES TO WRITE IT – THAT'S WHY I DIDN'T DO MY CHORES.'

'Time for sleep now.'

'WILL HE GET TO READ MY LETTER?'

'Dylan, for the love of God, will you just GO TO SLEEP.'

The silence came again and so did the wee rats. It was as if

Mum was waiting for me to say something. But I was waiting for her to say something. Waiting kills me. I hate being in that place where I don't know what I should be doing or how I should be acting or what I should be saying. Confusion world.

I did what I normally do: I tucked my ears inside themselves and twiddled Green between my fingers. Wow! They were so cold, the sensation was sensational. This was an a-mayonnaise-ing moment. My eyes were shut so tight that they made tiny white dots. I was laughing dead hard on the inside though because of Dad's brilliant word. Then *pop*! Out came my ears.

'Are you sleeping, Dylan?' Mum asked.

'COW, BITCH.'

'Dylan.'

'SH ... SH ... SHOUTER SL ... SL ... SLUT.' I held my breath. I wanted it to stop. Tears. Bloody tears. Big boys don't cry, but big boys who go to Drumhill Special School cry all the time.

'It's OK, Dylan. It's OK.'

'OK.'

'I love you.'

'THANKS.'

'I won't let any of this affect you.'

'LOVE YOU TOO, BITCH.'

'Night-night.'

'NIGHT,' I shouted and pretended to wait for a bus.

I waited for ages but no bus arrived. Nothing arrived. I waited until the rats had all gone to sleep.

The stars on my bedroom ceiling were losing their glowing power. I'd have to buy new ones. Amir said his cousin could get ones that never ever lost their power. He said they were made from bits of real stars, but there was no way on this God's earth that I believed him. Sometimes he spoke pure gobbledegook. I always thought about Amir when I was lying in bed at night (not in *that* way). I thought of some of the mad things he'd done that day or some of the eejit things he'd said. And there were usually loads because he went on and on about stuff, like cricket, whether I was interested or not. I thought Amir could be Scotland's biggest Pakistani stand-up comedian if he put his mind to it. He told two jokes at the *Drumhill's Got Talent* afternoon but nobody laughed. Doughnut shouted, 'That's pure shite' after the first one, which made Amir's second one bomb big time. To make things worse for the poor wee fella, Doughnut's comment got a bigger laugh. Amir was raging but I told him that Doughnut was a prick-licker and he'd get his one day.

I didn't say this to Amir's face but

Who invented knock knock?

Two wee chaps

was a shite joke.

The thing was, he had mega ones too, like:

What's the difference between light and hard?

You can sleep with a light on.

That cracked me up. Mr McGrain, the headie, would've kicked him on his bahookie if he'd told that one, however. Maybe I could be Amir's manager–agent. Then we'd be best buds forever *and* earn some quality cashino along the way.

Aren't you forgetting something, Dylan? that little nutty bastard reminded me. I slapped myself on the head.

It must have been tough for Mum, watching her only son, her only child, deteriorate before her very eyes. She was ultra-brave. George Cross brave. Usually she'd come into my room to give me some soggy pecks, a mega hug and tell me how much she loved me. And the nights when she'd been on one of her booze cruises she'd slobber all over my face like a big St Bernard dog who'd just discovered me in some manky crevasse deep in Swiss mountain territory. This was just Mum's way of showing me that she loved me like a crazy woman and had nothing to do with the fact that the whopping amounts of booze guzzled that evening had shattered and scattered her emotional inhibitions. (We were doing the Alcohol module in Social and Health Education.) Booze cruise or no booze cruise, she was *Bravo Two Zero* saying she'd protect me from all this palaver and won't let it affect me. It made me feel Mr Guilty as I was the one who should be doing the protecting. Mums are the best things in the world. I often wondered what it would be like being a Mum. I don't have boobs so it isn't ever going to happen. Although I think it does in America.

When I looked at my dimmed stars, I began to think more and more about Michelle Malloy and how I could get her to do the jiggy. Having a top blether would be a start. Women like chatting about stuff and all that. She was soooooooooo beautiful. By far the coolest, grooviest, hippest, sexiest chick at Drumhill. I was sure that if Michelle Malloy went to a proper school she'd be the coolest, grooviest, hippest, sexiest chick there too . . .

The next morning I had to cut my own banana slices and plonk them in the porridge before putting it in the microwave. Mum was still in her kip. I was a raging bull because Mum knew how much I hated taking anything out of the microwave.

'MICROWAVE PRICK.'

The microwaves can jump on your brain and kill you stone dead right there and then. Zoom! There have been cases in America, Bulgaria and Ecuador. But it didn't matter any more so I took the porridge out myself. Nothing happened, so I munched the porridge.

12
Match

I always loved it when September came along. Not because the sweltering summer sun had finally buggered off to somewhere else. That was me being *ironic*, as I live in Scotland, which is not Papua New Guinea or Torremolinos. A hee-hee moment! No, I loved September because it was the time of the year that men became men and all the girls did arts and crafts. September was when THE FOOTBALL SEASON started in school. And I, Dylan Mint, was a first-on-the-team-sheet key member of the Drumhill School Football Team.

First game: local rivals, Shawhead.

Bring it on.

If you didn't want to do arts and crafts or pretend-reading in the library, students could watch the game and cheer like maddies for the Drumhill boys. It was that numpty Amir who egged me on to ask Michelle Malloy if she wanted to watch me playing the game.

'It's perfect,' Amir said.

'Not sure, amigo – the whole football thing wasn't part of my master plan.'

'*Plant some groovy seeds*, you said, so time to get them out.' Amir wiggled his fingers, all ten of them, in front of my face, like he was planting his thoughts in my brain.

'Amir, she'll see my legs.'

'So.'

'So there's no hair on them.'

'That's coz you're a white boy.'

'She'll think I'm, like, twelve or something.'

'Twelve isn't so bad – you know what they say about twelve-year-olds . . .' Amir winked and smiled.

'No, what?'

'Erm . . . I do-do-don't know really.'

'You're not helping, Amir. It's OK for you – your legs are like an orang-utan's; girls like seeing those, not two baldy wee twigs like mine.'

*

And then, without any strategy or an Action Jackson plan, the chance came.

Location: outside the Senior Toilets.

Activity: I'd just done my biz (pee). Michelle Malloy was just going (hopefully for a number one. The image of Michelle Malloy doing a number two was mega distressing and a potential deal-breaker).

Heart condition: it didn't have much time to think about it, but torpedoed into action as soon as I spied her.

Hands: moist.

Hair: OK. I fixed it in the bogs' mirror, pulling it over my eyes. I was trying to get it more cooler, like some of the dudes at the normal school. Twitching shifted my hair away from my eyes. No hands! One–nil Tourette's.

She came towards me without any warning. Like an angel out of the mist.

'Hi, Michelle.'

'What are you up to, Mint?'

'Erm . . . noth–'

'Hanging around the bogs, are we now?'

'No . . . I was . . . I was . . . DOIN' A SHITE . . . NO. I wasn't, Michelle, honestly. I was doing a pee. I was only doing a pee. BIG GIANT SHITE.' It blasted out of my mouth. I couldn't stop it happening.

'OK, so you've done your piss, now piss off.'

I laughed at Michelle Malloy's joke. 'Piss off, that's good,' I said.

'What planet are you on, moon man?'

'Erm, Planet Earth.' I felt for Green in my pocket and rubbed him as hard as I could.

'What in the name of fuck are you doing there, Mint?'

'What? Where?'

'*There!*' Michelle Malloy pointed to the pocket where Green was. 'Mint, if you're fiddling with yourself in front of me, I swear to God I'll cut that fucker off and shove *it* and *you* back up your mother.'

Wow! I didn't know how she'd do that, but it sounded painfully sore for everyone involved.

'No, it's my stone, Michelle. Look, it's only a wee stone. See?' I took Green out of my pocket.

'You better get that fucking thing out of my face, Mint, if you want to keep your nose.'

'I was just wondering if you're going to watch the first game of the season next week? We're playing Shawhead. DICK-CHEWER SHITE-DOER . . . Shit, sorry, Michelle.'

'You want me to watch you playing football, Mint?'

'Yes.'

'Mint, I'd rather wank a sheep.'

'A . . . sheep?'

'Now, get out of my way.' She made her way to the toilets.

'BIG GIANT SHITE,' I shouted, whooped a few times and then headed back to class in a massive daze. No Way, José Amir was getting wind of that chat.

We kicked off.

Ping.

Ping.

Ping.

The Barcelona of the spazzie world.

Goals galore.

A dodgy penalty decision.

Criminal refereeing.

Then it *really* kicked off. *Kicked off* is a football phrase clever-clog people use instead of *fight* or *scrap*. The thing was, we were playing football at the time – mad or what?

It actually all started because Snot Rag (aka Terence Trower) had to dash like a crazy man into hospital for emergency kidney stuff, which left Drumhill's football team without a first-choice goalie.

Holy Moly, no goalie! What were we to do?

I came up with a quality eureka moment: tell the bold Amir to hit the sticks.

I pushed for him to get the nod because cricket skills equal catching balls at sonic speed, a top-notch asset for any goalie to have.

It wasn't.

He was rank rotten.

Worse than rank rotten.

Pish.

Pure pish.

Pure heavy yellow pish.

We lost 7–4 to Shawhead. Total redneck at this level. The majority of the Shawhead team was full of proper spazzies too. And I mean spazzies who struggle to walk, so playing football for them was, like, a miracle. Yet they did manage to rap seven past Amir. Utter, total, complete, scarlet redneck.

It all kicked off like a Ross Kemp programme.

With the score at 6–4 Shawhead got a butter-soft penalty. One of their club-foot guys fell over in the box and the ref, Mr Comeford, pointed to the spot. It was so obvious to everyone that the guy just lost his balance and keeled over; Comeford blew out of pity more than anything. Shocking decision.

'If you don't save this, I'm going to boot your Paki balls up your arse,' Doughnut screamed at Amir.

'Eh?' Amir asked.

'You'd better save this or else,' Doughnut shouted. Amir looked at me all confused face. 'You couldn't catch syphilis in a Paki brothel.'

'Wha-wha-what?' Amir asked again. I wanted to say 'what?' too because I had no idea what syphilis was ... or what a Paki brothel was.

'Are you deaf, Pak-man?'

'No, I'm n-n-not deaf.' Amir didn't really get these types of questions. His answer threw Doughnut's brain cells into a tizzy. Doughnut got confused quickly when his mind was thrown into a tizzy, meaning his anger grew to mercury level. You should have seen Doughnut in class when teachers asked him mad hard questions – he's like an exploding space hopper.

'Just fucking save it or you'll be shitting your balls along with your curry tonight.' I could tell that Amir didn't have a clue what all this meant as he was still coming to terms with everyone (including me) shouting and screaming at him for being the crappiest goalie the world of football had ever seen.

'OK, I'll try,' he said, as if Doughnut had made a proper footballing request.

This huge Shawhead player with a mega limp ran up (or limped up) and blootered the ball towards Amir's goal. The ball blasted off the underside of the bar, scudded Amir on the back of the head and bobbled into the net. Amir hadn't the foggiest what had happened. Comeford blew for a goal. The Shawhead players celebrated. And Doughnut headed straight for Amir.

'You're one proper Paki fanny.' Doughnut was seething mad with steamy ears and nostrils.

Amir half ran away.

'Come here,' Doughnut said, walking after him, ready to do a hate crime.

'No,' Amir said.

'Don't make me chase you, Pak-man.'

'I didn't d-d-do anything,' Amir said.

'Exactly, you dick. Come here.'

Doughnut was within an arm's reach of Amir, while I was within an arm's reach of Doughnut.

'Leave me alone.'

'Yeah, leave him alone. He hasn't done anything wrong,' I said. Bad move. Major bad move.

'You stay out of this, Tic Tac, or I'll knock you into the middle of next week.'

I hated that name. Amir shook and growled, which made me shake and growl too. It was like we had that weird twin thing going on between us. Twin dogs. Twin dingo dogs. Doughnut grabbed Amir by the neck, shoving him to the ground. Then, I swear to the baby Jesus, he was setting himself up to take a penalty kick into Amir's napper.

'WANKER FUCKER!'

'Arrrrrrrhhhhhhh,' screamed Amir. The sound was like a newborn baby wailing and it made everyone turn towards the incident.

'BASTARD FUCKER.' The next thing I knew I was on Doughnut's back, arms curled around his neck, tugging him to the grass. 'FAT CUNT BAMPOT.' I couldn't hear what anyone was saying or shouting at all. What I heard was a *ssszzzhhhoooooooooooo* sound ringing in my head, like a washing machine spinning dead dead fast trying to get the thick dirt out of the muckiest clothes from the muckiest town in the muckiest country in the world.

Ssszzzhhhoooooooooooo.

Ssszzzhhhoooooooooooo.

Ssszzzhhhoooooooooooo.

Then the spin cycle slowed right down to a

stut

stut

stutter

stutter

stutter

stut

stut

stut

tut

tut

tut

tu

tu

tu

t

t

t

nt

nt

nt

int

int

int

Mint

Mint

Mint . . .

'MINT!'

'MINT!'

'MINT.' Mr Comeford ripped my football jersey as he pulled me off Doughnut. It was A-OK though because it was the school's football shirt. 'STAND OVER THERE, MINT, AND DON'T BLOODY MOVE,' he snarled at me, pointing to the goal Shawhead had just scored into. 'THOMPSON, YOU GET YOUR BLOODY CARCASS UP OFF THE GROUND AND STAND OVER THERE,' he said, pointing to a part of the field that was far away from where I was. 'MANZOOR, STOP ROLLING AROUND IN THE GRASS LIKE A BLOODY STUPID STRAY DOG AND GET ON YOUR FEET, SON.'

I heard him say, 'Fuckin' ******' under his breath as Amir was getting up. I wasn't one hundred per cent sure if the '******' was *Paki*, *darkie* or *spazzie*, but I was almost eighty-five per cent sure that whatever it was, it was a shocker word. A word like that could have made the papers, coming from a teacher. I don't think Mr Comeford cared that much for the students at Drumhill.

'GAME OVER,' he shouted into the air, then blew his whistle really loud.

The Shawhead teacher shook his head as if this was a ploy to have the game abandoned. But the game was abandoned for real. Would that mean we wouldn't lose the points?

As the Shawhead team was hobbling off to get their bus back to their school, Doughnut dished out some flying kung fu kicks to any Shawhead player near him. Skittle and Snot Rag weren't too far behind him, but they were just dishing out pretend kicks, as if they were playing the Keeping Up With The Joneses game. Being a lover and not a fighter, I decided to do no violent acts.

But I couldn't stop me being me.

'FUCKING SPAZZIES . . . SHAWHEAD SPAZZIES.' My hands were hurting because of all the tight fist-clenching. 'KNOB SUCKER,' I screamed at Comeford. My knees hurt from the banging; two wee twigs crashing against each other, sore as Hell. 'KNOB NUZZLER.' It was painful but the words kept coming.

'YOU, GET INTO THE SCHOOL,' Comeford said, pointing his finger at me, and wiggled towards the school building. 'NOW, MINT.'

And I sprinted there like a young Allan Wells (who won the gold medal for Great Britain in the 100 metres at the Moscow Olympics in 1980 with a time of 10.25 seconds, which is a rubbish time that wouldn't even get him into the semis nowadays. And he only won gold because all the good sprinters boycotted the games – well, their countries did – because the Soviet Union in 1980 was a place for mentalists). When I got into the school building, I didn't know what to do or where to go or who to speak to. The place was silent. I took myself to the nearest corner and stood really close to the angle of the corner's V shape, counted to ten, said all the consonants in the alphabet, then tried to say an animal beginning with each consonant, did my breathing exercises, played a tune from the air that was streaming out of my nose. *The William Tell Overture.* We do that in music with Miss Adams – well, we try to but we end up sounding like the Bonkers Orchestra for the Deaf. I wished I had Green to move between my fingers, but it was in my blinkin' school trousers.

No one came for ages. I was on the letter X.

Tap.

I was on the letter X for ages.

Tap.

I couldn't think of an animal with the letter X. Or a word.

I thought of Michelle Malloy because X reminded me of the word *sex* and Michelle Malloy reminded me of sex.

Tap on the shoulder.

Woman smell gusted up my hooter: make-up and perfume mixed together.

Boy, was I glad to see Miss Flynn. So glad that I flung my arms around her neck, like when I score a goal. But there was no goal joy. I belted it all out into her chest. Which was mega weird because I could feel her boobs against my own boy boobs and I was worried in case my willy was going to get angry, but this took my mind off the incident with Dough-nut. I continued to bubble though. Just in case. I wanted to be in Miss Flynn's office sitting on her big comfy chair, listen-ing to the groovy tunes she played to *soothe* me. She also put up these wacky posters to get us *reflecting* and help us feel better. *That which does not kill us makes us stronger* by some dude called Friedrich Nietzsche was my numero uno. Friedrich Nietzsche's job was to sit around THINKING about all this pure mad stuff.

Bonkerinos!

I could do a job like that.

*

Mum was lying on the couch with two cucumber slices covering her eyes. I could have eaten a scabby dog, because playing high-energised performance sport does that to the body. What I needed was carbs. Or a Pot Noodle. But I could have quite easily dived on Mum and eaten her cucumber eyes, I was so Hank Marvin. I wasn't sure if she was sleeping or not. She didn't move a muscle. Her belly went up and down so I knew she wasn't dead.

Phew!

The TV was on. Some guy was making a pasta dish with eggs and bacon. My belly rumbled, making a noise like a little embarrassed fart.

'There's soup in the pot,' Mum said, without even looking up or removing her cucumbers. She must have heard my belly fart. I didn't want soup.

'Mum, why do you have cucumbers on your eyes?'

'I was tired, Dylan.'

'Did you sleep with cucumbers on your eyes?'

'My eyes are tired. Cucumber helps.'

'Does it soothe them?'

'Yes.' It was ultra-weird talking to Mum while she was like this. It was what I'd imagined Martians to be like. 'I really need some sleep, Dylan. You can heat up the soup and have that for your dinner. It's tomato. There's some bread in the cupboard.' At least it was tom-tom soup.

'Did the school phone?' I asked.

'They might have but I didn't hear anything.'

'OK.'

'Why would the school be phoning?'

'Erm, just . . .'

'Have you been in trouble?'

'No.'

'You better not have been.'

'I wasn't.'

'I've got enough to worry about.'

'I wasn't in trouble, Mum.'

'OK, so go and have your soup and let me sleep.'

'Do you want me to bring you fresh cucumbers?' I asked. I felt guilty about lying.

'No, it's fine, Dylan, but if you have tea don't throw the tea bags away.'

'No problem, Mrs Mint.'

I saw her belly make a wee shudder, like a chuckle. Tom-tom soup is class. No other word for it.

Class.

Well, you could say fandabbydozie.

Amir wasn't allowed to have anything out of a tin; his mum made everything from scratch and used all-fresh produce that you could only get in special supermarkets, which ponged like a super skunk that had pished itself. He didn't know what he was missing though. Nor did Mrs Manzoor. Scooby-Doo would have been proud of me, the way I licked and licked the bowl. Crystal clean. If Mum had been there, I would have told her not to bother putting it in the dishwasher. Then the phone rang, making me jump out of my hickory dickories.

'Hello, 426258 . . . Hello?'

The person on the other end didn't say hello back. Rude. Maybe they were deaf as a post.

'Hello, 426258.'

Still nothing. So I said nothing for a bit as well.

'Dylan Mint speaking . . . Hello?'

I waited.

Zilcho.

I put the phone down because I had made a jumbo blunder. I had only gone and told the person on the other end my name. My full name. If this person on the other end was a murderer or someone who wanted to ride teenage boys, they knew how to get hold of me now. What an eejit. I went back to the kitchen. Then it rang again. My heart went thump, thump, scud, scud. I didn't want to wake Mum. And I certainly didn't want to get murdered or ridden. I couldn't work out which was worse.

It kept ringing.

Flippin' heck.

I slapped my head before I picked it up.

'Hello.'

No voice arrived.

'Hello. Who is this please?'

I could hear breathing. Not pervert breathing – normal breathing.

'State your desire. I know you're there. This number can now be traced, my friend. The CIA will be all over this. My dad has this phone tapped.'

Still no reply.

'CHILD FUCKER,' I screamed in my other voice – but I didn't mean it to be so loud – before slamming the phone down.

'Dylan!' Mum shouted. 'Was that the phone?'

'I think so.'

'What do you mean, you think so? Was it the phone or not?'

'Suppose so.'

'Yes or no?'

'Yes.'

'Who was it?'

'They didn't say.'

'Who didn't say?'

'They didn't say anything.'

'Who?'

'The person on the other end.'

'What person on the other end?'

'They only breathed a wee bit.'

'Breathed?'

'No words, just breathing.'

'Did you not ask who was speaking?'

'I did, but they didn't reply.'

I could hear Mum muttering to herself. Not like a mad mentalist, more like she was raging bull about something.

'Go and get me some used tea bags, Dylan.'

13

Date

I had to spring into action. No Coke or chocolate injection would do for this dude, no siree. October's leaves were yellowy red and scattered all over the ground making my front garden look like one massive pizza.

I was lying in my scratcher staring at the ceiling and thinking that Michelle Malloy was one funny bunny. One funny minx of a bunny. The chat outside the toilet was good for several reasons:

1. She cracked a joke.
2. She didn't hit me.
3. She said the word *wank*, which is capital letter CRAZY as she's a girl . . . but not just any girl!

It was time for this knight to spring into action and slay that dragon once and for all. Eminem sprang me into action. It was time to tackle the *Cool Things To Do Before I Cack It* list. And, as Fräulein Maria says, let's go to the very beginning . . . or something like that.

Number one: have real sexual intercourse with a girl. (Preferably Michelle Malloy and definitely not on a train or any other mode of transport. If possible, the intercoursing will be at her house.)

I couldn't drink booze or smoke the wacky baccy so it was up to Eminem to give me some Dutch courage. I don't know why they use this phrase because I haven't met any courageous Dutch people yet. I bopped around my room to the song *Business*. It was tough trying to sing along though. Scottish people singing rap is a bit like black American bagpipe players. Totally weird as! I only rapped the odd word here or there. Mum hated the rap music I listened to; she said it polluted the brain cells and would turn me into a NED, or a G-man. (Mum didn't actually say G-man.) When it was blaring, I had to pretend to be a loopy Tourette's guy so I could sing along to all the swear words.

'Turn that bloody racket off, Dylan,' Mum shouted, banging on the wall between our rooms.

'Sorry, Mum,' I said, but I wasn't that sorry.

'Don't be sorry, just turn it down . . . or preferably off. I've told you what that stuff can do.'

'OK.'

I put in my earphones instead and blasted *Cleanin' Out My Closet* into my lugs. I rapped for a wee bit but at the end of the day Eminem wasn't working for me – I think he was too close to my brain cells. In its place I searched for the perfect song that would brilliantly capture this momentous moment, something that could sum everything up in a three-minute tune. I flicked through billions of songs on my iPod until I found it: *This Is The One* by the Stone Roses. If you lob away the verses of the song, this was what I was feeling in my head. Also in my head was the dreaded fear, and when the dreaded fear enters the old napper that's when the tics and the howling start too. And sometimes the hitting. And the more I try to rid my head of the dreaded fear, it builds up more and more and more, like a giant snowman being built from a tiny snowball. But I sort of knew that that's what would happen. There's not really much I can do about it when it gets to that stage. It was something I had to find 'coping mechanisms' for, as Miss Flynn kept telling me. My coping mechanism was my pal.

When the day came to slay Michelle Malloy, Amir said he would be a best bud and meet me before we got to school in order to help me calm the jets or cool my beans. I suspected this was in case Doughnut tried to jump him at the school gates and nothing to do with me.

'WANK, AMIR . . . Shit, sorry, Amir. PRICK-FACE . . . Shit . . . Sorry . . . DICK-BAWZ.'

'Nervous?'

'Just a bit.'

'You'll be grand-a-mundo.'

'Hope so.'

'Just walk tall and Michelle Malloy will be glue in your hands, man.'

'Putty.'

'What?'

'Putty in your . . . Oh, never mind, Amir.'

'Have you gone over your sp-sp-spiel?'

'Until I'm bloomin' blue in the face. SLUT DOG . . . Don't laugh, Amir, it's not funny. I'm shitting it here. I need help.'

'I'm not laughing at you, Dylan – there's no way I'd do that.'

'I know.'

'It's just the thought of your first words to Michelle Malloy being sl-sl-slut dog.' He had a point. I did a pained laugh.

'I'm buggered, Amir. What am I going to do?'

'You don't need to talk to her today, you know.'

'I do.'

'No you don't.'

'If I don't make my move now, someone else will get there before me and cut my blinkin' grass.'

'What, to have it o-o-off with her?'

'No, not to have it off with her . . . Good Golly, Miss Molly, Amir, sometimes I think that's all you think about.'

'I think of other things too.'

'This might be my last chance to ask her if she wants to go to the Halloween disco with me.'

'You'd better not hairy balls it up then.'

'Aw, cheers.'

'No, I mean you need to make a big giant effort.'

'But what if I'm ticking all over the place?'

Amir took this on and thought really hard about it. 'She'll think you're a suicide bomber.' He giggled like a wee devil on my shoulder. I could have punched him full force on the arm. 'I'm only j-joking, Dylan.'

'Well, don't!'

'OK, OK. Allah on a bike!'

'What? Who's Alan?'

'Allah, not Alan. You're allowed to say "Christ on a bike" so I'm allowed to say "Allah on a bike".'

'This is no time for any shite, Amir. This is a super-duper crisis.'

'Sorry, Dylan, I was just trying to take your mind off things.'

'But what if I do?'

'Do what?'

'Tick all over the joint?'

'What about it? She knows what you are and what you have.'

'I suppose she does.' I hadn't thought about it like that.

'And you also know what's wrong with her, so what's the big problem?'

Already I felt better. Amir was stepping up to the plate. Which is a baseball analogy. It would be a-mayonnaise-ing if I could do a cricket one in Amir's honour. Amir put his arm around my shoulder, which was very nice of him. He was the tops. I'd sure as Hell miss the fellow.

'Just be yourself and her pants will fall down around her a-a-ankles,' Amir said.

I sniggered. 'You mean her knickers will drop?'

'Knickers . . . pants . . . same thing.'

'Pants are more like boys' knickers.'

'Well, whatever. You know what I mean.'

The school bus rattled past. On the back seat with his face mashed up against the back window was Doughnut.

'There's that tube Doughnut,' Amir said.

It was the first time we'd seen Doughnut since the football match. He got suspended for trying to kung fu the shite out of the whole Shawhead team *and* the coach. Doughnut put his right index finger through a hole he'd made with his left hand, like a car piston, as if to suggest that Amir and I were having it off gay-boy style. He must have clocked Amir's arm around my shoulder. Then he stopped doing the having-sex motion and turned both his middle fingers up towards us.

I smiled and waved.

Amir didn't; he put up his left hand and slapped the back of it and started shouting 'spazzie, spazzie, spazzie' in a mentalist tone so it sounded like a real spazzie's voice. It was the same voice the people who go to the proper school use for us. I was just shocked that Doughnut had decided to ride the spazzie bus. He was a tube.

'I hate that stupid kiddie wanker,' Amir said.

'You can't say that, Amir.'

'Why can't I?'

'Because he could take you to court for slander.'

'So? I don't have any money.'

'No, but your dad is minted.'

'Well, Doughnut should keep his crap to himself.'

'Don't let him worry you.'

'That's easy for you to say, Dylan. You're not the Pa-Pa-Paki that everyone pure slags all the time.' I couldn't disagree with the bold Amir. In a way I was grateful to Doughnut for taking my mind off Michelle Malloy. 'This is why I get a lift every day, to avoid tits like Doughnut. I'm sick of people calling me *nigger* or *black bastard*. I mean, I'm no black and my dad still lives at home with us.'

'Well, I'm Man United delighted you're here, Amir. That's what best buds do.'

'Cheers.'

'So that makes you, like, the best of the best buds.'

Amir shrugged.

I sang *This Is The One* by the Stone Roses in my head. I wanted to psyche myself up before the big event. I'd seen all those footballers psyche themselves up by listening to music while getting off the team bus and they had gladiator looks about them. Dad used to say they were overpaid twats who couldn't string a sentence together between them if their life depended on it and that a good stint in the army was what most of them needed. He said he'd like to see them with no food, water or sleep in the jungles of Sierra Leone for five days and see how fucking cool they looked then. That wasn't part of a conversation me and Dad were having – that was just Dad being Dad. I preferred to watch football alone in my room.

'What are you going to say to her then?' Amir asked.

'I dunno . . . Ask her out straight, I suppose.'

'Bad move.'

'What do you mean, bad move?'

'That wouldn't be the approach I'd take.'

'Tell me then, Valentino, what would you do?'

Amir gave me one of the looks he gives when he doesn't know what I'm talking about, which is loads of times. I know that Amir look like the back of my hand.

'Who's Va-va-valentino?'

'Some ancient guy from Italy, I think, who did it with heaps and heaps of cracking-looking women.'

'Over ten?'

'I think so.'

'Wow, he must have had some size of tinkle.'

'I'll say.' You could see that Amir enjoyed being in the same sentence as Valentino. 'So what's your advice?'

'Well, if I were you, I'd try and make some small talk before diving right in.'

'Small talk about what?'

'Oh, I dunno. Talk about bands or shoes or films . . . Films are a good one to talk about.'

'Could be,' I agreed.

'What's your fav film?'

'Easy. *The Sound of Music*.'

'Maybe don't talk about films then. Talk about *Britain's Got Talent* and all the pure mad mental crap people who go on it.'

'That's a shite idea, Amir. No, I'm going with Plan A.'

'Which is?'

'Just be myself.'

'Are you sure?'

'Yes.'

'Fair doos.'

From miles away I saw Michelle Malloy's cool red Adidas trainers and her dinky Converse bag. The trainers looked all duffed up and the bag was decorated with all this graffiti stuff. If my new bag and giant shoes had been in this state,

Mum totally would have gone crackpot and probably scudded me around the dome and forced me to take a plastic bag to school as a punishment and screamed at me something like, 'Do you think money grows on trees, Dylan? Well, do you?' And I'd have stood shaking my head and trying not to swear at her. It's IMPOSSIBLE for dosh to grow on trees as dosh is a non-living thing and therefore CAN'T grow anywhere, never mind trees. Parents always ask these weird stupid questions. 'Do you want the back of my hand on your jaw, Dylan?' 'No, Dad, I don't.' Silly billy! Michelle Malloy's mum must have been chillaxed out of her nut about these things.

My heart was beating so fast it was as if it was trying to escape from my body or some tiny person inside me was using it for trampoline practice. Amir whooped but I couldn't understand if it was an Amir whoop or just a whoop of delight. In any case it made me want to shout something really bold boy bad at him. So bold boy bad that I couldn't even say it out loud. Mr Dog was trying to make me howl 'SLAPPER' and 'BUCKET CUNT' to Michelle Malloy. AAAARRRRHHHH! It was Torture with a capital T trying to keep it all in. My head twitched from side to side. I flicked at my ears, tucked them in. Rubbed Green till my palm became sauna hand.

I wanted to Usain Bolt.

I wanted to cry.

I wanted to be normal.

I wanted to go to the other school.

I wanted to chat to girls without screaming 'SLUT', 'COW' or 'WHORE' into their face before I'd even said 'howdy'.

I wanted Mum to start loving and snuggling me again.

I wanted Dad to come home and be a family man once more.

I wanted the docs to find a mega cure for me, then the cure finder and I would become worldwide celebs and be on the celeb scene and go to all the celeb parties and be given lavish gifts like DVDs and mobile phones and get to meet other celebs like Simon Cowell and Kevin Costner.

No doubt this was the biggest case of cacking myself that I'd ever had. Even more than when I did shit myself for real in my first year at secondary school. How the Devil's haircut do real players do it?

'I can't do it, Amir.'

'You can. Be br-br-brave.'

'I can't! My heart is pounding so much it hurts and I want to swear out loud like a mofo.'

'So swear then – she's heard it all before,' Amir said in an aggressive voice. 'Look, if you don't I will.'

'What, ask her out?'

'No, you dumpling, I'll ask her out for *you*.'

We were now in the school canteen watching all the poor people queuing up for their free breakfast: mainly smelly fruit that supermarkets chuck out, dry eggs, soggy toast and porridge. Yuck-a-duck! The noise was humongous. All these mad maddies in the same place making a major racket. It was worse than the worst disco on earth. Thank the lucky stars I wasn't poor enough to ever have to come in here for scran; God bless the good old-fashioned packed lunch.

Michelle Malloy was sitting in a corner with her hooter deep in a magazine. Probably a magazine about cool fashions or groovy pop bands or hot hunks or make-up. A magazine I would know heehaw about.

'There she is,' Amir said, shoving me in the back.

'All right, Amir, I'm not Stevie Wonder.'

'Go,' he said, shoving harder, dead excited.

'Calm down to a riot, Amir.'

'Go.'

'A player's got to play it cool, you know.'

'Well, you better hurry up or you'll miss the opp-opp-opporchancity.'

'I'm just composing myself.' No tics, no swearing, no slapping. Just a wee bit of nerves and heart hammering, that was all.

'Come on,' Amir urged. 'I didn't get out of my scratcher mad early for bugger all. Go on.'

I shuffled towards her. All the noise, all the deadbeats, all the pongo of the stinking breakfast food disappeared. It was only the two of us: Michelle Malloy and me. Just like a dual from the Western films that Dad liked to watch when he came home from the pub with his takeaway. In my head I kept thinking, *Just say hello, just say hello* over and over again. And before you could say, 'Hey, Big Mamma!', I was standing at her table.

Time stopped. Frozen stiff. I could hear nothing at all except my own head. It was as if I was playing statues. Michelle Malloy didn't look up to welcome me; she just kept reading her magazine as if it was the last thing in the whole wide world with words in it and she only had two more minutes left in the world to live. BIG GIANT WAVE coming with a naked surfer riding on it. Nightmare. Amir, bud, please come and rescue me Pakistan-superhero style!

'SNOBBY BITCH . . . Shit . . . Fuck . . . Sorry, Michelle, I didn't . . .'

'What do you want, Mint?' she said, not taking her peepers off the magazine.

'FUCKIN' TEASE . . . Shit . . . Sorry, Michelle . . .'

'You'd better get it out, Mint, because I've no time for your Tourette's crap.'

Amir was spot on about her knowing what I had and not really caring too much about it. She was mega cucumber. I was a turnip.

'I was just wondering what magazine you were reading.'

She looked at me. Wow! Michelle Malloy was sooooooooo close to me right now that I could have reached out and stroked her. I could have smudged her bright red lipstick and

116

dark mascara with my thumb. Man alive, I could have flicked her earrings with my pinkie. My super smell sense told me that her deodorant was the same as Mum's, Sure for Women. I was one hundred and seventeen per cent Sure of it. When it wafted up my snout I didn't think of those minging breakfast smells any more.

'Go away, Mint. Don't you have some puerile stuff to be getting on with, with that friend of yours?'

What did *puerile* mean? What an incredible babe. But this was *Cool Things To Do Before I Cack It* so I had to get a move on. I had to get my game head on.

'You mean Amir?'

'I don't give a shit what he's called.' She flipped a page over in her magazine.

'What's your magazine about?'

She looked up at me again. Oh, my good God in Heaven! Those eyes! They were like two wee jewels peeking through her black eyeliner. Emeralds. But Michelle Malloy didn't have sparkle happy eyes.

'Why do you care?'

'Just interested, Michelle.'

'Well, don't be.' My heart was boom boom booming about all Joe 90. 'Look, what is it you want, Mint? I've no time for all this crap.'

'It's just . . . I'm dead interested in your magazine . . . Magazines in general.'

She puffed out in the same way athletes do when they finish a tough old sprint.

'It's about body art.'

'Really?' I said, as if I knew what she was on about.

'Happy?'

I was happy so I nodded my head.

'Now piss off.' This wee honey said some great stuff, so she did.

'I just wanted to ask you something else, if that's OK with you?'

'What?'

But I couldn't get it out. I needed to scream something, to shout at her or to slap myself on the noggin. I could feel my face burning with trying to hold it in. To normal people it would have been like trying to speak with a ginormous gobstopper stuck in their throat. That was every day for me.

'I'm waiting, Mint.' And she waited.

I tried, I really tried.

She waited. 'See, this is the problem with you, Mint. You just can't get it out there, can you? Why don't you just go back to your weirdo pal?'

Then it all came out like projectile vomit. I had entered the Speed-Speaking World Championships.

'Would-you-like-to-come-to-the-Halloween-disco-with-me? FUCKING BITCH.' Oh, please tell me she didn't hear that last bit. But there was No Way, José she didn't. Michelle

118

Malloy stared at me for what seemed like yonks. I was rubbish at staring games.

'If, Mint, by some chance, I have a lobotomy and decide to go to the Halloween disco – which I'm not going to anyway because it's for major losers, but if I *was* going – there is no way on this earth I'd go with someone who calls me a bitch and a tease every second sentence.'

'But I didn't mean –'

'Now blow town.'

'I only ever say those things when I'm nervous, Michelle, you know that.'

'Whatever, Mint. I'm still not going to some infantile Halloween disco. Now make like Michael Jackson.'

'What?'

'Beat it!'

'We don't need to go to the disco. BIG VAG . . . Sorry . . . SOCK-FACE . . . Sorry.' Oh, someone please put me face up on a guillotine right now.

'Not even if you were the last man standing, Mint. Not even if you –'

'But I don't have much time left.' This was a silly line as it made me sound crazy mental. Michelle Malloy shook her head, the very same shake you do to pathetic people when you think they are super-thicko stupid, but for a nano-nanosecond I was about to tell her that I was soon to perish.

'Yeah? Join the club,' she said, and waved me away with her hand. 'If you'll excuse me, Mint, I have a multitude of miscellaneous crap to do before class.' And, just like that, her eyes flipped to her body-art magazine.

I plodded back to Amir. The long walk of shame. Everything in the canteen was in super slo-mo, all the voices were muffled and I sensed everyone's blurry peepers gawking at me. Then I felt Mr Dog coming again, a great big giant of a dog. Only this time he was coming to bite the dome straight off me in one gulp. My head twitched and almost shook straight off its shoulders. I couldn't control anything. Sweat soaked my stomach. Was this the moment the doc was on about? Was THIS my time? Without me achieving any of my wishes?

I made out the figure of Amir walking slowly towards me. He was major easy to make out. His teeth were chalk white with a big banana smile. You'd think he'd scored the winning goal in a cup final, or saved a last-minute penalty with a salmon leap to the top corner (or 'postage stamp' as Dad calls it). There was more chance of winning the EuroMillions lottery though.

'Well, is she?' he said, all googly excited. 'Is she going to have it off with you?'

Nada came out and I walked straight past him. I'm not a million per cent sure but I think I might have growled at him as well. Anyway I Usain Bolted out of the school gates for home, to *The Jeremy Kyle Show* in bed.

Then I realised why everything was blurry like Dad's car's windscreen when it rained all torrential. I wiped the tears away from my peepers.

14
Car

When I reached my street, the shaking, twitching, tears and shouting had all gone. Phew! But I was now terrified in case the school knew I was on the mitch. When they found out, they'd phone Mum to ask where I was. Or, worse, they'd tell her that I'd been seen entering the school gates and then exiting them. I hated how Drumhill always phoned parents when students were a nano-nano-nanosecond late for anything. Amir said it was in case anyone had had a heart attack or fallen on the ground with foam pouring from their mouths on their way to school or had been touched in their privates by pervert people in the bushes. I knew for a fact that this wasn't the case in the normal schools. If students didn't bother their arses attending from day to day, the schools didn't give two flying fishes. I wished Drumhill didn't give its fishes.

I hoped that Mum was out buying grub for dinner or having morning coffee with some of her friends who didn't do any paid work. If she was out, I could sneak up to bed to watch the saddos on *The Jeremy Kyle Show* and put my head under the covers and pretend I was inside a tent or an igloo or a teepee and feel super safe and comfortable. I could imagine I was on an exotic holiday or on some important adventure or leading a crucial expedition to find a cure for all those poor souls living in Tourette's Hell Hotel. (This would be tough as the doc had told Mum and Dad that there was no cure.) More likely I'd fall asleep and forget the whole Michelle Malloy conversation.

There was a maroon car in Dad's space. It wasn't Mum's because she couldn't drive and therefore didn't need a car to get her from A to B. Mum failed her driving test five blinkin' times. Imagine that. Dad always teased her about all her failed attempts behind a wheel, saying she 'couldn't drive a bargain', which is a pun, which is a thing people do when they're playing with words in order to make themselves seem funnier or cleverer than they actually are.

My favourite puns are:

I'm reading a book about anti-gravity. It's impossible to put down.

And:

I couldn't remember how to throw a boomerang, but then it came back to me.

But I'm not clever or funny.

It was similar to the kind of car that plain-clothes cops or the CID drive around in; a type of car that police want the public to believe is your average John Doe's car and not an actual police car so as to pull the wool over criminals' eyes and lead them into a false sense of security . . . then the clink. This ploy was rubbish because anyone streetwise and *with it* knew what an unmarked police car looked like straight away. And this thing sitting outside my house, in my dad's parking space, looked like an unmarked police car. *Ding! Dang! Dong!* I thought. What if the school had called the police and asked them to tail me for the crime of mitching school or, major head-wrecker, sexually harassing Michelle Malloy? Maybe I'd be frogmarched down to the station for some serious strip-searching interrogation. I'd have to get a brief in case they wanted me to do a stretch: five to ten in the pen. I didn't know what to think. I was all over the place. One part of my brain was at the shop while the other part was running home with the change. Jeeze Louise! If they did huckle me to the station for questioning, I'd tell them that Michelle Malloy was soooooooooooo cheeky and soooooooooooo insulting to me that her remarks actually made me cry and I was in such a state of emotional bouncy castle that there was No Way, José that I could've even considered sitting behind a desk all day, and if they made me I'd have probably launched it against the

124

classroom wall and quite possibly injured an innocent class-mate. I didn't want to do that so I walked out of the school gates for the safety of everyone.

My plan was to tiptoe up the stairs and sneak into bed without as much as a squeak or a creak being heard. I held my breath as I put my key into the door, twisting it the same way an iceberg safe-cracker would open a reinforced bank vault. If bones could breathe, I would have held my bones' breath too. My body tensed when I carefully closed the door behind me. One wee toe was on the bottom stair ready for the big climbing expedition.

'Is that you, Dylan?'

I held my breath and felt my face redden because this action was dead hard to do, meaning I would have been a terrible lifeguard or deep-sea free-diver if that was my chosen career path.

'Dylan?' Mum sounded upset – probably because I was driving her into an early grave – so I took my toe off the step and turned my body towards the kitchen. That's where her voice was coming from. 'Dylan?'

'Yeeeesss?'

'What are you doing home from school?'

I wondered if this was one of those questions that don't require an answer or one that did. If Mum wanted an answer, it meant that the school hadn't been in contact with her yet and if she didn't want an answer it meant I was for the high jump. I shushed myself and said zilch. Then there was a stand-off, just as the good and bad lads in the Wild West have from time to time. A silent stand-off. I was about to hot step it up to my room, when I heard another voice coming from the kitchen. Mum and this voice were having a whispering conversation. I didn't recognise the voice, and it was a man's. No mistake, sugar cake. Then I thought about it and . . . Jesus, Mary and Joseph! Maybe it was a policeman. A copper. The Old Bill. Five-O. At this moment my heart could have provided the beat on a rip-roaring drum 'n' bass track.

'Mum,' I said.

There was more whispering and I was sure I heard Mum saying, 'NO.' But she said this in her weird shouting-in-a-soft-voice way. She does this in the shops when I ask again and again and again if I can have random things, like chocolate, football stickers, special dishwasher tablets and razors (even though I haven't started shaving yet). Mum looks at me and softly shouts, 'No, Dylan, enough is enough.'

There was no answer from the kitchen.

'Mum, are you OK?'

That's when I thought the whispering guy in the kitchen could have done something evil to Mum. I could easily have interrupted him in the middle of a sickening and sordid ordeal. He could have been holding a blunt butcher's knife under her neck urging her to come clean about where all the goodies in the house were stashed. And the mad thing is, even though I was the man of the house, I didn't know what to do in a situation like this, or who to scream to, or who to phone. I didn't really know how to fight.

I whistled really loudly. I whistled to a flock of imaginary birds.

'Dylan, I'm OK.'

I kept whistling, getting louder and louder.

'Dylan, I'm OK, honestly.'

But I didn't believe her so I hotfooted it straight for the kitchen to make sure the whispering man hadn't been pressing the knife into Mum's throat, forcing her to say those things to me. This beast obviously thought Dylan Mint would roll over and say, 'No problemo, Mum', head up to bed and play some tunes while *he* was playing Devil in the kitchen. This geezer thought Dylan Mint was some sort of eejit.

'EVIL CUNT PAEDOPHILE.' I burst through the kitchen door and scowled at the man. Twitched like crazy. This fellow wasn't holding a blunt butcher's knife in his hand nor was he raping Mum. In fact Mum and the whispering man were sat at each end of the table having a nice cup of tea. Confused dot com. My head was fuzzy. I punched my thigh four times. Twitched three times. The whispering man stood up from the table and extended his hand for me to shake. I didn't. I kept my hands firmly at my side. No stranger was touching me. I'd have him locked up in solitary forever and ever. He'd

127

become someone's bitch behind bars if he didn't watch his step. Super rapido, he would. Face down in the showers.

'You, young man, must be Dylan?'

I looked at Mum. She smiled as if she'd done something incredibly wrong.

'Are you from my school?' I asked him, which was a stupid question because if he'd been from Drumhill I'd have seen him cutting about the corridors from time to time. He laughed. I was fed up to the back teeth with people laughing at me.

'Not exactly.'

'The school phoned by the way, Dylan,' Mum said. 'They told me you walked out, just like that.' On the *just like that* part Mum clicked her two fingers in the air. I must have looked sheepish because she didn't seem too angry or pure mad mental. 'We'll talk about this later, OK.'

I wasn't sure if she wanted an answer to this.

'OK,' I said. 'Are you a policeman?' I asked the man.

He was still standing. He was majorly tall, enough to be a policeman. Not CID or Special Branch though. I'd place this maniac outside a football stadium checking people's tickets. In my mind that would be a horrendous job, beaten only by waving heavy traffic through polluted streets in the wind and rain because the traffic lights have failed for the gazillionth time. He laughed at my question.

'UGLY PIG FILTH FUCK . . . Sorry . . . I'm . . .'

'That's OK, Dylan. And no, I'm not a policeman, Dylan.'

'Is that your car outside?'

'Yes it is. Do you like it?'

'It's in Dad's space.'

'I didn't know there were allotted spaces for residents on this road.' I made a mental note to look up *allotted* in the dictionary, but I had a fair idea what it meant. I'd remember this and impress Mrs Seed.

'Are you a doctor?' It all made sense then. This man was some sort of specialist doc sent by the NHS. The good news man. Maybe they'd realised that the other doc was terrible at his job and everything he said to patients was pork pies pish. I'd then have to sue his arse for the emotional rampage he had caused us.

'No, I'm not a doctor either, Dylan,' he said, still smiling away like a big massive cat from that town in England where cats smile all the time. He looked at Mum and flashed his eyes towards the ceiling as if to say, *Heaven forbid*.

'Dylan, stop asking so many questions, will you.' Then she rolled *her* eyes skywards at the man as if to say, *I did tell you what he was like, didn't I?*

'So why is your car in Dad's space if you're not from the school or a policeman or a doc?'

'Dylan,' Mum said, 'this is Tony. He gave me a lift back from the shops.'

'But it's too early to go to the shops.'

'Don't be so silly – it's never too early to go to the shops.'

'But you never go to the shops in the morning.'

'Well, I did this morning.'

'What did you buy?'

'Dylan, what's the problem with me going to the shops first thing in the morning, eh?'

'It's just a bit weird, that's all.'

'I just gave your mum a lift back because she had lots of bags, Dylan,' the tall man said.

'You're not my dad.'

'DYLAN,' Mum shouted.

'Well, he's not.'

'Tony knows that.'

'So tell him to get his car out of Dad's space then.'

'I'll do no such thing.'

'Look, Moira, I need to be going anyway,' the man said.

'At least finish your tea first, Tony.'

'I've got an airport run in half an hour anyway,' he said.

'Are you a pilot?' I asked him.

'No, Dylan. I'm a cabbie.'

'A what?'

'A taxi driver.'

'So that car outside is a taxi?'

'Yes, and it will be out of your dad's space in a jiffy.'

'Does that mean soon?'

'Dylan, will you please stop being rude to Tony,' Mum said. The anger had returned to her voice.

'But taxi drivers aren't supposed to come into passengers' houses for cups of tea,' I said.

'I couldn't agree more, but your mum and me go back a long way.'

'We were old school friends,' Mum added.

'But how come I've never heard you talking about him?'

'Well, that's because –' the taxi man butted in, but I didn't let him finish.

'Me and Amir are school pals and we see each other all the time and talk about each other when we're not at school and his mum and dad know well who I am even though I'm not allowed in his house.'

'Tony and I just rediscovered each other recently by accident.'

'At the shops?' I said.

'Online,' the taxi man said.

'On Facebook,' Mum said.

'But you said that Facebook was for freaks, Mum.'

The taxi man laughed and so did Mum, like they were sharing some secret joke. I hated them both.

'Many of the people who use it are, Dylan, but there are nice folk who use it as well.'

'Someone posted an old school photo on my wall and your mother was tagged in it,' the taxi man said. I didn't use

Facebook so I didn't really understand what the bloomin' Nora he was on about. 'So I sent a friend request and then we were writing on each other's wall talking about the old times and that.'

'But we don't have a wall,' I said.

He laughed again. 'It's not a real wall, Dylan. It's what they call your page on Facebook,' he said.

'Why don't they just call it a page?' I asked.

'This young chap's a right character, Moira, a real live wire.'

'That's not even the half of it,' Mum said.

'Right, listen, I'd best be off – got to get that fare.'

'Are you sure, Tony?' Mum said. She sounded disappointed.

'Afraid so. It's a biggie.'

'Yeah, right, Tony,' Mum said.

I felt both their peepers on me. I wasn't moving for no taxi man.

'See you, Mr,' I said, and there was this dead long pause.

'OK, Moira, I'll, er . . .'

'BYE,' I said.

Then he headed for the front door.

'I'll see you out, Tony,' Mum said, jumping from her seat. '*You*, stay here.' She had this witch's croak in her voice, making me feel scared. 'I mean it, Dylan. Stay here.' She said this in one of her angry-soft-voice ways.

So I stood like a pure mad plank in the kitchen looking at the half-empty mugs of tea. At the front door there were more whispers and a wee giggle from Mum and the taxi man. Then nothing. Hush. Dead time. That's when my mind went into a tailspin.

'TAXI BASTARD TAXI BASTARD.'

The door slammed shut.

Bang!

'Get up those stairs,' Mum shouted.

'Why are you friends with that man?' I asked.

'It's none of your business who I choose to be friends with.'

'But –'

'But nothing, Dylan. Get up those stairs. I won't tell you again.'

'Why?'

'Why? For skipping school, that's why. I'm fed up to the back teeth with all this.' She pointed to the stairs.

'Sorry for skipping school, Mum,' I said as I made my way towards the bottom step. 'I was having a mare of a morning.'

'Some of us have mares every morning, Dylan, but we don't run away.' Tears were in her eyes.

'Sorry for being rude to the taxi man.'

'His name's Tony, and it's too late for sorrys, isn't it?'

When I was at the top of the stairs, Mum shouted up to me.

'I'm thinking of going and having a word with your school, so you'd better watch your step from now on, Buster.' She only calls me Buster when she's mega angry, which meant that I was pressing all her wrong buttons.

'Fuck's sake,' I muttered to myself.

I lay on my bed, held on to Green tighter than ever and rocked myself exactly fifteen hundred times from side to side. Exactly fifteen hundred times. A record. I was rocking in time to songs by Sigur Rós because these guys knew how to churn out chilled peaceful music. I couldn't work out why Mum wasn't worried about me any more and why she was treating me like a Goddamn leper child given the race against time she had with me. Most mums in her position would have been carting their sick children off to a stunning sandy beach somewhere or to an adventure park that had a mandatory helmet-wearing policy or one of those safari parks you drove through to see all the wild animals roaming around. Although Mum didn't have a car and she usually relied on taxis, I couldn't make out why some taxi driver was in my house drinking out of our mugs and parking his jalopy in Dad's space. I couldn't make out why, when the taxi man left, Mum seemed to be angry or sad or disappointed. I was terribly confused, so I was.

It would have been incredible if Mum had come into my room, lain down beside me, stroked my head and said everything was going to be all right on the night. I would have given my right arm to be called *sweetheart* or *cuddly bum* or *Dylsy pops* again or for Mum to attack me in one of her giggle fits before licking my face and for me to go: 'Yuuuuuuuccccckkk, Muuuuuuummmmmmm, that's Disgusting with a capital D' and for her to say, 'Love ya, snookins'. Or was it *snookims*? When I was rocking, counting, slapping or whatever it was I was doing, Mum was always there to rub my back, run me a bath, to tell me everything was going to be 'hunky-dory' and she was sorry if she'd upset me. But not that time.

I lay there trying to think about anything other than the thing I was really thinking about. But as hard as I tried to imagine what Michelle Malloy looked like in her knick-knacks all I could think about was the big D word. WHAT WAS IT LIKE AND HOW WOULD IT HAPPEN? Would I just lie down on a really soft duvet, close my eyes and let my body sink into it? A bit like going into a big scanner, except more fluffy, comfortable and more exciting? I hoped Mum would buy a new one for me; I didn't want to bow out in the old scabby one I used coz it was like having Ten Ton Tessie on top of your body. Would it happen while I was asleep? Then my life (or death) could become, like, this amazing dream that never ever ends. All I'd be doing is floating from one groovy place to another. That would be Utterly Butterly A-mayonnaise-ing if that was to happen. I did an upside-down capital C grin when my eyes were closed as if I was actually in that dreamland.

Then my grin turned all the way around and I was in sad-face thought-time. I was thinking about all the ways Dad could go. Like if it was an IED, which is army talk for Improvised Explosive Device, it would be a disaster because it might take ages to find his legs, arms or torso. We might not get to see him in the coffin because they could only find his head, one leg and half an arm. If he went in Friendly Fire, which is what American soldiers call it when they accidentally kill their own buddies instead of backslapping them or saying hello – those bloody Yanks! – at least we'd get to see Dad in his coffin all peaceful and heroic. I swung my legs off the bed and fetched Dad's letter. I read it for the eighty-nine millionth time.

And I thought I had it bad!

Eventually I got back on to Michelle Malloy.

Phew!

15
Kidneys

When my mobile blared out *No Sleep Till Brooklyn* I woke up. Sun sneaked through my bedroom window, meaning that I had only been snoozing for a few hours. I knew who it was straight away because I have all my friends specially programmed in my phone. When I say all my friends, what I mean is that I have my mum, whose mobile song is *Mama Said Knock You Out*; I have my dad, whose mobile song is *King of the Swingers* (but that never rings because Dad can't use his mobile in case the crazy infidels track him down, cart him off to some deep dark cave in the middle of nowhere and torture him for the top-notch secret state information he has stored away in his head); and then I have Miss Flynn, whose mobile song is *Good Vibrations*. But that's just for emergencies. Even though today was a type of emergency I didn't hear *Good Vibrations*.

hi dylan, itz amir here. r u goin 2 skool 2 mor? Amir always started his texts with telling me who they were from even though I'd told him a billion times that *No Sleep Till Brooklyn* meant that I knew it was him. I even played his message tone to him. He was some man, Amir was.

Probs, dont want 2 tho

dont wory about MM

Im no

shez a carpet muncher anyway. lol

so iz her maw. Lol

lol

lllloooolll

r u still goin to disco?

dunno.

Itll be brill ... cum on?

Ill think about it.

we cud go as laurel and hardy

ur the fat one

or cagney and lacy. Amir was always watching the old programmes on Sky.

bags cagney then. Lol

wot about susan boyle and mrs seed? lol.

thot u wer goin as oor m8 doughnut?

na hez a fat cok gobbler

lol

lol rite bak at u

so r u goin then?

may b

think about it

I will. only got 17p credit left

c u 2mor then

okeydokey

Mobile phones are possibly the greatest invention the world has ever seen. My top four inventions are:

1. Mobile phones.
2. Sky+.
3. Football.
4. Dialysis machines.

Come to think of it, Michelle Malloy had to have a dialysis machine strapped to her kidneys so she didn't pee herself all the time. Or was it so her kidneys didn't go on the blink? Basically I wasn't one hundred per cent sure as I was too scared to ask her about it. She went to hospital loads for it – well, for that and her big-leg-wee-leg issue. Maybe that was why she was so grumpy: she could have been suffering dialysis machine withdrawal. Maybe being a crabby chops is a symptom of this – who knows how these dialysis machines work? I certainly don't. I wouldn't mind getting my grubby hands on her mobile number – I could send her nice text messages without having to listen to her slagging me off or calling me hurtful names. I'd send her text messages full of ???? so she'd have to return my

???? with answers. Amir did this and I ended up spending all my credit having text chat with him. He was a blast. I regularly fell asleep chuckling away to myself because of some daft thing he'd written. I lay in bed LMAO. Sometimes it was sooooooo funny that I was LMFAO. (The F is a bad word.)

It must have been really difficult in the olden days when they didn't have mobile phones. What did people do for fun in those days, I wondered? Questions like this often ripped my knitting and regularly kept me awake at night, tossing and turning and groaning, because I couldn't find answers to them. How come there were no black champion skiers? How come when I was in Torremolinos with Mum and Dad the dogs in the street could understand Spanish much better than I could? Who was it that decided that a table was going to be called a *table* or an ear was going to be called an *ear* or yellow was going to be called *yellow*? Aaaaarrrrrhhhhh . . .

You could never find these answers in any books, not even in *The Monster Book of Facts* or in *The Monster Book of Facts Volume 2* that we had in our school library.

The teachers didn't know the answers and they all told me to stop asking questions like these. That's how I got to know the meaning of the words

banal
futile
obtuse
facile.

16

Classmates

I thought Amir would be pleased as Punch and Judy to see me when I went back to school the next day.

He wasn't.

I thought he would do the high five, pulling away at the last minute just as I moved in to slap his hand and shout, 'Howdy, best bud.'

He didn't.

I thought he might put his hand lower and say, 'downstairs', then fire it away for a split second before I hammered mine down leaving him to say, 'too slow'.

He didn't.

I thought he might say his Special Occasion Amir Greeting to me: 'All right, D-d-dildo'. The word dildo sounded a wee bit like Dylan and coz we both knew it was a really dirty woman's word that always made us howl with laughter.

But he didn't do this either.

In fact Amir was like a bear with a sore toe when I saw him sitting in our tutor class.

'All right, farty pants,' I said.

He was pretending to be reading a book about lions, but I knew he was doing fake reading because Amir wasn't the world's number one reader. He couldn't pull the clothes over my eyes.

'All right, baw-jaws,' I said, in case he really was in fact reading the book and was in fact pulling the clothes over my eyes.

But he said nothing. No LOLs or LMAOs today.

'Are you all right, amigo?' I asked him.

I put my hand on his shoulder and he put his head on the desk. I knew that something was up as best buds tend to know when their buddy is feeling like shite.

'Amir, what's wrong, buddy?' I asked him again.

'I hate this st-st-stupid fu-fu-fucking shitey arse place,' he said. That was the point I knew something had gone massive boobs up.

'Amir?' I said.

'This school's full of dicks and arseholes,' he said, before launching the lions book across the room like the best ultimate frisbee player in Scotland. It almost hit the only other person in the class, Charlotte Duffy, full force on the napper. She hardly moved. She never did in the morning. That was when she was given all her drugs to eat. She was like a mad spacer in the morning time.

She turned in our direction and said, 'Watch it, you, or else I'll . . .' And after that she just muttered something under her breath that I couldn't make out, but her face was all scrunched up; it was like she was talking to her desk. Round the twist or what?

'Sorry, Charlotte, that was an accident,' I said.

'I'm going to get you one of these days.' And then she said something that made my hands tingle and my face bendy. Something that made me want to jump on her *Teen Wolf* style and yank a big chunk out of her cheek.

She called me a 'Paki shagger'.

'What did you call me?' I asked her.

'You heard.'

'Say it again.'

'*Say it again.*'

'Say it again – I dare you.'

'*Say it again – I dare you.*' I hated it when people did the imitation voice stuff; it made my inside kettle hiss. I was totally hissed off at this stage.

'You're off your head, Charlotte.'

'We're all off our heads, daft arse. That's why we're in this shithole.'

143

'Buzz off, desk-licker.'

'Is your ear sore?' she said.

'What?'

'Is your ear sore?' she said, tugging at her own ear.

'What have they been feeding you?'

'It's a simple question. IS YOUR EAR SORE?' she screamed.

'I think you'd better take another pill coz I haven't a clue what –'

'Rubber ear.'

'What?'

'Rubber ear.'

I didn't know what to say. I screwed up my face.

'Big rubber ear.'

'What are you on about, headbanger?' I said. Off-the-radar chats happened every hour at Drumhill – that was why there were always people shouting, screaming, crying or trying to hurt either themselves or each other. On one side of our classroom was Amir with his head down hugging the desk, at the other was Charlotte Duffy doing an impression of the bonkers girl from *The Exorcist*. Add another forty or fifty people to the mix and you had a typical day at Drumhill Special School. No wonder people actually shat themselves all the time.

'Michelle Malloy gave you a big giant rubber ear. HA!' Charlotte said, a witch cackling.

Charlotte Duffy and Michelle Malloy weren't big boob-buddies so I didn't know how she knew all the juicy goss. I'd say that Michelle Malloy's brain was way too advanced for her and Charlotte Duffy to be anywhere near friends. I was positive Charlotte Duffy's brain was half the size of a normal brain. She used to pick at her bogging ears and chew the wax, and before that she used to say to the boys in the normal school that she'd yank their ying-yangs so hard that their goo-goo would come out. Crazy with a capital C.

I couldn't Adam and Eve it that she knew about Michelle Malloy. News spread around school like a gaggle of WAGS' legs.

'Who told you that pish?'

'Everyone knows.'

'Bet they don't.'

'Bet they do.'

'I don't give a hairy arse, Charlotte.'

'Yes you do.'

'No I don't.'

'Do.'

'Don't.'

'DO!'

'DON'T.' I think my shout silenced her a bit.

'I don't blame her. I mean, look at the state of you,' she said.

'Look at the state of you,' I said.

'*State of you.*'

'State of you.'

'STATE OF FUCKING YOU!' she roared.

'STATE OF FUCKING YOU!' I roared back. The pressure was rising. Mr Dog was simmering. I'd never wanted to scud a girl as much in all my puff.

'Look at you. You've got a face like a painter's radio, Mint.'

'So, you've got a fanny like a ripped-out fireplace.'

'Shut up.'

'You shut up.'

'NO, YOU SHUT UP.'

'YOU'VE GOT AN ARSE LIKE A BAG OF WASHING,' I shouted for real – it was nothing to do with Tourette's. I didn't mean to say these awful things. I only said them because Charlotte was being vile to me. I wasn't even the one who threw the lions book at her in the first place.

'SHUT UP, HORRIBLE BASTARD!' she screamed, before smashing her head on the desk. I think she was bubbling away to herself; her shoulders were doing the crying boogie dance. I felt the opposite of a love song but Charlotte Duffy bloody well deserved it. It wasn't my fault that she'd decided she was going to be in a mental mood all day. Before I had the chance to turn back to Amir she popped her head up from the desk and bawled, 'DYLAN MINT, YOU'RE A DIRTY FUCKING SHITBAG

AND I HOPE YOU DIE!' She would regret saying that when March came.

I didn't know what annoyed me most, being called a 'Paki shagger' or everyone knowing that Michelle Malloy had given me a Big Knock-back. I wasn't an expert in social things, but I was pretty sure Charlotte Duffy was being an atrocious racist beast when she said that I was a 'Paki shagger'. I'm only saying this because I don't think she meant that I had actually shagged someone from Pakistan, which I haven't and that's not because I'm racist – I just hadn't met anyone, other than Amir and his family, who I hadn't officially *met* met, but I knew they were from Pakistan and I knew for a fact that I hadn't shagged Amir or anyone from his family. So far I hadn't shagged anyone from any country or any city in the world. *Cool Things To Do Before I Cack It: Number One* clearly said this. I did hope Charlotte Duffy didn't think Amir and me were bare-arse boxers. I hoped nobody in the school thought that way.

Aaarrrghhh. I was boiling mad.

I closed my eyes and clenched my fists because I didn't want to pounce on Charlotte Duffy, kick her desk, lob chairs at her or introduce her to Mr Dog. I kept my eyes tightly closed. Miss Flynn told me to try to solve random problems in my head when I got stressed out or felt like I wanted to freak out with my hands or tongue. Since I was rank rotten at maths I did other problem-solving things. Miss Flynn called them brain-gym exercises.

So with my eyes in the darkness, to cool the jets, I did some brain gym. I tried to find another team in the Scottish, English, Welsh and Irish football leagues with the letter J in their name – apart from St Johnstone, that is.

I couldn't find any.

With my head on my desk I imagined scoring the winner for Scotland in the World Cup final after diving to get my noggin on the end of a rapido counter-attacking move. I knew this wasn't a brain-gym exercise or the solving of a difficult problem but it put a super-charged brake on my jets.

*

When I opened my eyes I noticed that Amir's shoulders were also doing the crying boogie dance.

'Are you OK, Amir, me old mucker?'

'I can't believe you said that to her.' He was giggling; his shoulders were doing the *cheery* boogie dance.

'Said what?'

'That her fa-fa-fanny was like a ripped-out fireplace.'

'Did you not hear what she said to me?'

'Classic.'

'She deserved it.'

'I know.'

'What was up with you this morning?' I asked him, which seemed to bring back all his memories from earlier.

'Same old shite.'

'What same old shite?'

'All the stuff about curry breath and stop stealing our jobs and Pakis can't play football. I'm sick of it.'

'Who was it? Doughnut again?'

'No.'

'Who then?'

'Snot Rag and Skittle.'

'Snot Rag and Skittle?'

'Skittle mainly.'

'Really?'

'Yes.'

'Don't take any crap from him.'

'What can I do?'

'Just nudge that wee clown and he'll fall over.'

'It's every day now.'

'Why didn't you tell me, Amir?'

'Because you have your own things to worry about.'

'So?'

'And Michelle Malloy gave you a big rubber ear.'

'OK.'

'Well, she did.'

'OK.'

'I'm just saying –'

'I heard you, Amir, for the love of f . . .' I said.

'What can I do, Dylan?'

'What about?'

'All the Paki stuff?'

'Oh, yeah. Well, you could have a square go with Skittle.'

'Have you seen me fighting, Dylan?' Big miserable face had returned to Amir.

'I wasn't serious, Amir.'

'I don't think I want to come to school any more.'

'Don't say that.'

'I wish I was a top scrapper then I'd just give them a dink to the jaw and that'd be the end of it.'

'They never say anything to you when I'm around,' I said.

'They wouldn't dare,' Amir said. 'Can I ask you something?'

'Go.'

'Do you think I smell of curry?'

Boy, oh boy, oh boy, oh boy, oh boy, oh boy, what a question for one best bud to ask another best bud. If I gave my honest answer, it would have made a meteor dent in our best bud days. My eyes flicked like a camera.

'Do you?'

'Erm, of course not.'

'Really?'

'Don't listen to any of those plebs, Amir.'

'So, no curry smell?'

'No, none.'

'You m-m-mean that?'

'Course I do.'

'So I don't stink of curry then?'

'No, Amir, you don't stink of curry.'

'But Skittle said –'

'Next time *you* just ask *them* why they always reek of grease and chips and pish and farts, then see what they have to say.' I had to tell porkies through my teeth so Amir wouldn't tell me that he didn't want to be best buds any more, which was too scary to think about.

Imagine it!

I'd be left to kick stones about the playground on my own and I'd have nobody to send text messages to and nobody to talk dirty to either. I had to porky pie. Mine was a white lie. I felt rubbish after saying it to him, but the *truth* truth was that the bold Amir came to school loads smelling like he'd just popped out of Korma Chameleon's kitchen after a twenty-four-hour sweaty shift. I didn't mind – I quite like the smell of curry in the classroom. It was one of my fav foods anyway and the reek always got me in the mood for my din-dins. The curry smell sure as Hell beat the constant whiff of bum pong that hovered about the school. Almost every student at Drumhill reeked of something ming, like cabbage, farts, grease and damp towels. Give me Amir's smell any day. I used Lynx Africa every day, sometimes twice a day, so I was all right in the pong department.

'But why does everyone keep saying it, Dylan?'

'I think it's the colour of your skin, Amir.'

'The colour of my skin?'

'Yes.'

'What's up with the colour of my skin?' Amir asked, as if he didn't know. Honestly, butter wouldn't have dissolved in the mouth of that laddie.

'I think some people don't like it.'

'But why?'

'Some people are scared of it.'

'How the bloody Hell can you be scared of someone's skin?'

'I don't know, mate, but some people seem to be offended by other people's skin colour.' Amir looked at me similar to the way I look at Mum when the sad clouds float over me and she makes everything A-OK by giving me one of her hug specials. I wanted to give him a hug special, then perhaps he'd return to sunshine and happy Amir. If I did hug him though, Charlotte Duffy would probably put it all over Facebook that I was a Paki shagger for real.

'But how can you be offended by something like skin, Dylan?'

'I don't know, Amir, but some evil people are.'

'But skin doesn't even t-t-talk?'

'It's crazy, I know.'

'You bet it's crazy, Dylan. You bet it in the nearest bookie shop it's crazy.'

'It's Billy Bonking Bonkers.'

'I j-j-just don't understand it.'

'It's like one of those mad questions that we can never answer,' I said to Amir.

'Like why do we have the same word for bark on a tree and bark for a dog's talking?'

'Or why *gay* means to have it off with another guy and to be dead happy?'

'Exactly, Dylan. Exactly.'

'I mean, how can you be dead happy if another guy is putting his ting-tang in your bu-bu-bumbaleery? Eh? Answer me that, Amir?' There was no answer as the world was off its rocker.

'I don't really know, Dylan,' he said.

Sometimes me and Amir would go off on one and say the barmiest things that would never ever enter the minds of normal human beings. 'Normal people don't ask such things,' Mrs Seed always said to Amir in class when he asked his Whack Attack question.

'No, I don't know either, I suppose.'

'I do know it's not normal to hate people just because of their skin,' Amir said.

'I know.'

'I mean, you'd need to be mentally retarded to hate skin.'

'But Skittle and Snot Rag *are* retarded, Amir,' I said.

'Suppose.'

'See? No need to worry.'

I knew we were all retarded but those two were more retarded because they did extra-retarded things like seeing who could hold their pee in the longest before shooting it out pretending that it was a fireman's hose, or seeing who could pee the highest in the bog cubicles, or seeing who had the smelliest finger after sticking it up their own bum. Me and Amir never did anything as batty as that.

'Yeah ... but ... still.'

'I agree, it's not right.'

'I think I want to go home,' Amir said.

'Don't do that, Amir.'

'You did it when Michelle Malloy gave you a massive ru-ru-rubber ear.'

'Aw, cheers.'

'Sorry, but you know what I mean. I'm fed up with it all.'

'Yes, but I got into mega trouble and I didn't really do anything when I went home.'

'What did you do?'

'Mainly sat in my room.'

'Doing what?'

'Thinking.'

'About what?'

'Nothing really, just random stuff.'

'Nude girls?'

'No.'

'Bet you were.'

'Bet I wasn't.'

'I bet you were all over the internet.'

'Bet I wasn't.'

'Bet you were looking at blow jobs and pumping,' he said, looking around before he said the words *blow job* and *pumping*, which he whispered.

'Bet I wasn't.' This was a proper LOL moment, but I didn't LOL.

'Bet you were.' I was just about to give Amir a dead arm, in a best bud way, when out of the corner of my left eye I saw him.

Skittle.

He hobbled into the class dragging his wonky legs behind him. Amir put his head on the desk. Charlotte Duffy took her head off her desk and blew me a colossal raspberry and did a man-fiddling-with-himself gesture with her hand as if to say that I was a masturbator.

I twirled my index fingers around my temples in return.

Touché, Charlotte Duffy!

I walked over to Skittle's desk. The bell was about to go and people were streaming and shuffling into the room. I had to make this quick. Darn snaptastic quick. I still had to keep my promise to help my best bud Amir and remember *Cool Things To Do Before I Cack It: Number Two: make Amir a happy chappy again instead of a miserable c***!* This was a perfect moment to prove to him what I was all about, to show him what he'd be missing when I was gone.

'Skittle, I've got a wee bone to pick with you,' I said, trying to act all cool and hard like the T-Birds from *Grease*.

'What?'

'What's with you taking the piss out of Amir all the time?'

'What?'

'You heard, Skittle. You've been ripping the piss out of Amir.'

'What are you on about, you mongo?'

'You'd better well pack it in,' I said, putting on my best Hard Man Who Doesn't Take No Shit From Nobody face, which we learnt to do in Mr Grant's drama class.

'Or else what?'

'I'm just saying, pack it in, all right?'

'Shut your gub, cock-bawz.'

'If I see you doing it again . . .'

Then Skittle stood closer to me and puffed his wee chest out like people do when they want a piece of the action or want to go to town, which we also learnt in Mr Grant's class. Come to think of it, Mr Grant's class was all about standing up for yourself and taking no crap from no one and having a go and duffing up folk.

'. . . Or what?' he said.

This was exactly the same as our drama class improvisations (which I loved), except this was for real. I could smell the grease off Skittle's breath. *Oh, sugar of a shitey stick*, I thought. *What now?*

'I'm telling you, Skittle . . .'

'What are you going to do about it, Dildo, eh?' he said, and moved even closer so that we were touching man boobs.

That was when Skittle made me majorly nervous. I'm not that comfortable with people I hardly know being so close to me. I cleared my throat so aggressively loud it made him back off a smidgen. When I say cleared my throat, it was more like a wolf pack clearing their throats. When Skittle backed off a smidgen, this told me that I had the upper hand in our tussle, and I remembered that Dad always told me whenever I had the upper hand in tussles: 'Never NEVER back down. Stand your bloody ground and then always ALWAYS advance.' This was invaluable advice from the military, coming direct from top brass, so it had to be good advice. I took it. Just like Dad when guys inside and outside the pub 'fucked with his karma'. Bad move to do that when military experts are involved.

'I'll knock your bloody racist block off, that's what I'll do,' I said. At the same moment my head started twitching and ticking.

'Shut up, Tic Tac, and go back to your fucking monkey,' he said, nodding to Amir.

'What did you say?'

'I said . . .' He moved closer to me again, meaning my advance was rubbish. '. . . Shove it up your mum's stinking kipper, Tourette's Boy.'

Wow!

Wait a blinking minute!

Hold the Goddamn press!

Un-be-liev-able.

A comment like this was a red carpet to a bull shopping in a place that sells nothing but mountains of cut-glass crystal.

Always advance.

'You gammy-legged wee twat.' I cat-pounced and grabbed him around the neck with one hand so tight I felt his Adam's apple wobble in my thumb. I squeezed hard until his face went alcoholic-nose red. Then I booted one of his gammy legs below the knee and that was it. Skittle fell to the floor like a sack of spuds.

Crash!

Bang!

Wallop!

Amir was groaning and whooping up the back. Charlotte Duffy screamed and was pulling at her hair, mad excited. Mentalist.

'What do you have to say now, you wee tosspot?' I shouted down at Skittle.

He was curled up in a ball and shaking uncontrollably. I was thinking of taking a penalty but that would have been taking liberties and I am not a liberty taker. In any case before I could cock back my left foot (that's my strongest), Mr Comeford roared, 'ENOUGH, DYLAN MINT!' into my face, grabbed me full force by the collar and huckled me really aggressively out of the room Flash Gordon style. My shirt collar ripped. And, because I tucked my shirt into my pants, my pants got yanked right up my bum and my bum and ball-sack hurt like a mofo. I thought of having Mr Comeford charged with GBH and the ripping of private property and the hurting of my bum-hole–ball-sack combo. But damn! Blast! Mum and I didn't have a brief or the brass to get me any of the top legal minds in Scotland. The upshot was, I didn't do anything else about the issue of Mr Comeford's assault on me. But the more I thought of it, the more I could have had that man's arse on a plate. I could see the headline: *Teacher Tampers With Terminal Teenager.*

Again I was left to stand with my face millimetres from the V in the corner of the wall outside Miss Flynn's office. All because I tried to help my best bud out of a spot of racist bother.

I did brain gym.

I fiddled with Green in my pocket.

I counted how many clubs had the colour green in their

football strips. I made this harder because I counted from *all* the leagues in Europe. Olympic brain gym.

I didn't really remember too much about the scrap with Skittle, but I did remember that when I was being led out Charlotte Duffy twirled her index fingers around her temples at me. That image actually made me laugh because it was a top-notch touché moment.

Grade A to Charlotte Duffy.

Mentalist.

17
Millionaire

Miss Flynn called Mum to see if she could come and pick me up from school. She said I'd got myself into 'a bit of a pickle'. When she was on the phone, Miss Flynn winked at me. If we'd been at a wicked club or hip bar and I was ten years older and she winked at me in the same way, I'd have sauntered over and bought that chick a half pint of lager. Then she handed me the receiver and Miss Flynn's phone ear was touching my ear; it was hot and perfumey, which made me feel gooey down below.

'Look, Dylan, I'm tied up with something. Can you make your own way home?' Mum said.

'Are you mad at me?'

'No, sweetheart, I'm not mad, but I have to go.'

'Will we have soup tonight and watch the telly together?'

'Sounds like a plan.'

'I'll pimp the soup if you want?'

'Brilliant. Can't wait. Put Miss Flynn back on.'

'OK, bye,' I said, and handed the phone to Miss Flynn, who made a date for Mum to come into school for a good old-fashioned chinwag.

*

I knew most teenagers didn't like hanging out with the oldies, but doing it some of the time was OK. And it was A-OK when me and Mum ate our soup and watched *Who Wants To Be A Millionaire?* together. Either I'd shout 'IT'S STARTING!' or Mum would if we weren't both in the living room already.

'What's in this, chef?' She called me chef because that was what I was like when I was pimping soup. Mum knew not to come into the kitchen when the heat was on.

'So, tonight we have tomato soup . . .'

'Of course.'

'. . . with some paprika, black pepper, basil leaves, a tin of mixed beans . . .'

'Mmm, it smells delicious, chef.'

'. . . oh, and tarragon.'

'Oooooo, tarragon,' Mum said, widening her eyes. 'Who's after a Michelin star then?'

I laughed because they only give, like, the world's best

pimpers of food a Michelin star and it takes donkey's years to get one, and you have to work all the hours God sends and risk losing your wife and kids because you never get to see them, and then your liver becomes mushy with all the pressure booze you drink. And all for a blinkin' Michelin star. I didn't want one, no siree. Maybe I could be a No Michelin Star Chef when I was older. No, wait – I couldn't because of you-know-what. Sometimes I have sieve head.

'Taste it,' I said.

Mum slurped the soup. 'Oh, Dylan, it's delicious.'

'Really?'

'Totally love it, chef.'

'Fantastico,' I said, and slurped my first spoonful. It was delicious. 'Shizenhowzen!'

'What?'

'I forgot the crusty bread.'

Crusty bread isn't big red onions so I couldn't blame crusty bread for making my peepers stream. No. It was thinking about me and Mum having quality time together that made them waterfall. I had to lob the third slice out as some snot dripped on to it while I was cutting it. In that moment I could see Mum staring at me while I was lying peaceful in my coffin. She was in bits. Screaming and screaming. People had to drag her away from the coffin in case she pulled it down on top of herself. Then I imagined that I rolled out of the coffin and did a massive roly-poly down the church aisle and Mum had to go on her hands and knees in order to catch me. I didn't want Mum to be sad.

'IT'S STARTING!'

'OK.' I splashed my face and blew my hooter.

The thousand-pound question was a complete doddle for Mum.

Q: *The TV series* Sex and the City *is based on a book by which writer?*
a) *Carrie Bradshaw*
b) *Candace Bradshaw*
c) *Candace Bushnell*
d) *Carrie Bushnell*

'Would Dad be your Phone-a-Friend?' I asked Mum.

'He can't get to a phone, Dylan.'

'I know, but for talking sake. Would he be?'

'Depends on the question, doesn't it?' she said, and dipped some crusty bread into her delicious soup.

'The bold Amir would be my Phone-a-Friend,' I told Mum, 'especially if I had an epically hard cricket question.'

Mum was on a major roll: she answered the two-thousand-pound question right. The five-thousand-quid question was no probs for Big Chick Mint.

The roll stopped: she didn't know the ten-thousand-pound question.

50:50?

Phone-a-Friend?

Ask the Audience?

Not on your nelly.

Enter Dylan Mint with his brain after seventeen hours at the gym.

What a stonker of a question, right up my *strada*:

Q: *Which football club was the first to introduce the dugout in the 1920s?*
a) Arsenal
b) Airdrieonians
c) Aston Villa
d) Aberdeen

When I said, 'D, Aberdeen. Final answer', I got a wee flutter in my belly. Me and Mum were ten large in the red. God, imagine if we had ten large for real – I'd suggest a no-expenses-spared family holiday to Torremolinos again, or Kavos.

'Yeah, way to go, Dylan!' Mum said, and we high-fived. What could be better than high-fiving your mum?

Ding! Dong!

'Was that the door?' Mum asked.

'I didn't hear anything,' I lied. Who, in the name of the wee man, would be calling just as the twenty-grand question was about to be asked?

Ding! Dong!

'It *is* the door,' Mum said, and got up.

I puffed my cheeks out and phewed!

'Don't answer it,' I said.

'It could be important, Dylan.'

'But it's the twenty-thousand-quid question.' If we'd had the proper telly package I could have paused it and waited, but because we were stuck with antique crap telly there should have been a ban on house visits after eight o'clock at night.

Mum was at the front door doing her wee giggle. Then a deep voice came in. Then no voices.

I peeked out of the blinds and saw it. WHAT THE . . . ? In Dad's space again. The cheeky bugger. Me and Amir should acid attack that maroon shite heap then he'd get the message and know not to park in Dad's space again. Maybe this taxi bastard was a real-life stalker, harassing Mum all the time and being a total sex pest? Maybe Mum was at her rock bottom with this taxi creep trying to enter her zones. If he tried any funny business, I'd be out there with my piping hot soup and he'd be getting it flush in the mush. Filth monger.

More giggling and hushed voices.

I had too much brain frazzle to focus on the question. I didn't know the answer anyway. *The Bauhaus movement.* The what?

'Look who it is, Dylan,' Mum said.

I stared at the telly. The 50K question came and went. My concentration was shot to shit.

'Hi, Dylan,' the taxi man said.

'We're watching telly so we don't need a taxi,' I said.

'Tony was just passing,' Mum said.

I did muffle voice, like a baby.

'What was that, Dylan?'

'We live in a cul-de-sac so it's impossible to be *just passing*.'

The taxi man laughed.

'TAXI CUNT.'

'Dylan!'

'He's right, Moira. How can you be passing in a cul-de-sac?' The taxi man smiled at me.

I looked away. Perv.

'FAT LIAR.'

'I'm warning you, Dylan,' Mum said. 'That's not involuntary.' She knew when it was easy for me to bring it out. Mums *do* know everything.

'You're dead right, Dylan. Actually I was dropping someone off nearby and I thought I'd pop in, say hello.'

'Hello. Cheerio.'

'Did we not speak about this, Dylan?'

'Maybe this was a bad idea, Moira.' The taxi man whispered into Mum's ear.

'No, Tony, he has to learn. He's not ruling the roost here.'

Mum tried to whisper super silent, but my bionic hearing heard it all. 'Sit down, Tony.'

Tony the taxi driver sat in Dad's chair. Who Wants To RUIN A Millionaire?

'CHEEKY FUCKER.'

'Dylan, I'm warning you.'

'I can't help it.'

'Oh, I think you can,' Mum said. 'Apologise to Tony.'

'What for?'

'Honestly, Moira, I understand.'

'I'm waiting, Buster,' Mum said with folded arms.

'Sorry.'

'Ah, you're OK, Dylan. No harm done.'

'You're in Dad's space again,' I said.

'Am I?'

'Yes.'

'I'll fix that next time and park up a bit,' the taxi man said. Listen to him: *next time*. Not on my watch, Buster!

'No, the chair,' I said, and pointed.

'Stupid me,' the taxi man said, and tried to stand up. 'I'll move over here so.'

'You will do no such thing,' Mum said to the taxi man. '*Stop it now!*' she said to me.

I counted to twelve and a half in my head.

No one spoke during that time.

Talk about spoiling the mum–son atmos.

'Your car's maroon,' I said.

'Yes, do you like maroon cars?'

'But if you're a taxi driver why isn't your car silver or beige?'

'I don't know, mate. Haven't really thought about it.'

He was shooting blanks if he thought I was his mate.

'Most taxis are silver or beige unless they're Hackneys,' I said.

'Yeah, you're right.'

'Do you have a Hackney?'

'No.'

'Why not? They're way cooler than that maroon thing.'

The taxi man started laughing. 'I agree, Dylan. But Hackneys are used more in London than they are up here.'

'I've seen them on *Eastenders*,' I said. 'They make too much noise anyway.'

'That's why I like driving my maroon car.'

Mum sat down because she felt that we had cooled the jets. Now it was like a triangle of weirdness in the living room. I looked at Mum, who looked at the taxi man, who looked at Mum. Then I looked at the taxi man, who looked at me and grinned. Then we all looked at the telly.

'What are you watching?' the taxi man said.

'*Who Wants To Be A Millionaire?*' I said.

'I love that show,' the taxi man said.

I bet he didn't love it and was just saying that to get

into Mum's knick-knacks. I bet he was thick as old rope and wouldn't even get past the five-hundred-quid question. I bet he didn't know anything about *Sex in the City* or football dugouts. That was the reason he drove people around all day, because you didn't need brain cells to do a job like that. Playing *Who Wants To Be A Millionaire?* with the taxi man would be as useful as a willy on a lesbian.

'We love it too. It's become a bit of a ritual for me and Dylan,' Mum said.

'I bet it has,' the taxi man said.

'Dylan's pretty good too, aren't you, Dylan?'

I said nothing, just kept staring at the telly.

I read the 150 Gs question.

Q: *Who coined the phrase 'That which does not kill us makes us stronger'?*
a) *Friedrich Nietzsche*
b) *Immanuel Kant*
c) *Jean-Jacques Rousseau*
d) *Friedrich Wilhelm Joseph Schelling*

I read it about four times. My hands tingled. I knew it. I knew it. The bloody 150 Gs question and me, Dylan Mint, who went to Drumhill School, knew it. This was a new record for me. The taxi man would soon know that he was in the presence of the real deal brain in this house. Miss Flynn, you and your office posters were legendinas.

'I know it, Mum, I know it,' I said.

'Yeah, I think I know it as well,' the taxi man said.

WHAT THE F . . . ?

'Bet you don't,' I said.

'Bet I do,' he said.

The contestant asked the audience, who were fifty shades of thick.

'BET YOU DON'T KNOW IT,' I shouted.

'Dylan!'

'OK. After three we'll say it together, OK?' the taxi man said.

'OK,' I said.

'Moira, you count to three.'

'OK, ready?' Mum said.

'We only shout out the correct letter,' I said.

'Gotcha.'

The contestant decided to Phone-a-Friend, who sounded as though they ate soup with a fork. Clueless.

'One . . . Two . . . Three . . .'

'A.'

'A.'

We said it at the same time.

Wow!

The taxi man knew the answer.

'How did you know that?' I said.

'I'm reading a book about him at the moment.'

'About Friedrich Nietzsche?'

'Yes.'

'Any good?'

'I'll let you borrow it if you want.'

'Erm . . .' I didn't know what to say.

'That'd be nice, Dylan, wouldn't it?' Mum said.

'Erm . . .' I was still biting my tongue.

'That's nice of you, Tony,' Mum said.

'It'd be my pleasure,' the taxi man said.

'What do you say, Dylan?'

'Erm . . . Thanks.' That would be nice, I thought.

'No problem. Just as soon as I finish it, I'll pop it over.'

'Will I understand it?'

'I'm sure there's not much you don't understand, Dylan,' the taxi man said.

I wasn't sure if that was a compliment or not, but I smiled just in case. We never got to see the next question because the contestant's loaf was still in the bakery.

18

Counselling

'Mrs Mint, we've noticed that Dylan hasn't been himself these past few weeks,' Miss Flynn said.

'To be honest I've noticed it myself,' Mum said.

Well, big WOW, Mum and Miss Flynn!

Of course
OF COURSE
OF COURSE
I haven't been myself.

A tremendous bomb fell from a great blinkin' height and smashed into me.

ME.

REMEMBER?

Not YOU.

INTO ME.

Dylan (No Middle Name) Mint.

But I didn't cry, not once.

OK, OK, I admit it: I cried at the start when I found out, because I was trying to *be myself*, trying to keep it real. And I cried when Michelle Malloy gave me a rubber ear, but those tears were nothing to do with you-know-what, therefore the Big Knock-back tears from Michelle Malloy can't be counted.

PPPPPHHHHHEEEEEWWWWWW!

'He's just not been the same bubbly Dylan,' Miss Flynn said, looking at me and then Mum and then me again, with a wee smile on her face. Cutey-pie face.

'You're telling me,' Mum said, looking at me then Miss Flynn then me again, with a scowl on her face.

Then Mum and Miss Flynn looked at each other and I was a big elephant in the room.

'It's becoming an issue, I'm afraid, Mrs Mint.'

'Moira.'

'It's becoming an issue, Moira.'

'Oh, you don't need to tell me. I'm his mother – I see it every day.'

Again I was being seen and not heard so I bit the nails on my thumbs; my jaw a pneumatic drill grinding away at them. Then I swallowed the nails and started on the skin below the parts that look like half-moons. They bled so I sucked all the blood back into my bloodstream in case I keeled over due to litres and litres of lost blood and urgently required a blood transfusion.

I'M HERE!

HELLO!

OVER HERE.

DOING MAD WAVING.

I'M NOT REALLY STARING AT THE CARPET. I'M LISTENING TO EVERY WORD YOU'RE SAYING AND I CAN TELL YOU I DON'T LIKE WHAT I'M HEARING.

SEE ME?

How the dog's bollocks could I *be myself* after hearing that news from the doc?

Miss Flynn's office was super-duper cool with enormous leather chairs that you sank into, huge plants that almost touched the ceiling and nice pictures of beaches, rainforests and waterfalls hanging on the walls. Sometimes she played music to calm down students who acted all loony head cases. She'd tell us to sink into the chair, sip some water and listen to music. It worked a treat for me. That day after our football game when it all kicked off she played Sigur Rós especially for me. They're a band from Iceland and some of them have got beards and they wear winter clothes cause it's totally freezing in Iceland, and when it's not bloody brass monkeys it's full of volcanic ash and people who are much more skint than Mum because they've had a whopper of a dosh crisis and everyone is now gloomy grumpy pants over there.

'Is there anything we should know about?' Miss Flynn asked.

Mum shuffled in her leather chair like she was trying to scratch her bum without anyone detecting her. My peepers were on fire.

'Well . . . Erm . . . There's . . .'

'SHUT UP. NOTHING. GGGGGGGRRRRRR.'

'Dylan, don't interrupt,' Mum said.

'Would you like some water, Dylan?' Miss Flynn asked.

I shook my head. Negative, miss.

'FUCK WATER TITS.' I *meant* to only shake my head. At that moment I wanted to sniffle because I was fed up with that voice, that animal, that other person, that rat living inside me. I was fed up not just to the back teeth, but the front, sides and gums as well.

Then Mum said in her whisper voice, 'Well, there's the situation with his dad.'

'I understand,' Miss Flynn said in her own whisper voice, which I'd never heard before. 'It must be tough for everyone concerned.'

'It is tough.'

TOUGH?

Of course it was TOUGH.

There was Dad, lying deep in enemy territory being blasted at by rebels on a daily basis, and Miss Flynn and Mum were calling it 'tough'. What a blinkin' insult. Brave Dad was fighting against the forces of evil in order to build paths for a country's freedom and these two were sitting on big soft chairs drinking sweet cold water and saying how TOUGH it must be.

INCREDIBLE OR WHAT?

If 'tough' was a tiny tent then Dad was a mammoth skyscraper. In fact I'd have gone further and said he was a supersonic space-scraper.

It would've been much better if I'd just stopped listening and thought about other things, like Amir stuck in English class without me. Mrs Seed was doing mad hard past tense verbs and he was shock shocking at verbs. He was shock shocking at grammar in general, but that didn't make him a bad person. He'd be rocking on his chair in agony because he didn't know the past participle of the verb *to eat*. His dad would be Mr Angry Pants because the bold Amir was never going to be a doctor, lawyer or engineer. He'd make a brilliant waiter or kitchen helper though – he loves home economics.

'This isn't funny, Dylan. This is deadly serious,' Mum said.

'What?' I said.

'I wouldn't be laughing if I were you, young man.'

'I'm not laughing.'

'Take that smirk off your face this minute.' Mum said this through her gritted teeth.

'Dylan, this isn't a time for laughter,' Miss Flynn said. 'Do you understand that? Dylan?'

'But I'm –'

'We want to help you,' Miss Flynn said.

Why weren't they listening to me? Who were these heart-less people?

'Look at him, Miss Flynn, sitting there sniggering away. He's got no respect for anyone any more. He's a cheeky little runt . . . You're a cheeky little runt.'

'I'M NOT FUCKING LAUGHING.' This wasn't in the other guy's voice and certainly not in the dog's either; it was all mine. When the stares and silence came, I sank deep into the comfy leather chair, folded my arms, breathed through my nose and thought of all the football teams in the Scottish, English, Irish and Welsh leagues that didn't have any of the letters F, O, T, B, A, L in their names.

Now this was TOUGH too.

'See what I have to put up with, Miss Flynn?'

'Call me Sandra.'

'He hasn't really had a father figure in his life,' Mum said in her whispering voice.

'Is that situation likely to be resolved any time soon?'

'God only knows, Sandra. We're still waiting on word.'

'And that could be a while, I presume?'

'Yes.'

'Shame.'

'These things seem to go on for an eternity.'

'I can imagine.'

'It's just one thing after another.'

'And he still doesn't . . .'

'No, he doesn't.'

'Probably for the best, Moira.'

'I think so.'

They looked at me with big floppy hound-dog eyes.

'Yes, probably for the best,' Miss Flynn said again.

'It is.'

'Indeed.'

'Anyway, he's got enough to worry about without me landing *that* on his lap as well.'

'I think you're absolutely right, Moira. Better for everyone.'

'It is.'

'He probably needs protecting from it.'

'Oh, he does.'

'Yes.'

'Look, Sandra, I know he can be a wee bugger at times and I lose my patience with him, but deep down he's a good lad and he's not got long to go here now, as you know.'

AS YOU KNOW *WHAT*?

Miss Flynn knew?

Jeeze Louise!

Was there nothing sacred any more?

'No, I suppose he doesn't have long to go here, which, I may add, we're all sad about. Dylan will be a great loss to our school when he eventually leaves.'

Really? Was Miss Flynn talking about me leaving school? Or *leaving* leaving?

'I'll make sure he pulls his socks up.'

'We'd appreciate that.'

'Oh, don't you worry about that.'

'The fighting and aggression is something we can deal with in-house, but the truancy can be problematic.'

'Oh, he'll be in school all right, even if I have to drag him here myself every morning.'

'It's just that Dylan would be placing himself in a vulnerable, if not precarious, position if he was wandering the streets all by himself instead of coming to school, you know?'

'Oh, you don't need to tell me, Sandra.'

'Drumhill is a sanctuary for students like Dylan.'

'My nerves are shattered with the thought of him all alone . . .'

'Exactly.'

'People laughing at him and teasing him . . .'

'Yes.'

'No, you mark my words, Sandra. He'll be here every day from now on.'

'That's all we ask, Moira.'

'And if there is anything – anything so much as a sniff of something – you'll let me know straight away?'

'Of course I will.'

'DUNDEE, DUNDEE, DUNDEE,' I screamed, semi-bouncing off the comfy leather chair.

'What's the big fascination with Dundee, Dylan?' Mum asked. This wasn't one of those rhetoric questions.

'Dundee is the only team with no letter F or O or T or B or A or L in its name.'

'Well, that's just wonderful, Dylan,' Miss Flynn said.

'No, you don't get it. Dundee is the ONLY team in the Scottish, English, Irish or Welsh leagues with no letter F or O or T or B or A or L in its name. The ONLY team and I got it all on my own. Amazing.'

'Really?' Mum said in her I-couldn't-give-a-flying-fahoola voice.

'You don't believe me?'

'Of course we believe you, Dylan,' Miss Flynn said in her you-are-wired-to-the-moon-young-man voice.

I'd heard both these voices many times before.

'That's what I call major brain gym, miss.'

'It certainly is, Dylan, it certainly is.' Miss Flynn seemed impressed with my brain-gym exercise. She'd have felt pleased as brain gym was her gift to me.

'You should try it, Mum.'

'Maybe on Sunday when the papers arrive I will,' Mum said.

'But that's Ronan Keating. That's not fair.'

'It's perfectly fair,' Mum said.

At that moment I wished I could press the massive *Family Fortunes* buzzer. The one that makes the *you're so wrong that you're a pure redneck* sound.

'That wouldn't be a proper brain-gym exercise.'

'Nonsense.'

'It would be Ronan Keating,' I said.

'It would not be Ronan Keating, Dylan,' Mum said.

'OK, I'm confused now. What's Ronan Keating got to do with anything?' Miss Flynn asked.

'Oh, it's the rhyming slang Dylan likes to use. *Ronan Keating* means *cheating*,' Mum said.

'Oh, I get it.'

'It's like our own language, miss,' I said.

'That's fabulous. Do you know any more?' Miss Flynn asked.

'Cristiano Ronaldo.'

'Which is?'

'That's a killer to get. It means *hot*, because *caldo* means *hot* in Italian, which rhymes with *Ronaldo*. So that's like a Portuguese–Italian–English one, which is for advanced rhymers.'

'Oh, very clever.' Miss Flynn seemed thrilled.

'Then there's Richard Gere.'

'Which is . . . ?'

'Beer.'

'Well, you're a man with a bag of tricks, aren't you,

Dylan?' And she widened her eyes towards Mum, like what adults do when ten-year-olds ask them what the meaning of *fanny* is.

'Then if I go to the dentist, I'm going for a Bob Dylan.'

'Oh, I like that one.' Miss Flynn was flying with enthusiasm.

'But I never go to the dentist.'

'Aw, well, but it's still a good one. Maybe I can use it.'

'If you want.'

'Know any more?' Miss Flynn asked.

'If a man and woman are guzzling glasses and glasses of wine, then afterwards they might want to have a Billy Bragg –'

'Enough, Dylan!' Mum jumped in. 'His mind is in overdrive sometimes.'

'Aren't they all at that age?'

'That's his father's influence right there.'

'Right. So, I think we'll wrap it up there, Moira.'

'OK, right you are.'

They both got up from their seats. That was my cue to get up also.

'And is everything OK with you, apart from . . . ?'

'Yes, why wouldn't it be?' Mum seemed annoyed at this question and she was short with Miss Flynn.

'Oh, no reason. Just thought I'd check, Moira, that's all.'

'Well, I'm fine.'

I was getting a wee bit red and sweaty with wanting to say, 'Shut up, Mum.'

'Oh, sorry, I didn't mean to pry.'

'Thanks for seeing us, Miss Flynn,' Mum said, and put out her hand.

What happened to Sandra? Adults are weird sometimes.

'Thanks for coming in.' Miss Flynn shook Mum's hand.

'Not at all. And remember: if he steps out of line you know where to find me.'

'I won't hesitate.'

'Well, thanks again for seeing us, Miss Flynn.'

'You can probably run back to class now, Dylan.'

'Can I not go home with Mum?'

'Do what Miss Flynn is telling you to do,' Mum snarled.

'But it's only verbs we're doing.'

'Exactly, and how important are they?' Miss Flynn said.

'But I know them all.'

'Even phrasal verbs?' Miss Flynn said. She was a crafty little devil.

'What are those?' I asked.

'Exactly,' Mum said. 'Now do what Miss Flynn is telling you or I'll take you there myself.' Holy Moly, that would be the biggest redneck ever!

'No, I'm going.' And I was out of there Speedy-Gonzales-On-Speed super fast.

Whhhhhhoooooosssssshhhhhh!

The past participle of the verb *to eat* is *eaten*.

Some verbs are awesome, which is a word used by excited daft Americans. I discovered that you could use verbs that made you sound like you were speaking Chinese when you said them dead fast, like *sing, sang, sung*. Awesome.

19
Rap

Dear Dad

What's up, dogg? That's what some rappers say when they bump into each other in the street or at an awards ceremony. It means 'How are you doing, friend?' Sometimes they say 'Word up?' or just 'Word'. But my favourite is 'What's up, dogg?' although I do quite like 'Word up, dogg?' as well. But if you say any of these in a Scottish accent people will think you have just come out of the loony bin, or you are soon to be carted off to the nearest loony bin. LOL. This means Laugh Out Loud. Get it? It's an acronym. Mrs Seed taught us that the other week in English class. You can say lots of cool stuff in acronym speak. For example LMAO means Laughing My Arse Off and ADIDAS means All Dames In Denmark Are Sexy. You can make your own up if you want. It's dead easy.

School is crazy these days. Caa-razy with a crazy capital C. We were stuffed at football by Shawhead, and you know how rubbish they are, right? Then I got into a fight. Well, not a fight exactly, more like a scuffle with this big guy from our school. But only because he was going to batter Amir and Amir is my best bud, and I remember you always advised that I should lamp anyone who was threatening me. Give them the old knuckle sandwich, you said. This guy wasn't threatening me directly, but he was going to take a penalty into Amir's head. So he was kind of threatening me because if any fella says something evil to Amir, even though he is the worst goalie on earth, they may as well be saying something evil to me too, and that's why I jumped on this big guy's back and held on to him like a man possessed by a rabid dingo dog. Then all Hell broke loose and the next thing I knew I had my face against the wall waiting for Mr McGrain to come and give me a good old-fashioned talking-to. They said I tried to bite him on the back of the head, which is a load of old crap. But I've promised to be good from now on in.

I did a really bonkers thing though ... I bet you're wondering what it is? I asked this lassie to go to the Halloween disco with me.

Like, on a date. It was terrible because I was shaking like the guy who sells *The Big Issue* outside Asda when I asked her. I only did it because it was on my list of things to do before I ... But I haven't told you about my list yet. I thought with you being over there stuck in a war zone it would be bad enough without me ranting about my own problems. Anyway the girl said NO, which sort of puts a damper on school at the moment. It's a chief pain because she's really nice-looking too. Maybe I'm just not her type.

Not much else has been happening except that Mum has taken to putting food in her eyes, which is the weirdest thing she's done since making us a mixture of beans, tuna and sweetcorn mush for our dinner. Remember that?

DIS-

Gusting!

So

DIS-

Gusting

that you threw yours against the wall.

That was a LOL moment if ever there was one.

Also, some mad person has been phoning the house and refusing to talk. Whenever I pick it up they say nada on the other end. I think it's a man because of the breathing, but I can't be too sure. We had a talk in school about the dangers of online gangs of perverts grooming boys and girls for illegal activities, so I'm thinking he could be part of that gang. Everything's A-OK though, you don't need to worry – I haven't been on the net talking to gangs of perverts or meeting strangers in parks or outside underground stations. I have my head screwed on.

Oh, I almost forgot. I saw something totally out of left field. (That's a baseball analogy.) Mum was out doing the shopping and was too lazy to walk home (I said that the exercise was as good as anything she'd get in boot camp though) so she flagged a taxi. And the next thing you know, abracadabra, the taxi driver's in our kitchen guzzling down a hot cup of tea. But don't fret. I told him off for parking in your space. His car wasn't as good as yours either. His was not silver with spoilers and gleaming chrome alloys that could go zero to sixty in no time. Zoom!

I loved that car. It's a pity we're not allowed to keep things like that when you're away at the war. I've never understood that. It's one of those bonkers questions that keep me awake at night ... along with many others. I hope they let you have it back when you return. Any idea when that will be? I think we should take the beast for a spin up to Loch Lomond when you get home. Fingers crossed it's before March. It has to be! We can go after all the parties and fanfare people will throw for you. I suspect you'll want to get some well-earned shut-eye before such a long drive also.

Anyway I'd better go and let you get some Little Bo Peep. You must be cream-crackered after dismantling bombs and shooting terrorists all day long. I know I would be. I'd love to hear all about your manoeuvres and secret missions, but I know the score. Mad people could intercept your letters and come after Mum and me.

That would be a total nightmare situation for us all. I have an idea – you can tell all the stories to me on our drive to Loch Lomond.

Before I go I just want to let you know that I have been listening to some of your old rap CDs, though Mum doesn't like me listening to them so much. My favs are N.W.A. and the Beastie Boys. They kick ass, dogg!!!

Speak soon, señor. (That can be Spanish and Portuguese [I think] *and* it's Alliteration.)

Dylan Mint xxx

As always I put Dad's name on the envelope along with his rank (Sgt, which is an abbreviation of Sergeant, which is one of the top jobs in the ground force) and then gave it to Mum so she could send it off to the special military forces post office, who would then give it to the special military forces postman, who would then give it to Dad, who would then read it, smile and have a massive lump in his throat when he folded it away and put it back in its envelope. I liked to follow the journey of the letters. Post was mind-boggling. *Cool Things To Do Before I Cack It: Number Three: get Dad back from the war before . . . you-know-what . . . happens* was sooooooooo mind-boggling that my head was all waltzer wacky when I'd finished my letter.

20

Costume

At school everyone was yapping on about the Halloween disco so much that their chat was giving me major sore napper:

'What are you going as next week?'

'Don't know. What are you going as?'

'I haven't decided yet. What are you going as?'

'Not got a clue. What about you?'

'Well, I don't know, but I was thinking of going as . . .'

BALLS, BALLS, BLAH, BLAH.

Not on your nelly did I ever want to go to the school's Halloween disco in the first place, but as soon as Mum said, 'There's no way on this big round earth, Dylan, that you're going to any Halloween disco after your behaviour over the past few weeks. You must think I'm up a gum tree or something, young man', I wanted to go so much that it hurt my stomach. I was desperate to go. I would have done the dishes and scrubbed the toilet bowl until March if only I could go. I didn't know what she meant by being 'up a gum tree', but I giggled at the image of Mum sitting up a tree doing all the stuff she likes to do, drinking wine and watching *Come Dine With Me*, *Eastenders* and *Who Wants To Be A Millionaire?* Then Amir kept texting, pestering my life to go. Almost every night my phone would play *No Sleep Till Brooklyn* at least five or seven times, always with some Billy Bonkers idea of what we should dress up as.

simon cowell + louis walsh?

no way, josé

batman + robin?

blow town

jedward?

r u up a gum tree?

a wot?

nuting

After the tussle with Skittle, Amir's good books had me all over the front covers. I was, like, his bestest best bud. Better than his family even. The daftest bit about the Skittle scrap, which made me happy as Homer Simpson at a hot dog festival, was that everyone seemed to forget all about my Massive Knock-back from Michelle Malloy. The talk now was all about how I had put Skittle in his place and how Dylan Mint didn't take any shite from anyone. And even though I felt like Ralph Macchio from *The Karate Kid I, II* and *III*, I didn't want anyone to think I was a guy who didn't take any shite. I didn't want to be Dylan Mint the Psycho of the School.

The groovy idea flashed in my head when I was seeing how long my ear could remain tucked inside itself. One minute forty-three seconds. Not long enough to get the *Guinness World Records* on the blower, but a tremendous starting point. My aim was three minutes.

wot about reservoir dogs?????

wot u on about?

itz a film

havnt seen it

watch it then

I will

thats wot we r goin as

sure?

sure

gr8

reservoir dogs it is so

reservoir dicks!!!

lol. U r mad amir

we all r . . . lol

21

Argument

'DYLAN,' Mum screamed at me from the bottom of the stairs, in her mega mad voice. The same voice that made my heart go faster and faster. 'DYLAN!'

Boom!

Boom!

Boom!

Went my heart.

I put my head into ultra-flashback mode wondering if I had done anything grand scale to annoy Mum. I had done my chores, she hadn't shouted because of 'the state of my sheets' in ages nor had she gone ballistic after doing her *Cagney and Lacey* when looking at my internet history.

'DYLAN, IF I'VE GOT TO COME UP THOSE STAIRS . . .'

'What is it?'

'DON'T YOU "WHAT IS IT?" ME, YOUNG MAN. GET DOWN HERE NOW.'

'Okey-dokey,' I said, hoping Mum would hear that my voice had no guilt.

As soon as I came out of my bedroom I saw Mum standing at the bottom of the stairs. She was holding something in her hand, waving it over her head like infidel rebels do when they are surrounded and have no way out of the shit they are in. I recognised it straight away. If there was a word better than BOOM, then that was what my heart was doing.

'Dylan, get down these stairs right now.'

'What have I done?'

'What have you done? Get down here and I'll tell you what you've done.'

I took wee baby steps down each stair, dragging my hand over the wallpaper pattern. Mum put her eyes all over me. I think my throat swelled up. I knew she wouldn't skelp me because of my condition but her eyes were spitting firebombs and tornadoes.

'What's this?' she said.

'What's what?'

'This.'

'What?'

'THIS,' she said, and fired the thing she was waving above her head right at me. And my reactions aren't, like, spitfire quick, so before I could dive out of the way of the flying object it rattled me bang on the chest.

'Aaaarrrrhhhh.'

'Oh, shut up, Dylan. It's not sore.'

'It *is* bloody sore,' I said, but it wasn't really bloody sore; the shock made me go 'Aaaarrrrhhhh' more than anything.

'It's only a piece of paper,' Mum said.

I recognised the wiggly squiggly handwriting. Mine. I recognised the paper also. 80 g/m^2. Magnolia. My paper. My letter. My letter to Dad.

'Explain that,' Mum said, with a finger ET-pointing directly to the letter lying on the floor. I thought the finger thing was a bit stupid because I didn't need my eyes tested and I could see the letter no problemo.

'Explain what?'

'That.' And she did the pointing thing again.

I was mega confused by this stage but my anger rose because Mum wasn't meant to read the letters I sent to Dad. Mum had carried out a seriously serious crime act. If I wanted, I could have had her frogmarched to the nearest police station, and then prison, for abusing my privacy. I thought about doing it, but in a clear mind moment I decided *not* to have her banged to rights because that would mean I'd probably have to go to live with a foster family, who had, like, nine dogs, five cats and four headbanger foster kids all living under the one roof, and I'd hate that. So

Mum could count herself lucky on this occasion. Mrs Seed said that I would be banged to rights if I continued on the path I was going on.

'That's my letter to Dad,' I said.

'Oh, I know it's your letter to Dad.'

'You shouldn't be reading it.'

'I'm your mother.'

'It's against the law.'

'Don't be stupid, Dylan.'

'It is.'

'Well, I'm glad I did read it. I will be reading all future letters you write to your dad.'

'I won't give them to you.'

'They won't get posted in that case.'

'I can post them.'

'Not at the military place. You're not allowed.' It was true. Only mums or dads were allowed into the special post office to deliver fresh mail. I would have been a chief security risk on my own. All the military stuff would wreck your head. 'I need to check them before they're posted.'

'That's snooping.'

'Why did you write that strangers were phoning the house?'

'Cause they were.'

'When?'

'That day you were lying with cucumbers on your eyes.'

'And why didn't you say anything to me?'

'I did, but you were hiding under the cucumbers.'

'How many times have they phoned?'

'About three.'

'Your dad doesn't need to know these things, Dylan.'

'I'm just trying to make him feel like he's here.'

'Well, he's not here.'

'I know . . .'

'And we need to learn to live with that.'

'But he's probably dead sad where he is.'

Then Mum turned her face to the left and said out of the side of her mouth, 'Don't bank on it.'

'He's still my dad and I want him to know things.'

Mum stared at me; I could tell that the little thought cars in her head were all crashing into each other like one of those Indian cities during rush hour. She wanted to say something, but she bit her tongue instead. We had a stare-off. A glare-off. I won cause she spoke first.

Ha! Ha!

'And this crap about the taxi driver.'

'What crap?'

'Why are you blabbing your mouth off about that, eh?'

'Cause taxi drivers aren't supposed to go into the passengers' houses.'

'It wasn't just a random taxi driver, Dylan.'

'Well, I just thought it was a bonkers story that would have made Dad laugh when he was going to sleep at night, instead of thinking of all the Talibans who are out for his blood all the time.'

Mum didn't say anything for a while. 'I doubt it would have made him laugh, Dylan.'

'Why?'

'Because your dad has a different sense of humour from you and me, that's why.'

'No he doesn't.'

'Trust me, he does.'

'Why are you saying that?'

'Because it's true.'

'Dad's got a right to know who was in his parking space and who was drinking tea in his house. He's got a right to know.'

'And I have a right to invite whoever I want into my house.'

'But a big taxi driver? That's just weird.'

'His name's Tony and he's a friend of mine, so tell me what's weird about that?'

'He should just drop you off and not scrounge tea from us.'

'He's a friend, Dylan.'

'He's a taxi driver.'

'I don't mind you writing to your dad, but I don't want you telling him about every Tom, Dick or Harry that steps over the door.'

'Why not?'

'Because I said so, that's why.'

'All the neighbours will think bad things if they see taxi drivers in Dad's space all the time.'

'Oh, shut up, Dylan.'

'They'll think you're a filthy whore,' I said. I knew I shouldn't have said this, but I was at boiling point and mercury was bubbling, and Mum shouldn't have raised her hand as well. Being the big responsible one, she should have cooled the jets. She should NOT have raised her hand. No Way, José.

'DON'T YOU EVER, EVER SPEAK TO ME LIKE THAT AGAIN.'

I let out a bark and growled at Mum.

'Don't you dare pull that stunt, young man.'

I growled and barked some more.

Louder.

WOOOOFFFF!

'You're doing that on purpose, Dylan. Do you think I'm daft?'

Grrrrrrrrrrrrrrrrrrrrrr.

'Do you think I don't know what you're up to?' Mum clicked her fingers. 'I want you to stop this minute.'

Grrrrrrrrrrrrrrrrrrrrrrr.

'You can turn that on and off whenever you like. Don't think I don't know what you're up to.'

That's what she thought, but she didn't know how

difficult it was, how tough it was to keep it all in, how I had to clench my fists and toes as hard as I could so that it wouldn't come out. How I squeezed my eyes shut so tight, hoping it would all go away, until I saw little white balls dancing around in the dark. I squeezed them so tight I gave myself a headache. And still nothing went away. Mum didn't know any of this; nobody knew any of this.

I picked up the letter, scrunched it into a ball and threw it at Mum. 'Keep the shitty letter.' I ran back up the stairs to get my jacket.

'And you can forget about going to any Halloween disco,' she shouted up at me.

I grabbed my new zip-up jacket, which I didn't really like too much. It felt like it cost a tenner and smelt like it cost a fiver. I remember she bought it the day after the taxi driver was drinking tea in our kitchen. I secretly called it the guilty jacket. Then I belted down the stairs.

Bang.

Bang.

Bang on each step, like an elephant learning to walk. I barged straight past Mum.

'Where do you think you're going?'

'What do you care?' I shouted.

'Come here.'

I didn't. I opened the front door and turned to Mum so I could get the last word in.

'I bet you and your taxi driver can't wait until March,' I said before scudding the door shut behind me.

Halfway down the path I heard cries of 'DYLAN, DYLAN'.

I kept walking until the sniffles faded into zero sound.

The zipper was caught halfway up. 'Cheap shite,' I said under my breath.

But after I'd said, 'Cheap shite', I said, 'Where the Pop-Tarts are you going, Dylan? It will be din-dins time soon.'

If it was school or the shops, I always turned right going out of the gate at the bottom of our path, but because I was so major cheesed off I decided to go left. The left was towards the park. Mum always warned me about the park: the park was full of nasty types, kids whose parents didn't know what they were up to or where they were. The local NEDs. Mum said the police should round up their parents for bloody neglect. Dad never took me to the park because he said it was full of people drinking tonic wine and smoking cheap-arse hash. I've never smoked cheap-arse hash nor drunk tonic wine so I could never understand why he refused to take me. I would have been A-OK if he had.

The only football pitch in the park had one of the goals smaller than the other and two wonky crossbars; whoever put the lines on must have been on the tonic wine and the cheap-arse hash because they were all squiggly wiggly. The pitch was lumpy but, still, when I was walking across it I dreamt of scoring a scissor-kick sizzler into the top pokey from outside the box on the volley. I imagined myself running down the line of the crowd with my jersey pulled over my head, slapping hands. Everyone would be there screaming and singing my name like a bunch of maddies. My dad, Michelle Malloy, Miss Flynn and all the students from the normal school would be there. That would be a real brilliant thing to do. I wished that my football team was actually good enough to play for all the top prizes, like the Regional Schools Challenge Cup. Instead we played in a crap round-robin tournament for special schools only, the Spazzie Schools Super Cup . . . and we couldn't even win that.

'FUCKING SHITE SPAZZIES' just popped out.

I was inside the box next to the penalty spot, which was nowhere near the twelve yards regulation distance from the goal. This penalty spot was about nine point five yards. I know this for sure because I counted out the steps.

And it's going to be left to none other than Scotland's finest player, Dylan Mint, to take this last-minute penalty. A penalty that will undoubtedly see Scotland win their first World Cup. With gazillions watching around the world, Mint looks calm and composed as he places the ball on the spot. He steps back from the ball, puffs out his chest, waits for the referee's whistle. He blows. The world holds its breath. Mint approaches . . . strikes it left-footed . . . The ball flies right . . . The England keeper dives . . . and it's a . . .

'All right, Dildo.'

'Are you talking to yourself again, spazzmo?'

These two headers went to the normal school at the other side of the park. I knew them because we were in the same primary school class for a few months before Mum took me out when I was eight and moved me to Drumhill. The taller one, Fritz, had braces on his jeans, which I didn't understand because his jeans were so tight on his legs that they were never in a month of Saturdays going to fall down. His Mohawkian hairdo scared me a wee bit. His mate, Gaz, had no hair at all, but not like Kojak or cancer people. His was shaved to the skin; I could see the scars on his head, like little bits of marble. I couldn't tell if the scars were from football – because Gaz could play football much better than anyone in our area – or from bottle fights. His jeans were rolled up to the top of his burgundy Docs.

'What are you doing, Dildo?' Fritz said.

'Nothing, just . . .' I said.

'Just talking to yourself again?' Gaz said.

'No, I was just going home.'

'But you live that way,' Fritz said, and pointed in the direction of my house. The opposite direction of where I was going.

'I was just looking at the pitch before I headed home,' I said.

'But nobody's playing, nobody's here,' Fritz said.

'That's what mongos do,' Gaz said.

'Are you some sort of mongo, Dildo?' Fritz asked.

'No,' I said.

'Why are you always talking to yourself then?' Gaz asked.

'I'm not,' I said.

'Everybody knows you do. You swear at people in the shops and all that, like some fucked-up mongo,' Fritz said.

'Only mad mental mongos would do that,' Gaz said.

I couldn't tell if they were pulling my leg or deadly serious.

'It's a condition I have. I don't mean anybody any harm by it.'

'Well, if you swear at us, we'll glue your fucking eyelids closed.' Fritz took out a tube of glue from his jacket pocket to prove that this was the real deal.

Wow!

These guys meant business. Ringo Starr rattled at my heart. I said nothing.

'Start shouting some of your mad shit now,' Gaz said.

'What?' I said.

'Yeah, shout some mental mongo stuff,' Fritz said.

'It's all right, we won't do anything to you. We just want to hear something,' Gaz said.

'Yeah, it's OK this time. We just want to hear some mental stuff – it'd be fucking hilarious,' Fritz said.

'I can't. It happens when it wants to; I can't just make it happen,' I said. And if there was one time I hoped something would come out it was this time. I wanted to swear and scream at them, but nothing was happening. I always tried to force it in; it had never entered my head to force it out.

'Come on,' Gaz said.

'I can't just –' I said.

'You fucking better.' Fritz's voice had changed, like a G-Man you see on telly. That was when I decided to fake it. I wished I hadn't argued with Mum now.

'Move it, Dildo. Do something,' Gaz said.

I let the air fill my lungs and puffed out my chest then I rushed at them like they do in a bullfight.

'GGGGGGGGGGGRRRRRRRRRRRRRR. CUNT FUCKERS BUGGER CUNTS. GGGGGGGGGGGRRRRRRRRRRRRRR.'

Fritz and Gaz were in hysterics, running around, trying to dodge me, holding on to each other. They laughed so hard. They got out of breath quickly.

'You are one mental fucking mongo, Dildo,' Fritz said.

'That's bonkers! You need to come down here and do that for the rest of the lads.'

I knew then why Mum and Dad didn't want me going near the park. I promised myself never never never never to set foot in the park again.

'I'd better go,' I said.

'Wait a minute,' Gaz said.

'But I'm going to be late,' I said.

'Where's your wee mate?' Gaz asked.

'What wee mate?' I said.

'The coon,' Fritz said.

'The nig-nog,' Gaz said.

'I don't know any coons or nig-nogs,' I said, which was so true because no coons or nig-nogs went to my school or lived in our area, although Dad used to say that Glasgow was teeming with them now and that in ten years' time there would be all these guys with dead long foreign names playing football for Scotland.

'That smelly wee black cunt you know,' Fritz said.

'I don't know any black cunts,' I said, nodding my head and missing Mum, afraid that my eyelids were going to be glued down and terrified that I wouldn't be able to see again, and I wanted to see as much as I could before you-know-what happened.

'The Paki cunt,' Gaz said.

'Who? Amir?' I said.

'That's the one,' Fritz said.

'What sort of coon name is that anyway?' Gaz butted in.

'I think it's Pakistani,' I said, and they laughed.

'It's almost as bad as Dildo,' Gaz said.

'It's a coon name, that's what it is,' Fritz said.

'The name Amir actually means *commander*.' Amir had told everyone that one day in history when we were doing a class on what our names meant. Mine meant *great sea*, but I wasn't going to tell Fritz or Gaz this.

'Who gives a fuck what his name means, arse-bandit,' Fritz said.

'Can he command this?' Gaz said, putting his hand on his willy, rubbing and tugging at it really hard. He made a stupid Cabbage Patch Doll face, all screwed up and ugly. 'Can he?'

I thought this was a serious question so I answered it.

'Erm, I don't know.' Which I didn't.

'Does he shag his sister?' Fritz said.

'What?' I also scrunched up my face because this was a mega weird question to ask about someone. This was one of those deep stress moments I get myself into at times. I should have been doing something like counting or brain-gym exercises or curling up in womb baby position to relieve the pressure or fiddling with Green. There was no chance of me taking Green out – these two eejits would take it off me, lob it in the bushes and that would be the end of poor wee Green. Mind-bogglingly I wasn't having any tics, screaming fits or grunting noises. Strange, because my insides were like the percussion section of our school orchestra. I was in Normal Town.

'I heard that Pakis shag their sisters and cousins,' Fritz added.

'Erm . . . I don't think they do.' This was all new to me, a real eye-opener.

'Why do you hang around with that Paki?' Fritz said.

208

'Yeah, answer that one, Dildo,' Gaz added.

'Because he's my best bud,' I said, which made the two lads howl with laughter as if I was a comedian with some top-notch belly-shaker jokes.

'Best bud! Would you listen to that shite – what age are you?' Gaz said.

'Well, he is,' I said.

'He's a sister-shagging Paki, that's what he is, and you shouldn't be seen dead with him, Dildo,' Fritz said.

'Does he go to your spazzie school?' Gaz asked.

'It's not a spazzie school,' I said, but I knew deep down that it was.

'It's for mental twats who can't wipe their own arses and who piss themselves,' Fritz said.

Both of the lads laughed again.

I just stood there like a pure saddo spaz, saying nothing. It was hard to argue against what they were saying about Drumhill because every day pupils do have to get their arse wiped. I was not one of those. Nor was Amir.

'Do you piss yourself, Dildo?' Gaz asked.

'No.'

'Sure?' he asked again.

'Do you and your Paki friend ever piss on his sister?' Fritz asked.

'No. I'd use the toilet if I wanted to pee,' I said, because I certainly wouldn't pee on anyone, no matter how desperate

I was for a wazz. I'd tie a knot in it before I'd pee on someone else.

Again they LOLed out loud at my answer. These guys were a right pair of sniggering hyena eejits. They wouldn't last a minute at Drumhill.

'Have you ever seen a girl pissing?' Gaz asked.

My eyes shot up to the sky. At the same time my mind went into super-overdrive mode because, the thing was, at school I'd seen millions of girls peeing. For example, when I was in the second year I saw Marta Lenton squat down behind her desk, lift up her skirt and pee all over the floor just because the teacher was going to ask her to read out loud. The fear got the better of her bladder. Then one time I saw Suzanne Donnelly rooted to a spot on the floor with pee gushing down her legs leaving a puddle at her feet – it was in home economics class – just because she was scared of the carrots we were using. So in actual fact I could have answered yes to the question, but I didn't.

'No.'

Fritz asked yet another confusing question. 'Have you ever seen a woman's fanny?'

Now if we were in America I could have answered a crystal-clear yes cause *fanny* means *bum* across the pond and one time I got a swatch of Claire McManus's bum when she mooned me and Amir from the school bus for calling her a fat lezzie sock. But we weren't in America.

'No.'

'Have you ever sniffed a woman's fanny?' Gaz said, which was a really silly question to ask because if I hadn't even seen one how could I have sniffed one? Unless I did it blindfolded. These park guys made no sense to me at all.

'Why would I want to do that?' I said.

'Cause it's good,' Gaz said, and stuck out his tongue and sort of pretended to make a snake noise, or be a snake; I couldn't tell the difference. Confused or what! I didn't know what snakes and women's fannies had in common. The whole conversation was becoming Billy Bonkers and I missed Mum. I had lots to learn about stuff, that was for sure. Maybe this was what adults and teachers mean when they talk about intellectual conversations. As much as I would have loved to stay and chat with the guys, time was getting on and I knew for defo Mum would be at her wits' end searching for me, and that was not a place I liked her to be in.

'I need to go,' I said.

'No you don't,' Fritz said, his face changing from Laughing Boy to Glue Master expression.

'You'll go when we tell you to go, Dildo,' Gaz said.

Fritz nodded in agreement. 'We've got tons to talk about yet, Dildo,' he said.

'Like what?' I said, thinking that we had done all the talking for the day. And some interesting chat it had been too.

'Are you a fag?' Gaz said.

'I don't smoke,' I said.

More laughter.

'Do you and your Paki "best bud" ever ride each other?'
Fritz said.

'What?' I said.

'Do you shag each other?'

Then it was my turn to laugh. 'That's a Billy Bonkers question,' I said.

'A what?' Gaz said.

'A silly question,' I said, because Gaz and Fritz were obviously the thickos of the week.

'Do you suck each other's cock?' Fritz said.

'No, why would we?' I said.

'Cause you're a couple of bare-arse boxers,' Gaz said.

'We don't box,' I said.

'For fuck's sake, it's like talking to a pure and utter mong, Gaz.'

'He *is* a mong,' Gaz said.

More laughter. Louder.

'Honestly, guys, I need to go, but if you're here tomorrow or the day after we can chat some more if you like.' That was a total pork pie. There was No Way, José and his sister that I was coming back to meet these two spanners. What we spoke about was good for bed-thinking time but nothing else beyond that. Two things put me off: their hair and the glue. I wasn't too chuffed with what they were saying about Amir and his family either, but the only reason I kept schtum was so my eyelids remained unglued.

'Fuck that!' Fritz said.

'We can talk now, Dildo,' Gaz said.

'Unless you don't like us and want to run away,' Fritz said.

'No, it's just . . .'

'I don't think Dildo here likes us, Fritz.'

'I think you might be right, Gaz.'

'I'm offended by that, Fritz. The cheeky little mong twat doesn't like us,' Gaz said, taking a step closer to me.

'You cheeky mong twat.'

'I'm not being a cheeky mong twat,' I said.

'He's not being a cheeky mong twat, Fritz.'

'I bet he's a *dirty* cheeky mong twat, Gaz.'

'I'm not,' I pleaded.

'I bet he's a *filthy* little fucker, Gaz.'

Gaz came much closer so that I could smell his breath; it was so much worse than Amir's, any day of the week. I think Gaz had definitely been drinking tonic wine and smoking cheap-arse hash. Death breath! I pulled back from him a bit.

'I'm not filthy. I shower every day,' I said. These guys were blind as buttons as anyone could have seen that they were much filthier than I was.

'This bellend's hilarious, Gaz.'

'Fucking riot,' Gaz said. Then he backed off a touch.

'Tell us something, Dildo,' Fritz said.

'What?'

'Can you come yet?' Fritz said, waggling his cupped hand fast as anything in front of his own willy.

I didn't answer.

'Are you a mad mong hand-jiver?'

'Yeah, do you shoot your load all over your stomach every night, Dildo?'

'No,' I said, and stared at the ground. I knew one hundred and ten per cent what they were on about, but I was embarrassed to talk about things like this with strangers; even with Amir it would have been jeepers creepers to talk about stuff like this. I'd never tried to do what they were going on about. If Mum caught me doing something like that, she'd probably go to Hell and back. No one would want that to happen in the house.

'I bet Dildo here licks his own chipmunk, Fritz,' Gaz said, giggling.

'Do you lick your own chipmunk, Dildo?'

'In the name of the Wee Man! Why would anyone want to do that?' That's, like, the yuckiest thing on the planet; even thinking about it gave me the dry boak. These guys were beyond eejits. Licking animals. Madness.

'I bet when it scuds you on the face you lick it all off,' Gaz said.

The numpties were in hysterics again. That was the effect of the cheap-arse hash, I thought.

'Yuck!' This was all I said because that was the word I felt like when I thought about what Gaz had said.

'Have you had your hole yet, Dildo?' Fritz asked.

'Yeah, have you rode anyone yet?' Gaz joined in.

'I'm not telling.' I could have told them my intention of doing it with Michelle Malloy, but I didn't want to drag her name into the dirt, and the fact that we hadn't done the deed yet meant that I couldn't answer their question with a big fat yes. Maybe if I had said yes they'd have put their arms around my shoulders and fed me some of their tonic wine and cheap-arse hash.

'Come on, who have you pumped, Dildo?' Gaz said.

'Yeah, who got the mad mong boaby?'

'Someone at school?' Gaz asked.

'You shagged another spazzie?' Fritz said.

'That's pure mad as, man,' Gaz screamed.

'Big spazzie orgy,' said Fritz.

'Look, I have to get home asap as Mum has my dinner on,' I said.

'Listen to him, Gaz. Fucking mummy's boy.'

'Bet he shags his mum as well.'

'Yeah, is that it, Dildo? Do you shag your mum?' Fritz said.

Double wow!

This was what Mr McGrain at school called a preposterous question.

'It's against the law to do that,' I said, which sent the plebs into convulsions. Either I was the funniest guy in our scheme or these saps would cackle at a pair of knickers dangling on a washing line.

'Maybe his balls are too baldy to ride anyone, is that it?' Fritz said.

'Yeah, have you any pubes, Dildo?' Gaz asked.

'Why do you want to know that?' I said. Then it dawned on me that these morons could be a couple of sausage jockeys, especially if they really wanted to know about the hair around my willy and if I played the hand-jiving game in my spare time.

'We're doing a survey for school,' Gaz said.

'Yeah, so show us your pubes,' Fritz agreed.

'No.'

'What do you mean, no? Show us your pubes now, Dildo.' Gaz's voice had changed from being full of laughs and giggles to a voice that wanted to knock ten lumps of shite out of me. My evil radar was alerted.

'No, I don't want to show you,' I said.

'Get them out now, Dildo, or else this glue's going on your fucking eyelids.' Fritz's voice was now the same as Gaz's. The cheap-arse hash had obviously worn off and their laughter had evaporated like saltwater does in science class. Dad was one hundred and twenty per cent right about the hash.

216

'Yeah, and then we'll glue your hands to the goalposts so you'll never fucking escape,' Gaz said.

'And no one will find you,' Fritz said.

'And you'll fucking die right there on the goal line,' Gaz added.

'Like the fucking mongo boy you are.' They were like a bad double act. Cannon and Ball, or Little and Large, who were on UK Gold all the time, but I didn't think they were as funny as all those people in the audience thought they were, who went bananas over their rotten jokes.

'I really need to get home,' I said.

'Show us your pubes first and then you can go home,' Gaz said.

'Yeah, get them out,' Fritz said.

And he came towards me, pushing hard on my left shoulder and forcing his hands on the belt of my jeans, tugging

　　and tugging
　　and tugging
　　at my belt
　　and yanking
　　and yanking
　　and yanking

the belt up towards my belly so that the lining of my jeans hurt my willy, ball-sack and bum-hole. I let out a high-pitched yelp. Gaz egged him on. Both eejits howled with laughter. I couldn't make out what they were saying exactly, but I knew it was weird and not the right thing to do. Only people who are not right in the bloody head would do something like this. Gaz soon arrived to join in the fun. He came from behind, his hands on the back of my belt. Now they were both heaving me off the ground.

Up.

Down.

Up.

Down.

Up.

Down.

A blooming human booming trampoline!

My willy, bum-hole and ball-sack hurt like a mofo. This game could have been mega fun if it was played properly, but these maniacs were way too rough. The pain in my willy, bum-hole and ball-sack began to make my eyes water. A tricky situation.

The tugging and yanking then took second fiddle because all I could feel were little rabbit digs into my kidneys and hard squeezes on my willy and ball-sack. They were so sore that I wanted to scream like a wee hungry bambino.

I wanted Mum.

I wanted Dad.

I wanted my best bud.

My ears hurt.

My eyes hurt.

My heart hurt.

I gritted my teeth tight so I wouldn't cry. *Don't let them see you cry, Dylan. Don't let them see you cry, me old mucker,* I kept saying to myself. Then, for one billionth of a nanosecond, I thought that THIS was it, this was how it would end, with me having my willy and ball-sack ripped to shreds, getting my eyelids glued together and being left to wander around the park before collapsing in a heap near the penalty spot. Surely this wasn't the terrible end of Dylan Mint? It was still only October and March was donkeys away yet. This was an absolutely No Dice situation. I, Dylan Mint, wasn't leaving this world without my willy and ball-sack combo. Not tonight, Josephine!

I closed my eyes and felt a tear trickle down my cheek. I clenched my fists and bum.

I didn't know where he came from because I didn't feel him coming like I usually did; this time there was no surge. There weren't any clues at all. He just popped in out of the blue. Thank the lads in the sky that he did though because he quickly worked his magic. When the eejit spanner numpties laid eyes on him they let go of me immediately, backed off, stood a few metres away and watched Mr Dog, the Tourette's superhero, do his stuff.

I barked.

Bit out.

Growled.

Howled.

Wuff woofed.

Snapped.

Snarled.

Gnarled.

Gnawed.

Pawed.

It did work at first, but then Fritz raised his fist. So did Gaz. It was show time. I put my hands over my head to make a helmet. I waited for it all to come crashing down, like the snowballs in winter. I squeezed my eyes tight again. I waited and waited. I sang a made-up song in my head all about not being able to speak in libraries.

I waited.

Nothing happened.

I heard people chatting. Not chatting like pals do after school, or before and after football matches.

'You two, get yourselves to fuck before I kick your arses all over this park.'

'You're not allowed on here with a car, mister.'

'Gary Darcy, I know your dad, so if I were you, son, I'd get up the bloody road and less of the cheek.'

'You don't know *my* dad,' said Fritz.

'No, Paul Fitzgerald, but I know your mum and she won't be too happy when I let her know what you've been up to the next time she's in the back of my car.'

'We haven't been up to anything.'

'Get moving before I radio the police.'

'But we're just talking.'

'Is that what you call it? Well, we'll let the police be the judge of that.'

'No, don't, mister.'

'We're going.'

'Piss off then, and if I see either of you messing about down here again I'll be on to the police right away. This is a public park, not some NEDs hang-out.'

That was when I had the courage to peek out from behind my fingers. I opened them slowly, like the Spanish lady's fan when we went to see this mad stomping dance in Torremolinos.

Holy Moly, pig on a pokey!

It was none other than the car that stole Dad's parking space. The maroon monstrosity. And Mum's taxi-driver tea buddy was in the driver seat with his window rolled down, staring at me. In the distance Fritz and Gaz were on their way home. They didn't look back or wave or anything.

'Are you OK, Dylan?' the taxi man asked me.

'What are you doing here?'

'Those boys friends of yours?'

I had to think long and hard about this question; the answer didn't come to me finger-click fast.

'Erm . . . I don't know. I'm not sure.'

Maybe we could have been friends if they didn't drink

tonic wine and smoke cheap-arse hash so much. Who knows? One thing was for sure, the games we played would have to come with clear rules if we were ever going to be playing them again. However, they wouldn't have wanted Amir hanging around because he was a Paki, and they hated Pakis, which meant that I could never in a gazillion years be pals with Gaz and Fritz. Anyone who was no friend of Amir was no friend of mine *and* anyone who hated Pakis was NO friend of mine either. So these two spangles would definitely be totally off the radar as potential new buddies for Amir after I'd taken the big bus north.

'In fact, no. I'm not friends with them. I don't like them at all. They are a couple of dicks.' And I laughed cause I'd said the word *dicks* freely in front of an adult.

'Good. Those boys are bad news, Dylan. You should keep well away from them.'

'I will.'

'Good man.'

'Cars aren't allowed on here, you know.'

'Really?'

'Yes, you could damage the grass and then all the games would have to be called off.'

'I'll bear that in mind, young man . . . Jump in and I'll take you home.' The taxi driver reached over and swung open the passenger door. 'Come on, I'll drive you back home.'

But I didn't move in case it was the shady deal of the

century. In case he was twisting my melon, man. In case he was being a pure head-wrecker and trying to mess with my napper or psych me out. In case he was the leader of a major paedophile ring, who wanted to trick me into getting into his car so he could blindfold me, drive me to the ring's safe house and video everything. Then he'd put the video on the internet and it would become a YouTube sensation then all the teachers and students at Drumhill would know that I had paedophile sex with a mega paedophile ring and they'd all rip the pure pish out of me. Michelle Malloy wouldn't touch me with a pole vault after that incident, I could tell you that.

'I don't really know you,' I said.

'We met twice at your house.'

'I know, but this is the park.'

'I was having tea in your kitchen, remember?'

'Yes, I do.'

'We watched *Who Wants To Be A Millionaire?* together, remember?'

'Yes, I do.'

'I parked in your dad's parking space, remember?'

'Yes, I do.'

'I said you could borrow my book on Friedrich Nietzsche, remember?'

'Yes, I do.'

'I'm a friend of your mum's, remember?'

'My mum and dad told me to never on your nelly get into a car with a stranger, no matter how friendly they are.'

The taxi driver smiled. 'Well, that is very good advice, Dylan. Maybe you should stick to it.'

'I think I will.'

'If you want to walk, that's all right with me.'

'I think I will.'

'What if you bump into those two clowns again?'

Aaaarrrrgggg! The taxi driver had me by the short and curlies. I had no answer. I one hundred and twenty-seven per cent didn't want to bump into any more clowns on my way home.

'. . . Erm . . .'

'Look, your mum phoned me to ask if I could keep an eye out for you, try and find you.'

'She did?'

'She was worried sick about you, Dylan.'

'She was?'

'Worried sick,' the taxi driver said again.

This made me feel sad and happy; sad because I didn't like the thought of Mum being sick as a parrot because of me and happy because she loved the bones of me no matter what. And you know what? I loved the bones of her as well. I guess I'd have been sick as a parrot if Mum was down the park hanging out with tonic drinkers and cheap-arse hash smokers. I could see where she was coming from. All I wanted now was one of Mum's hug specials. I vowed to squeeze her so tight that the blood flow would stop circling around her belly region.

'But I wasn't out for long.'

'She likes to know where you are, I suppose.'

'So Mum asked you to look for me?'

'She phoned me.'

'Why didn't she come and look for me herself?'

'Maybe she thought it would be quicker in a car.'

'Suppose . . .'

'And I was out and about so it was easier.'

'Suppose.'

'So what do you say, buddy?'

'Nothing.'

'No, what do you say about a lift home?'

The taxi driver had done a convincing job so I decided to go with him. If it turned out to be one huge hoax and I was whisked off to some shady paedophile shack, I'd curse my bloody luck and have no one to blame but myself for making such crap choices in life. Miss Flynn said that I had to get better at making the right choices in life. *Here goes*, I thought as I approached the taxi driver's maroon car.

I looked for signs of criminal activity and paranormal behaviour in the taxi driver's car; it was so hard for me not to pop the glove compartment open to see if he had a hammer in there. He'd also have needed a rope – just enough to go around the neck – a few black bin bags and perhaps, most important of all, some chloroform. Next week's Halloween disco was now appealing to me.

'You shouldn't have run off like that, Dylan,' the taxi driver said.

'Well . . .'

'Your mum's at her wits' end.'

'How do you know?'

'I told you, she phoned me to –'

'No, how do you know when Mum's at her wits' end?'

'I could hear it in her voice.'

'But how do you know what her wits' end voice sounds like?'

'Well, I was just trying to gauge her emotions.'

'I'm the only one who knows what her wits' end voice sounds like, and Dad as well.'

'OK. Well, kiddo, I know that she was really annoyed when you ran off like that.'

'She shouldn't have read my letter then.'

'What letter?'

'My letter to Dad.'

'Oh.'

'Mum read it.'

'Did she now?'

'And that's what made me run out in a bonkers mood.'

'I see.'

'She shouldn't have messed with my privacy.'

'I agree.'

'What?'

'I agree that she shouldn't have messed with your privacy or read your letter.'

'You do?'

'Of course. What's written between two people in a letter should be sacrosanct.'

'Try telling Mum that.'

'I'll have a word with her.' Then the taxi driver pressed his stereo button and on came some sounds.

I looked at him.

'Don't you like music?'

'Yes, I'm not weird, you know.'

He laughed, but in a different way from the two bellends earlier. 'I know that. What I mean is, do you like this music?'

I put my ear closer to the stereo and listened intently for thirty-three seconds. The singer had a dreamy steamy creamy voice, a bit like eating a Wispa bar.

'Erm . . .'

'I can change it if it bothers you.'

'No, it's OK. I think I like it.'

'Thank God for that. I thought for a minute I had a Take That fan in my cab.'

'Who is it?'

'It's old school.'

'Don't think I know them.'

The taxi driver laughed again; his smile was as wide as the Clyde.

I smiled and mine was wider.

'No, old school means they're from back in the day.'

'Like the eighties?'

'Try earlier.'

'Who is it then?'

'Ever heard of Pink Floyd?'

'Don't think so.'

'Well, Dylan, Pink Floyd are probably the best band ever.'

'Never heard of them.'

'Heathen!' the taxi driver said, which I didn't know the meaning of, but I giggled so as not to appear stupid.

Then he started singing a song, about being numb and comfortable, which made me want to be anywhere else but there. I promised I'd search for this Pink Floyd band online, if Mum hadn't banned me from using the internet.

'I thought the Beatles were the best band ever,' I said to the taxi driver. Dad was, like, the biggest Beatles fan ever and we always listened to them in our house when he was there. As well as some kick-ass rap.

'Rubbish, the Beatles were just the Take That of their day.' He chuckled.

I pretend-sniggered like I do when people tell mince jokes and I don't want to offend them. I gazed out of the window, watching the rows and rows of identical houses pass by. Each one could have been a twin of the other. I was glad when we turned the corner into our street – it meant the taxi driver wasn't going to take me to a manky den and present me on a platter to his merry band of paedophiles.

As soon as the car pulled up the curtains began to twitch. Nosy Nora stood behind them. Sometimes we called each other Nosy Nora if we were peeping out of the window and trying not to be seen. Mum was Nosy Nora on this occasion. I didn't have the faintest idea who this Nosy Nora character was in the first place though. She must have spent all day peeking out of windows; she probably didn't have a television. He'd gone straight into Dad's parking space again and pulled the handbrake, which made a sound like a high-pitched fart.

'You're in Dad's space again.' Could you believe this taxi driver?

'It's only for a minute, kiddo, that OK?'

'I guess so.' I nodded.

'Cheers, wee man,' he said, and soft-punched me on the thigh. 'We'll just tell your mum I found you wandering in the park, okey-dokey?'

'That's what I was doing anyway.'

'No, I mean we won't say anything about you bumping into those two head cases.'

'Erm . . . OK then.'

'No need to make your mum more worried.'

I looked out at Mum standing in the doorway with her arms folded. Her pure raging stance.

'That's a good idea.'

'Ready to face the music?' the taxi driver said.

'I haven't done anything major wrong, mister,' I said.

'Call me Tony.'

'I haven't done anything wrong, Mister Tony,' I said.

'I'm sure everything will be OK, Dylan.'

'Yes.'

'Ready?' he said, and flicked Pink Floyd off.

'Wait!' I said.

'What can I do for you?'

'Can I ask you a question?'

'Course you can, kiddo. Shoot.'

'Can you not call me kiddo or wee man?'

'Sure, no problem. Is Dylan OK?'

'Dylan's fine.'

'OK, Dylan, let's go,' Tony said, and went to open his door.

'Wait!' I said.

'Yes.'

'Can I ask you one final question?'

'Course you can.'

'What does *sacrosanct* mean?'

Mum gave me one of her hug specials right there on the doorstep, which was kind of scarlet-face embarrassing. Thinking of all the Nosy Noras in our street who were watching us hug was an utter redneck. The hug was tight and secure and I liked it. I loved Mum so much and could tell she felt the same way about me because my ribs were cracking under the pressure of this extraordinary jumbo hug. So, not only were my willy, ball-sack and bum-hole all aching to Hell's fire, now my ribs were as well. But I didn't really mind; I was just super chuffed to be home.

'Sorry about the letter, Dylan,' Mum said.

'That's OK, Mum. I'm sorry for scudding you with it and running out.'

'I shouldn't have read it, son.'

'I know, letters are sacrosanct after all, but, hey ho,' I said.

Tony was standing behind me and we gave each other a wee glance. This was what you would call an insider joke.

'You're dead right, Dylan, you're dead right,' Mum said.

'I don't want to fight any more,' I said, because I was doing far too much fighting these days.

'Me neither. Let's be friends again?'

'OK.'

'Good.'

'We shouldn't have another fight before March,' I said, knowing that this would pull her heart out of its socket.

'What?' Mum said, stepping back from me and flashing a glance at Tony.

'Nothing, I just mean that we should be friends again.'

'I agree,' she said, like the weight of ten dumper trucks had been lifted from her shoulders.

'I'm going to go up and have a bath,' I said.

'Good idea,' Mum said. 'Stay for a cuppa, Tony?'

'Why not?' Tony said. 'See you, Dylan,' he said, as I made my way up the stairs.

'Don't you have something to say to Tony first, young man?' Mum said.

'That's OK, Moira,' Tony said.

'Thanks for coming to rescue me,' I said.

'What do you mean, *rescue*?' Mum said, then she turned towards Tony. 'What happened?'

'He means *find*,' Tony said.

'Yes, I meant *find*. Find, rescue, it's the same thing. Anyway, thanks for finding me, Tony,' I said.

He winked.

I winked back, but just a reflex wink. Another insider thing. A need-to-know thing.

22

Characters

wot u up 2 dylan?

not much

wot u doing?

in the bath

who with? lol

yer maw. lol

i saw reservoir dogs earlier

and?

cool as

so u up for it?

u bet

brill, im mr blue then

im mr orange so

u have a suit?

my dad has one. wot about u?

Dad has funeral one i can blag

ties?

funeral ties. mine and Dads so i can give u one.

itz gonna be fabby dylan

i no

u gonna try pork MM at it?

dont know ... prob not amir ... prob not

u cood try pauline mcstay??

not even with urs. lol.

any word from the docs?

no, y?

just sometimes they have these mad cures for things

no cures for tourettes amir

sorry just thinking

better go, been a mad bonkers day and cream crackered

i hear u captain

wot u up 2?

in the bath as well

who with, yer da? Lol

yer maw. lol

see u the morra

OK best bud

by

by

When we stopped texting I jumped out of the bath, dried myself and thought how berserk towels were because towels, when they dry, actually get wet.

Life!

But the reason for jumping out of the bath was because the bold Amir had planted a mega seed in the old napper: cures. I went online and Googled *cures for Tourette's* and there were, like, forty trillion pages all about Tourette's. I checked about nine of them, but they all said the same thing, that there was NO CURE. NOTHING. NADA. NIENTE. BUGGER ALL. Some guy in America (always bloody America) became paralysed because he ticked so much that he damaged his spine. Now he had to suck hamburgers up through a straw and surf the net using a glockenspiel stick attached to his head. Some of his no-hands paintings were online too, which would have got a D in our art class. Then there was this woman who couldn't eat or walk in a straight line because her Tourette's was so bad. She was covered in bumps and bruises because she kept falling over. She'd broken her arms, her hip, her collarbone and her knees.

Christ on a cracker!

It wasn't those people's problems that scared the Jimmys out of me, no siree, it was them saying that when they were my age their Tourette's was 'manageable and low level'. So maybe it was a good thing that March was almost five months away as I sure as shit didn't want to be painting pictures with my head or being wonky donkey on my feet.

I read that some head-smart docs wanted to drill holes into people's brains and insert teeny-weeny electrical things in there that would help stop tics and jerks. No effing chance was I letting some doc drill holes into my napper. Did these docs think they worked on a building site or something?

Too many pages.

No Cure. No Cure.

When I closed my eyes in bed that night, I could see NO in my left eye and CURE in my right eye.

Life!

23

Funeral

In order to go to the Halloween disco we needed a plan. And, boy, did we have a plan. Our plan was watertight, although Amir didn't need a plan because he was actually allowed to go to the Halloween disco. He was just in it to win it. Mum told me that she was 'being true to her convictions and responsibilities as a mother' and was sticking with her decision of not allowing me to attend the Halloween disco. I could have thrown my toys out of the pram and written *bitch* on the toilet mirror with her lipstick or something equally childish, but I was trying to live up to my mum's title of being a 'much more mature boy'. She said it was time to grow up and put all my 'childish antics behind me'. I agreed. I was nearly seventeen after all. If you looked at it from Mum's eyes (which would be the coolest thing ever to do) you could see that I had been acting like a selfish rotten bampot over the past few months, even though I did have some good reasons for it.

The watertight plan involved borrowing Dad's funeral suit – that's what he called it – and pretending that Amir's uncle had suddenly died. I'd tell Mum that the pressure of owning a high-class Indian restaurant had got the better of him and he'd suffered a mammoth heart attack due to stress and the credit crunching. Amir was well in on the plan, which came direct from my own imagination. And if he got hauled downtown to give evidence against me, Amir would never crack under the fuzz's cross-examination. I trusted him and he was my best bud; he wouldn't be no stool pigeon. The only stumbling brick I could see was that the bold Amir was Pakistani, not Indian, and Glasgow didn't have any Pakistani restaurants that I knew of. This was the type of risk I was prepared to take, but I knew it was all going to be all right on the night because Mum didn't take the slightest bit of interest in Amir and she hadn't the foggiest about his family set-up either. She'd never find out the truth. I'd tell her that I wanted to go to the funeral to show my support for sad Amir.

'When did he die?' Mum asked.

'Two days ago,' I lied.

Mum went into her thinking-out-loud state. 'It's terrible what the bankers have done to people.' This wasn't a question.

If my insides could chat, they'd have said, *phew*!

'I know, it's pure rubbish. Amir is in thrupnies about it.'

'Thrupny what?'

'He's in bits. It's rhyming slang. It means –'

'I know what it means, Dylan, just speak properly.'

'Gotcha!'

'And when's the funeral?'

'Friday.'

'Halloween?'

'Weird, isn't it? I thought everything shut down on Halloween.'

'Don't be silly, Dylan.'

'DEAD PAKI CUNT! Shit, sorry.' It just popped out. I'd being doing so well. I didn't mean any of it. I hated saying things I didn't mean. The doc told me it was an 'unavoidable subconscious cognitive behavioural action'. Really he told Mum, who told me, and I wrote it down because I didn't quite know what it meant. Still don't, but I think this was the straw that finally broke the donkey's back.

'Are you sure you want to go?'

'Amir needs his best bud with him to show some support.'

'What about his brothers?'

'He doesn't have any brothers.'

'Oh, I thought they always had big families in that culture . . . Oh, well, never mind.'

'Well, he doesn't.'

239

'You learn something new every day, I suppose.'

'Can I borrow Dad's suit for it?'

'What suit?'

'His funeral suit.'

'What suit are you on about?'

'The black one.'

'What black one?'

'The one hanging up at the side of the wardrobe.' The reason it wasn't hanging up in the wardrobe, where it was supposed to be, was yet another of life's bizarre things I didn't really understand. It was like the towels in our bathroom that I wasn't allowed to dry myself with. Mum put them there just for show, so they become our Just For Show Towels. What was the point of that then? A wardrobe is for hanging things *in*, not *on*. A towel is for drying yourself *with*, not for looking *at*. How would staring at it make my hands dry? Things needed to change around here. I'd get Dad on my side when he got back from his TOD, which means Tour Of Duty. (Army guys use it all the time. And their sons.) Dad was good at getting things done the way he wanted. When Dad returned it would be *hasta la vista*, Just For Show Towels.

'Oh, that one.'

'Yes, that one.'

'Your dad's funeral suit?'

'Yes.'

'Who told you it was a funeral suit?'

'Dad did.'

'Figures. Does it fit you?'

'I don't know.'

'Have you tried it on, at least?'

'No.'

'That's a good plan.'

'Me and Dad are roughly the same build.' Most of our relatives said that I was the spitting image of Dad.

'You think so?'

'Uncle Terry said I was a chip off the old block.'

'God help us,' Mum said, not in a funny way.

'I can use my own funeral tie as well.'

'What funeral tie?'

'The one I got for Granda Joe's funeral.'

'Oh, I forgot about that.'

'It's still, like, brand new since I've only worn it once.'

'What about shoes?'

'I haven't thought about those.'

'Matalan are having a sale.'

'NO!' My days of wearing cheap-arse shoes were done and dusted. 'I'll just polish up some older ones I have.'

'Whatever.'

'So, can I try Dad's suit?'

'I suppose so.'

'Groovy.'

'You know something?'

'What?'

'I'm proud of you, Dylan,' she said. 'Ever since that letter misunderstanding thing you've been as good as gold.'

This made me look at the floor because I didn't want to be telling Mum pork pies and have her thinking I was good as gold; I wanted her to be proud of me for something deep, like taking the footie game by the scruff of the neck and pulling my team out of the Goddamn mire they had gotten themselves into, or because I got to play the part of Danny Zuko in our school's production of *Grease* instead of one of the non-singing and non-dancing guys who stood at the back and shifted things around when the top actors were getting into their costumes or positions for their next scene. A blinking slave. But no, now Mum was proud of me for telling pork pies.

'LYING CUNT SON . . . Sorry, Mum . . . BAWBAG'S LYING!'

'Want some tomato soup?'

'No, I'm good,' I said.

Mum did her gazing.

'Seriously, I'm top of the morning to ya!'

'Sure?'

'Sure.'

'Good,' she said, and smack-a-roonied me on the cheek. I didn't see them because it would have been impossible without a mirror but I knew her lips were still there like a rosy lips tattoo.

'Thanks, Mum, for letting me go to the funeral.'

'It's great that you want to stand by your friend at this time.'

'Yup.'

'It's a shame though because I was going to tell you that you could go to the Halloween disco after all.'

'Really?'

'Yes, really.'

'Why?'

'As I said, you've been my golden boy again, and I know these past few months have been hard on you . . . on everyone.'

'They have.'

'The last thing you needed was me giving you it from all angles as well.'

'I suppose.'

'Maybe I was too hard on you.'

'So, can I go to the Halloween disco then?'

'Well, you can't any more, can you?' The crap plan was starting to let in water.

'No, I guess not.' What a bloomin' klutz.

'Maybe I can ask Tony to pick you up from the funeral when it's finished.' By this time the plan was similar to Niagara Falls on the rainiest day in the monsoon calendar.

243

Noah and all his animals would have been the best bet to carry the rest of the plan out.

'No, that's OK, he doesn't have to do that.'

'He won't mind.'

'I'm not a big fan of his maroon car.'

'Oh, come on, Dylan.'

'His driving makes me feel sick and I wouldn't want to be sick all over his taxi cause then he'd be off the road for hours on end and he'd lose a ton of dosh, then his wife and kids wouldn't be able to eat good food. And, well, he plays crap music as well.'

'But you like Tony now.'

'No, it's not that. TAXI PRICK SHAGGER.'

'Dylan!'

'Sorry, no. It's just that we'll be at Amir's mum and dad's house afterwards and I don't know what time we'll finish eating and talking about dead people.'

'They probably do things differently, I imagine.'

'Amir said there'll be oodles of mad funky food as well.'

'Sounds lovely.'

'So, maybe Amir's dad will give me a lift home.'

'Amir's dad?'

'Yes.'

'But it's a funeral, Dylan.'

'And?'

'Won't he be a bit sozzled?'

'He doesn't drink alcohol, so he won't crash his car and kill anyone.'

'He doesn't drink?' Mum said, and one of those *!* things appeared in my head.

'It's against what he believes in, I think.'

'And what's that?'

'Don't really know . . . That all drinking is bad . . . And it's OK to marry, like, when you are ten or thirteen . . . And he starves himself lots because maybe he doesn't want his country to be full of obese people like America . . . And he thinks that you must pray on a Friday, always kneeling down . . . And he doesn't have Christmas. How cracked is that? . . . And I'm not really sure what else . . .'

'And what does Amir believe in?'

'I'm not forty-five per cent sure if it's the same, but I one hundred and fifty per cent know he hates racists.'

'Does he now?'

'Yes, and so do I.'

'Well, good for you.'

'I think his dad does as well. Maybe that's why he doesn't touch the demon drink cause all the racists drink like mad dogs.'

'Well, I don't know about those things, Dylan.'

Mum then went to the window and did her Nosy Nora thing. She didn't say anything to me and it seemed as though she was at the end of her tether with something or someone, but not with me because I was her golden boy again. I puffed out my cheeks and in my head I called myself a fucking eejit for the plan. Watertight = water-shite. I couldn't understand why Mum was gawking outside; I knew for a fact that nobody was hovering in the streets because the *X Factor* results show was on the television. Mum was watching absolutely nothing happen outside. Nada. Heehaw. Strange. Weird. Cloud cuckoo land. What was the point of looking at nothing?

'Dylan, son, can we talk about something?' she said.

And I was just about to say 'Shoot from the hip, big chick', thinking this was going to be one of those colossal Mum and Me Chats. My sharp-as-a-tack instinct had kicked in because Mum rarely called me *Dylan* and *son* in the same sentence without it being colossal. But, anyhow, I didn't get to say 'Shoot from the hip, big chick' because my pocket started bopping and singing *No Sleep Till Brooklyn*. I always got excited when Amir called because it meant there was something super serious to discuss. He probably wanted to be briefed on the developments of the watertight plan. We'd made a pact to only talk about it and never write anything in case our phone calls or text messages could be traced, or we had failed to delete anything incriminating (which means make us look like criminals). In this day and age phones of nobodies like us could be tapped easy-peasy. Not texting any information was what I called proper detective procedure. I ran upstairs with the phone.

A few natters later everything was hunky-dory. I sat on my bed slapping Green between my hands and staring at the orange, blue and grey sky outside. If I'd been a painter, this would have made a brilliant painting, but I'm crap at painting. I used to get billions of colour-by-numbers books for Christmas and they confused me to buggery. All the finished pictures seemed to be of horses as well. What was the point of herds of blooming colour-by-numbers horses?

I sat on my bed thinking of all those lined horses and how I'd never even petted a horse in my life (I'd be too scared anyway); how I'd never done a bunch of things in my life; of all the stuff I'd never get the opportunity to do. I realised that my *Cool Things To Do Before I Cack It* list was going down like a steel balloon, and if I couldn't do the skoosh things like bring Dad home without the need of a body bag, get Michelle Malloy to want to do things to me (apart from punch me) or get the bold Amir a new best bud, how in the world of big racist pigs was I ever going to milk a goat or paint a cool picture of a sky? I stuck my cold ears into my head and blinked hard so they would pop out again. Over and over I did this. I didn't want to return downstairs to Mum even though we were bestest pals again.

I knew what it was. She didn't need to Colossal Chat with me. I saw it. With my own peepers I saw it. So I knew what our Colossal Chat was going to be all about. The Goddamn letters. The curse of our house.

I spied it on top of the fridge.

Dear Mrs Mint. Blah blah blah. *Come to our hospital on 5ᵗʰ November at 10 a.m. Bring your son, Dylan Mint*. Blah blah blah. Signed: *the Doc.*

My doc.

24
Disco

Usually when there was any kind of student event at Drumhill it was Crap with a capital C. School discos were always the worst though because they were full of people who couldn't dance. Who really, physically couldn't dance, meaning everyone else just stood around the edges of the hall staring at a big empty dance floor or their shoes. The dance floor was our gym, which we used for doing roly-polies and being told not to climb on the bars. The DJ was always Mr Comeford. If his music was food, it would have tasted like shite. He'd say things like 'Come on, Drumhill, don't be square. Waggle yer wallies on this here dance flair'. There was lots of waggling, but we couldn't help that. Our school discos were no different to being at school, except you got to wear different clothes, rubbish doof-doof music played when you were trying to have some top chat with your buds and it was dark outside. It was funny to see the teachers in their going-out clothes. Miss Flynn wore a see-through blouse at the last one and you could see her bra underneath. It was black and lacy. Miss Adams wore these big shiny silver stilettos. Doughnut called them her Shag Me Shoes. Some of the teachers would drag the real spazzies up on to the dance floor and boogie with them. But they could only use their arms and waist so it wasn't actually, like, real dancing. It was a pure redneck for the teachers.

Wee Skittle told us he got into the disco at the normal school last year and it was full of people trying to get off with each other and everyone was dancing to banging hot tunes. He said that there were millions of stunning girls, full of the sauce, queuing up for man action. People were smoking the black stuff in the bogs, and the teachers were doing bugger all about it. Now *that* sounded more like it, apart from the wacky baccy in the bogs. It made our school discos look like a day out at confession.

The trousers of Dad's suit fitted perfectly but the jacket smothered me at the shoulders. Dad's muscles were way bigger than mine; his arms were like tree trunks and his shoulders like a really angry bouncer's. Dad pumped them up at the gym three times a week. Afterwards he had to go to the pub in order to hydrate himself or his gym efforts wouldn't have been 'worth a flying fuck to neither man nor mouse'. That was how it was in the army – there was no space for weaklings; weaklings would be left by the wayside. Or roadside, as it was known where Dad was. At least hydration problems didn't happen with brain gym. Dad didn't take me to the gym because he said I was too young.

Six attempts to tie the tie. When it was all done to my liking the tie and shades combo made the suit and me look Daddy Cool. Michelle Malloy would do a double take when she laid her sweet peepers on me. No, she wouldn't – she'd giggle and call me a horrible name that would make a lump in my throat and I'd want to cry and punch the nearest thing, like a wall or a hedge. I listened to the taxi driver's favourite band, who were singing all about these schools and how the teachers in these schools should bloody well leave the kids alone and not wreck with their heads. It was a humdinger of a tune. I played it over and over again until it was part of my brain.

'Is it not too late for a funeral, Dylan?' Mum said. She had good reason to ask – it was six o'clock after all, not exactly funeral time. I hadn't thought about this when concocting the watertight plan. Time for some sharp thinking.

'That's what time Amir told me to come. I think that's the normal funeral time for people from his country,' I said.

Mum didn't say anything to that; she lay on the couch watching a reality television programme all about trying to make ugly people look good by chopping their hair, slapping

251

loads of make-up on them and buying them bright-coloured clobber. It never worked.

'OK, phone me if you need a lift home and I'll phone Tony.'

'I will.'

I was surprised that Mum didn't ask for Amir's number. I guess she didn't want to be phoning Amir's house and trying to talk to his parents, which was good for me.

'OK, bye,' I said, and made my way to the door.

'Oh, do me a wee favour before you go, Dylan.'

'No problemo.'

'See if there's a cucumber in the fridge.'

Going near the fridge made me go gooey woozy because of that blinkin' doc's letter that was on top of it. I really hoped it wasn't for another scan experience. I made a mental note to find a better place for putting important letters that came to the house.

*

I had arranged to meet Amir near school at half six. On the way I felt everyone's eyes on me. Everyone who passed me by was doing something I didn't enjoy.

Staring.

Sniggering.

Pointing.

Whispering.

I really didn't want to scream something disgusting at them. I'd left Green in my other pocket. Disaster alert. A brain-gym exercise was required. I tried to think of football teams in Scotland that start and end with the same letter. A serious brain-gym exercise! I put my shades on to black out the people's faces and not clock their expressions while they were laughing at me. Usually I never wandered the streets at this time so it was probably barmy army for people to see that mad-hatter Dylan Mint walking towards them dressed all dapper and cool-like. If only they knew what I was going through, they'd feel guilt pain in March. Ha!

'LAUGHING UGLY CUNT.' A woman giggling away on her phone, not giving a shit about Dylan Mint and his problems.

Celtic. The easiest. One–nil Mint.

'FAT WHORES.' Two women carting their shopping bags around, laughing and squealing like wildcats. I saw a packet of biscuits popping out of one of their bags.

Kilmarnock. Two–nil Mint.

'SHUT IT, ARSE BANDITS.' Two guys in business suits walking behind me were talking massively loud to each other. I think their job was to show people around houses and try to get them to buy them. How dull would that be?

Dundee United. The first three were easy-peasy because they played in the top league. Three–nil Mint.

'TAKE A PICTURE, GINGER CUNT FUCKER.' A woman with red hair walked past me and stared and stared and stared. I think she liked the threads.

East Fife. That one was a toughie. Took a lot of thought and made me forget about many of the people walking past. Good stuff. Four–nil Mint.

'KIDDIE FUCKER.' A priest getting into his car looking at me and smiling.

I thought really really hard about the last one. Put my head to the ground and entered the brain gym.

East Stirlingshire. Wow! What a legend. Five–nil Mint. This boy simply couldn't be beaten. This boy's brain was way too advanced for a seat in the normal school up the road.

But, phew, I was chuffed to see Amir waiting on me.

'It doesn't look like we're dressed up for Halloween,' Amir said.

'That's the plan, Amir,' I said.

'It's not really fancy dress, is it? We should have gone as Transformers or a bunch of grapes or something. I feel as if I'm going to court in this clobber.'

'Stop being Moaning Minnie, Amir. We look Cool For Cats.'

'W-w-where's Wally would have been a good costume too.'

'He wasn't from Pakistan,' I said.

'Neither was Mr Orange,' Amir said, smiling because he

knew he'd done me over the backseat. He did his get-it-right-up-your-kipper face. 'Anyway, I decided not to go as Mr Orange.'

'Why?'

'Cause he's the police informer. I don't want to be a grass.'

'So who are you now then?'

'Mr Blonde,' Amir said, shrugging his shoulders up as if it was, like, dead cool to be Mr Blonde.

'But Mr Blonde is a mentalist.'

'I don't care if he is – he's way cooler than Mr Orange.'

'But he's more mental than anyone at our school and he dies in the end and cuts off some guy's ear and goes to set him on fire. I mean –'

'So?' Amir said, kicking his shoes off the ground, scuffing them up and looking dead *uncool*. I think Amir was nervous.

'Are you OK, Amir?' I asked.

'I just think we lo-lo-look rubbish.'

'We look the bomb.'

'But everyone will be dressed as famous people or super-heroes or sport stars. No one will know who we are.'

'Of course they will.'

'I was going to go as Sachin Tendulkar at the last minute, or Imran Khan,' Amir said.

'Who?'

'What do you mean, "who"? They're world fa-fa-famous cricketers.'

'But nobody would have a five-to-two who they are.'

'They would in Pakistan though.'

'But we're not in Pakistan, Amir, so I doubt the mongs at Drumhill will know who they are.'

'Whatever. Come on, let's go.'

'After you, DICKHEAD . . . Shite, I didn't mean that, Amir.'

''S OK. Sometimes I ca-ca-can be.'

'You're not.'

'Are you going to try and pork Michelle Malloy again?' Amir asked.

'She won't be there.'

'You think?'

'She's too good for Halloween discos at Drumhill.'

'Is she now?'

'She says they're for major losers.'

'Well, I'd say anyone who's on their sofa watching *Come Dine With Me* and not at the Halloween disco is the real major loser, if you ask me.'

'How do you know she's watching *Come Dine With Me*?'

'I have a good brain for these things, Dylan. Trust me, amigo, she'll be glued to *Co-co-come Di-dine With Me*.'

'If you say so, bud.'

'Who's the major loser now?'

'Well . . .'

'And who won't be getting the dagger tonight?' Amir said,

slapping me a cracker on the back. 'My main man, Dylan Mint, that's who.' An ouch moment.

'Let's get a move on.'

There was tons of activity in the playground. Two nurses were chatting to a scarecrow and a zombie. A cowboy and Bob the Builder were having a laugh with a hip hopper – or they could have been a rapper; I don't really know the difference – and a big giant iPod. A fireman was chasing an alien around with his pretend hose, using it as a big whopping willy. And a nun was trying to fix an oversized baby's nappy on her friend. It was bloody brilliant and bizarre. A bit like a Glasgow version of the bar scene from *Star Wars*.

An Amy Winehouse song was playing; we could hear it in the playground. It was the one about people trying to tell her to cut out all the drugs and demon booze in her life and get herself down to the clinic quick style so she could clean herself up from the mess she was in. Mum liked singing it when it was on the radio. I think Amy should have listened to all those people. I bet the poor girl just didn't have the time to make three parting wishes to herself. Shame! It wasn't a dance number though. Mr Comeford was probably trying to be all hip and with it.

Miss Flynn was semi-dancing at the door. She was obviously on door and make-sure-the-nutters-don't-do-mad-things-in-the-playground duty. Her feet were stuck to the ground but her hips jiggled a bit. She had her blouse on.

The one that you could see some of her bra through. Black. I bet she bought it in M&S or H&M or T.K. Maxx. I sometimes squinted my eyes to check out the lady section when I went to these shops with Mum. These shops sell all the silk and lacy stuff that make a woman feel sexy and important. We could smell her perfume when we got closer.

'Hi, guys. Let me guess,' Miss Flynn said, looking the two of us up and down.

'I bet you'll never get it, miss,' I said.

'No one will,' Amir said to me, not with a smiley face.

Miss Flynn was playing the game of fake-thinking, like she gave a flying fudball what we were dressed like.

'I think I've got it, lads,' she said.

'What?' I said.

'The Blues Brothers,' she said.

'Who?' I said.

'Who?' Amir said.

'Never mind,' she said, and then did her fake-thinking game again. 'Are you a couple of bouncers or minders?'

'Nope,' I said.

'Oh,' Miss Flynn said, with a wee bit of disappointment in her voice.

'Sorry, miss,' I said.

'These costumes are rank,' Amir whispered to me through his I'm-being-a-miserable-bastard-tonight teeth.

'One more guess, miss, and then we'll tell you.'

'OK, one final one,' Miss Flynn said. She pretended to be putting an invisible hat on her head and said, 'I'll need to put my thinking hat on for this one though', as if she was talking to a couple of four-year-olds or a pair of Drumhill's chief window-lickers. She made her eyes into two wee slits to show us that she was thinking like a woman possessed. 'I think I have it now,' she said.

'Who?' I said.

'Who?' Amir said.

'Are . . . you,' she started saying, but there was a dead long pause between the *Are* and the *you*. Then she repeated the words. 'Are . . . you . . . characters . . . from . . . a . . . famous . . . film?'

'Yes w-w-we are, miss,' Amir said, all excited.

I stood behind Amir and looked at Miss Flynn straight in the eye. Wowzers! I did some silent barking. Not Mr Dog barking; this was just me trying to give Miss Flynn a clue as to who we were. I really hoped that she had seen the film. Then I pretended to drink some water and did some more pretend barking. It was turning out to be, like, the worst game of charades ever. Miss Flynn looked confused.

'Who, miss? Who?' Amir said, as if he was about to pounce on Miss Flynn's see-through blouse with the excitement.

I pulled my ear out as wide as possible with one hand and with the other I pretended to slice the bugger off. Amir clocked me but he thought I was just doing my ear thing and luckily didn't say anything.

'Aw, lads, I knew right from the start. I was just pulling your legs,' Miss Flynn said.

'Who then, miss?' Amir said.

'Well, I'm not sure exactly which colour each of you are, but you're both definitely from the film *Reservoir Dogs*.'

'Brilliant, miss,' Amir said. 'I thought nobody would have a five-to-two who we were.'

'A what?'

'A clue . . . It's cockney rhyming slang, miss.'

'Well, Amir, everyone will know who you are, I'm sure.'

When we walked past Miss Flynn, the smell from her make-up–perfume blend made my nose wiggle. We gave each other one of those I-know-that-you-know-that-I-know looks. My favourites. I wanted to thank her. When we were well past her, me and Amir gave each other another one of those I-know-that-you-know-that-I-know looks. Then we put our shades on, ready for some serious disco action.

'It's hard to see with these shades on,' Amir said.

'So take them off.'

'Then I won't look so cool.'

We both took our shades off.

'I'm going to get a drink. Want a Coke?'

'Get me a lemon Fanta. I'm just going to hang here and see if the hot-hot-hotties come to me,' Amir said.

'Good luck with that,' I said, and plodded off to the bar.

Well, it wasn't exactly a bar, more like a couple of desks shoved together with rough white paper covering them; the same white paper that we put on the canteen tables when the school has its Christmas lunch. A square, metal money box and some plastic cups were on the *bar*. Mr Grant was barman.

'What will it be, sir?' Mr Grant said.

'Can I have a vodka tonic and a pina colada, Mr Barman?' I said.

'We've just this minute run out of vodka and colada, sir.'

'What about a G and T?'

'No G left, I'm afraid.'

'Give me a pint of snakebite then.'

'All the snakes have slithered away.'

'Shame, that. Give me a Bud?'

'Gone.'

'Becks?'

'*Finito.*'

'Wicked?'

'Out.'

'Water?'

'Now, *that*, we have gabillions of.'

What we were doing was called role play; we did this all the time in Mr Grant's drama class and I was quite good at it – he told me so. I was thinking that when I finished school maybe I could become the first actor with my syndrome to be on the silver screen or on *Eastenders*. But I tried not to think these thoughts cause that was when I became super sad and this was the big Halloween disco bash and the last thing I wanted to do was get all sad and misery guts. I laughed really loudly so that Mr Grant would realise our role play was over and done with. If I hadn't laughed, we could have gone on all night with it and there were far too many things to be getting on with for me to be standing and role playing with Mr Grant all evening. Also, he had to be a barman. For real.

'What can I get for you, Dylan?'

'Can I have a Coke and a lemon Fanta, sir?'

There was no fridge so all the sugar drinks were stacked up behind him. All warm and fizzy. In my mind some of the real zubes at Drumhill shouldn't have been mixing their medication with drinks like these. Could have been a disastrous concoction.

'One Coke and one lemon Fanta coming right up.'

Mr Grant put the drinks on the desks/bar and poured them into two plastic cups. I wasn't looking forward to the drinks.

'Thanks, sir.'

'Who are you supposed to be then? One of the Blues Brothers?'

'No, I'm one of the characters from *Reservoir Dogs*.'

'Oh, I see. Well, very good, Dylan, very good.' I could tell that Mr Grant had never seen the film.

The Beyoncé song where she talks about having a rock the size of a grape on her finger was playing. This was a song all the girls seemed to love; they loved it so much that they all pointed to their ring fingers when they were dancing as if all the men should go out and spend their hard-earned cash on a bloody silly sparkle ring. Stupid song. Stupid dance. Stupid message. And, as I expected, all the dudes and walking wounded hovered around the edges of the dance floor/gym hall with nothing to do.

'This is pure shite. There are no chickadees here,' Amir said.

'It's still early. Cool the jets, Amir.'

We checked out the dance floor, sipped our drinks and tried to sweat coolness. In America they would say we were working it or that we were damn fine.

'Look at the state of you two fannies.' The voice was so loud it boomed above Beyoncé. Doughnut was there with a couple of third-year guys. He was dressed as a punk rocker. The third-year guys were dressed as a pirate and the Pope. A punk, a pirate and the Pope. What a shower!

'Look at the nick of *you*,' I said.

'Yeah,' Amir said.

'So who are you supposed to be then?' Doughnut asked.

'*Reservoir Dogs* characters,' I said.

'Really?' Doughnut seemed impressed with this. 'Really? You're from *Reservoir Dogs*?'

'Yeah, really.' Amir was no longer scared of Doughnut since our football disaster.

'Cool fucking film, dudes,' Doughnut said. Scottish people shouldn't say words like *dudes* and *awesome* and *bitch* – it doesn't sound right. Singing in an American accent was OK, but Doughnut sounded like a pleb. Secret: I did it too sometimes, but never in company. 'So, what's happening, boys?' he asked.

Me and Amir looked at each other as if he was talking to someone else. Was Doughnut trying to be our Halloween disco buddy? He called us boys as if we were two of the boys or part of his gang of boys.

'Erm . . . Nothing much, just watching the dance floor,' I said.

'No bitches in here yet?' Doughnut said.

Amir laughed and I knew why.

Doughnut turned to the pirate and the Pope and said, 'Fudballs, go to the bar and ask that shirt lifter Grant to give me a Coke on the rocks.'

The two third years did what they were told. Fudballs. I'd never be a slave to anyone. Dad's advice was to scud someone full force in the coupon if they were taking liberties with friendship. I thought Doughnut was taking liberties here with the pirate and the Pope.

264

'What's your tipple, Amir?' Doughnut asked. For him to even say a sentence to the bold Amir without using the word *Paki* or *Pak-man* in it was a rip-roaring success. It made me happy inside for Amir.

'What?' Amir said. He spoke for me also.

'What are you drinking?'

'Erm . . . Just Fanta.'

'What kind?'

'Erm . . . Lemon.'

'Faggot Fanta!' Doughnut said.

'No it's not,' Amir said.

'No, I didn't mean you were a faggot, Amir. I mean your drink needs some jazzing up.' Then he turned to me. 'What are you guzzling, D-Boy?'

D-Boy? I guessed that meant *Dylan-Boy* and the *D* was an abbreviation. This was proper buddy talk. I wasn't quite sure of D-Boy as my new nickname, but I didn't want to tell Doughnut to blow town because he was making a real effort to act all chum chummy, even if it did sound like he was reading all his sentences from an American film script.

'Just Coke,' I said.

'Fuck that for a game of Scrabble. You want to put some of this in it, spunk it up a bit.'

Me and Amir sniggered at the thought of Doughnut spunking up our drinks. The image of it was rot rot rotten in the nap nap napper. Doughnut by this time had gone into the inside pocket of his punk leather jacket and produced two bottles. A half bottle of vodka and an odd-shaped bottle of something else.

'What's that one?' I asked, pointing to the odd-shaped bottle.

'Grappa,' Doughnut said.

'What the bloody Hell is that? It sou-sou-sounds like toilet cleaner,' Amir said.

'Crapper,' I said.

'It's fucking dee-licious. It's from Greece or Italy or some fucking spic country or other,' Doughnut said.

I wondered if he meant a clean country as in spic and span.

'Where did you get it?' Amir asked.

'I swiped the bitch from my dad's garage. He won't have a scooby – he's totally clueless.'

'And what do you do with it?' I asked.

'Are you serious, D-Boy?'

'I mean, do you put it in your drink or do you swig it neat?' Check me out, *neat*.

'Whatever floats your boat, D-Boy, whatever floats your boat. You guys want some?'

I flashed my eyes to Amir – he caught my eye – then to the bottles, and again to Amir. I could tell that he didn't want to be the one who backed down. Me neither. Neither of us wanted to be the one who was the weak son of a gun. But Mum would swing for me if she caught me drinking, as would the docs – it was super dangerous to booze while taking my type of medication. I knew for a fact that Amir's dad would gut him like a junkyard dog if he caught him pissed as a fart. I didn't think people like Amir or his family drank anyway. I scrunched up my face and looked at Amir. He understood the sign as only best buds do. Sometimes we had that ESP *Twilight Zone* stuff going on. Bonkerinos!

'Erm . . . I'm not sure, Doughnut. I'm not supposed to take any booze with my medication,' I said. That was my way out of the teenage humiliation of not being cool. I was Rubik's cube square.

'What about you, Amir? Your lot must like a bit of grappa, being foreign and all that.'

'No for me, man. My guts would be in bits all night and I'd have to spend the rest of the disco in the l-l-lavvy.' He didn't say that his dad would have knocked all the shite out of him if he got caught. He might even have kicked ten lumps of shite out of Doughnut too, but then he'd be in the papers for battering a spastic, which would mean they'd have to flee the country because of all the backlash.

'You want to lay off the curry, Amir. Anyway, your loss, boys, your loss,' Doughnut said.

Just at that point the pirate and the Pope returned from the bar and handed Doughnut his Coke on the rocks. Doughnut gulped down about three quarters of the Coke and then poured some of the vodka *and* the Grappa into the rest of it.

So much for the security. 'Right, I'm off to see what this shit-hole of a disco has to offer,' he said.

'See you then,' I said.

'Adios,' Amir said.

'What?' Doughnut said.

'Nothing, just saying ch-ch-cheerio,' Amir said.

'Well, if you change your mind and you want some jizz in your stomach I'll be floating about – unless I'm baw deep in some chick, that is.'

'OK, well, all the best with that,' I said.

'OK, see you,' Amir said.

'Right, boys, let's go and get ourselves some Drumhill pussy. I need to dip my wick,' he said to the little pirate and the Pope, who sloped off behind him through the – by now – busy dance floor. Everyone was dancing to Lady Gaga, who was chanting about the tabloid photographers. What the Hell was Comeford thinking?

'D-Boy?'

'What? Don't call me that, cock-balls.'

'Only teasing . . . Dylan?'

'What?'

'Do you think Doughnut *does* do it with chicks?'

'Not on your nelly.'

'Yeah, that's what I thought.'

'Too ugly.'

'And fat.'

We drank two more Cokes and lemon Fantas, both pissed twice, ate some monkey nuts, spoke to a selection of businessmen, tramps, robbers, footballers, Michael Jacksons, witches and geography teachers about our costumes and nothing else in particular. We stared at the dance floor, laughed at people's freaky dance moves, tried to see through Miss Flynn's blouse again and slagged off Mr Comeford's music selection. Then it got Channel 4 News boring.

'Want to dance?' Amir asked.

'With who? There's no one to dance with.'

'We could dance with each other.'

'Dance with each other?'

'Yeah.'

'Amir, people will think we're a couple of double adaptors if we dance with each other.'

'Why?'

'Cause they just will.'

'That's stupid, that is,' Amir said.

'Why don't you dance with a girl?'

'There's nobody I really want –'

'Are you scared?'

'No.'

'So go.'

'It's just . . .'

'Just what?'

'Just that I'm n-n-not a very good dancer.'

'Look around, Amir. Who is?'

'Yes, but I only know how to do bhangra dancing and there's no way I'm doing that here.'

'What about the *Slumdog Millionaire* dance?'

'Don't talk shite, Dylan.'

'What about her?' I said, pointing out a girl in the year below us. A cute girl right up Amir's street.

'Who?'

'That one who's dressed like a big cat.' I pointed.

'Priya?'

'Yes, that's her name. She's no bad-looking. I think you'd get on.'

'Cause she's a Paki?' Amir said. I didn't think he was happy.

'No, I didn't mean that. I just thought . . .' I DIDN'T MEAN THAT.

'She's no a Paki anyway.'

'She's not?'

'No, she's Indian.'

'Oh, right. Well, that's OK then, isn't it?'

'No, it's not, Dylan.'

'Why?'

'She's a Hindu from India and I'm a Muslim from Pakistan. What would my fo-fo-folks think? They'd go blinking ballistic!'

'Bloody Hell, Amir. I'm just saying you should dance with

her. I'm not saying you should invite her round to meet your mum and dad and have babies.'

'Well, that's not going to happen. I can tell you that for nothing.'

'There's no harm in a wee dance.'

'This song's crap to dance to anyway.'

'So wait till a better song comes on and then get in there.'

'I'll dance with her on one condition.'

'What?'

'You have to get her pal up to dance,' Amir said.

'Who?'

'That girl dressed as a butterfly.'

'What? Her?'

'Yeah, her.'

'No way, Amir,' I said. He was pointing to some wee dumpy girl with chemo hair and a really pronounced limp. I think she was born with a gammy hip. 'What's her name?'

'Is it not Sophie or something?'

Right on cue Comeford put on *Bonkers* by Dizzee Rascal, a top topper tune if ever there was one, by a billion miles the best song of the night and most *ironic*. I could have cut his DJ wires for doing that to me. If *Make Amir a happy chappy again instead of a miserable c***!* hadn't been number two on my *Cool Things To Do Before I Cack It* list the very thought of dancing with this lassie would never have taken place.

'Right, you up for it?' Amir said.

'Do I have to?'

'It was your idea. Come on.'

We put our shades on and headed for our women. The way to do things at school discos was to walk up behind the lucky lady and tap her on the shoulder and just start jigging. She'd return the dance if she was a cool cat. Easy-peasy. Well, that was the big plan. Amir didn't follow the rules – I should have known. Instead he leant forward and said something in his language to Priya, who smiled (it could have been more of a laugh, but it was hard to tell through her cat whiskers) and said something in the same language back to him. Before you knew it they were boogieing away all happy daze craze like a couple of good things.

I tapped Sophie's shoulder through one of her wings.

Tap One.

Nothing.

Tap Two.

Nothing.

Maybe she had lost the feeling in that part of her body.

Tap three. (More of a wallop.)

Something.

'For fuck's sake, what is it?' Sophie said.

'Erm . . . Sorry . . . but . . . erm . . . do you want to dance?' I said.

'No, I fucking don't want to dance. This song's shite

anyway. And if I did want to dance to this shite song it wouldn't be with you,' she said, storming off the dance floor. Well, hobbled off really.

Wow!

Completely round the bend.

I stood there like a pure plonker and didn't know whether to stand still or shuffle my feet to *Bonkers*. I didn't care what Sophie (or whatever her name was) said, it was a mega stonking song. What would Dizzee Rascal do? Me and Sophie weren't compatible. Mrs Seed taught me that word. She'd be proud of me using all her words. I should have been her Vocabulary King for that week.

Amir and Priya were doing weird dancing. I think it was the bhangra dance Amir said he wouldn't do. They were really good at it and loads of people were watching even though it looked as if they were swatting flies above their heads. I thought to myself, *Go on yerself, the bold Amir!*

They stayed dancing for the next song, *Radio Ga Ga* by Queen. I sloped off to the toilet. I didn't need a third pee – maybe only a half pee if I really forced it out – I just went to the toilet to kill time until *Radio Ga Ga* finished and I got my Amir back. When I heard *Last Night* by the Strokes slink under the toilet door I went back out. And would you Adam and Eve it – they were still at it, this time doing a mental freestyle dance. Amir was right – he was shite at dancing.

'Not dancing, Dylan?' Miss Flynn said.

I joined her at the door to see what the crack was like. Capital B Boring. I probably should have stayed at home with Mum, watching people on telly trying to lose weight. If she ever found out about the phoney funeral, I was going to get chucked in some huge dung heap. That's a *metaphor* . . . I think. I'd lied all because of this, this crap Halloween disco. Nobody knew who I was dressed up as, the girls were rubbish at being normal, the Coke was roasting hot and the music was painful. It was by far the worst disco I'd been to in my life. I couldn't believe that this could be the last disco I'd ever attend. I should have put *Go to a banging disco, where nobody wants to fight you, and get a groove on with some hot chick* on my list. Far too late.

'Nobody to dance with, miss.'

'Oh, I don't believe that. Have you asked anyone?'

'Yes.'

'And?'

'K-B.'

'Excuse me?'

'Knock-back.'

'I'm sure you haven't asked everyone.' That's when I gave her one of those looks Mum gives me, or Dad gives Mum. A look that says you think they're either Looney Tunes Thicko of the Week or that you want to belt them on the jaw.

'I'm not going to ask every girl in the hall to dance with

me, miss. What do you think I am, stupid or something?' And I tutted and shook my head four times because Miss Flynn annoyed me. She wasn't being what they call *tactful*.

'I'm not saying you are, Dylan. I'm –'

'What? Do you think I'm just going to go round and get a K-B off every girl in there? They're all socks anyway. FUCKIN' SHITE DISCO. PISH-FLAPS.'

'I'm sorry if I upset you, Dylan.' And she put her hand on my shoulder and I felt bad. Secretly I wanted her to hug me tight so I could feel her boobs sticking into me again. I considered crying but decided against it. 'Why don't you go for a wee stroll around the playground, get some fresh air about your lungs? Then go back in. Where's Amir?'

'He's been dancing with some girl for about twenty songs in a row.'

'Oh, well, that's exciting, isn't it?'

'Not for me it's not.'

'Aren't you happy for Amir?'

'I . . . erm . . .'

'He's your best friend, is he not? You should be happy that he's having a good time.'

'I *am* happy for him, miss.'

'Who's the girl?'

'The one with the strange Indian name.'

'Oh, Priya?'

'Yes, that's her.'

'Well, isn't that just lovely,' Miss Flynn said, but this wasn't said to me; this was said into the sky as though Amir and Priya were always meant to be and this was, like, the most romantic thing ever to happen at any Drumhill School event in the entire history of Drumhill School events.

'Lovely,' I said. 'I'm going for a walk, miss.'

'OK. See you later, alligator.'

'See you.' I knew I was supposed to say 'In a while, crocodile', but I was fed up with baby games. I wasn't a baby any more. I was Dylan Mint. A teenager. A young man dressed head to toe as a character from *Reservoir Dogs*, which is a sophisticated and mature film for adults and students. I also had a terminal illness, which is definitely not a baby thing to deal with and I thought I was dealing with it pretty fucking super amazingly and I wished people didn't tread on eggshells when talking to me. I *was* ultra-happy for the bold Amir. Get in there, my son. Give her one for the lads. Make sure you wear a Johnny-bag. Pump her hard, you mad thing, you. This was what I should have been saying to him, but us Drumhill students weren't meant to have thoughts like these, were we?

It wasn't a brain-gym moment and I didn't feel stressed or anxious. I just breathed the cold air into my lungs and blew some breath circles into the air. Pink Floyd sang about breathing in air and that song was playing in my noggin while I was out in the school yard. It smelt like Halloween. Dark, cold, smoky and fruity. It was jet black cutting around the playground, like *Scary Movie 1, 2, 3, 4* and *5*. Empty. Shadowy. Halloweeny. Cold. A perfect time for some perv willy-watchers to pull you into the bushes and touch your tackle. No need for a blindfold. In my head I was saying to myself, *Dylan, you've had enough fresh air to do you a lifetime – and the rest of your lifetime is just another five months. Time to head back in and take this Halloween disco by the scruff of the pants.*

The idea was to find my best bud – presuming he and that girl Priya had taken off their Velcro knickers – check out some more chickadees, hand Comeford a list of thumping beats to put on, hammer out some fat moves on the dance floor, go home, act all sad, go to bed and get warm and cosy under the covers. That was the idea swirling around. And that was when I heard the first groan – well, more of a moan really – coming from right under Mr McGrain's office window. It stopped me in my train tracks. I iceman froze, rooted to the spot like weeds in our garden. Then a grunt, a splat and a sound that I couldn't explain but if I had to write it down in Mrs Seed's class it would look like *aaarrrccchh-hkkktttssscccchhhtttcccchhhccchh*. For a billionth of a nanosecond I thought the paedophiles were making a charge on me, or worse, on the school's Halloween disco. I took out my mobile in case I needed to call the cops and ask them to send in a SWAT team asap. I dialled 999 and put my thumb over the button with the little green phone picture, ready to make the cops' number active in case one of the paedophiles tried anything risky frisky. Then a retch – like the dry boak – a splat and someone said, 'Fuck.' Not like a normal 'Fuck', more of a '*Fuuuuuuuuuck*'. It seemed to last forever. I clicked the big square menu button on my mobile, making myself a makeshift torch, put it in front of me and walked slowly to the sound of the '*Fuuuuuuuuuck*'.

What I saw knocked me for eighteen. When the doc told me all about the *degeneration* of my illness that only knocked me for ten, so you can imagine how much this knocked me. And anything over a ten is anxiety and psychological stress for me. Twitch twooing. Shaking. Whooping. Barking. Grunting. All that jazz.

'WHOOP. WHOOP.' My head and body shook like a Japanese earthquake. 'WHOOP.'

I directed my phone-light/torch gizmo. Dad would have been dead proud of me with my SAS skills. Maybe I could be an SAS cadet when this mission was over? Drumhill's playground had turned into a jungle, a war zone; I was deep inside enemy territory. There was no going back. With the help of the phone torch I first eye-spied the trainers, soles up, facing me. Someone was on their knees, which must have been as sore as a mofo on that stony gravel. The eighteen came when I recognised the trainers. Red Adidas high-tops. One big one. One wee one. Dangling beside each other.

NOOOO WAAAAYYYY, JOOOOSSSSÉÉÉÉ!

The Converse bag.

NOOOO WAAAAYYYY, JOOOOSSSSÉÉÉÉ AND ALL
HIS FAMILY!

The bag lay on the ground, half of it covered in puke soup.
Talk about yuckity yuck yuck. But Holy Moly, Jeeze Louise
and Gordon Bennett rolled into one. It was none other than
Michelle Malloy on her hands and knees, making horrendous
sounds and puking her guts up. Dad said that anyone who
was Uncle Dick (that's rhyming slang) was driving the porcelain bus. Well, if this was the case, Michelle Malloy was the
captain of the porcelain bus fleet. The poor lassie must have
eaten a dodgy candy apple.

'DISGUSTING SLUT. BITCH . . . Oh . . . Sorry, Michelle.'
I couldn't help it. It just sort of popped out. If Amir had been
there, he would've been in pure stitches at my greeting. He
loved that shit.

'Fuck you want, Mint?' she said. Charm alarm.

'Nothing. I was out for some fresh air and I heard the noise,
that's all. I came to see what it was in case it was . . . you
know.'

'Right, so you heard it, now fuck . . .' But she didn't have
time to say 'off' as all the diced carrots, squishy onions,
sausages and burgundy stuff erupted from her gub and
sprayed on the wall. Some of it splashed on her bag. I kicked
it out of the way. 'Don't touch my fucking stuff, Mint.' She

was on all fours, doggy style. The same style I'd thought about when I closed my eyes at night.

'I wasn't, I was just –'

'Well, don't just.'

'Did you eat something dickie dodgy?' I asked.

She didn't answer, preferring to do more boaking and groaning.

'Can I do anything, Michelle? SLUT-FACE . . . Sorry.'

'Can't you see I'm fucking dying here, Mint? What the fuck can you do?' Ah, a connection.

'Maybe I can get Miss Flynn,' I said.

'Do, and you're fucking dead meat, Mint.'

'Why? She'll be able to help.'

'Fuck her help.' Then she yanked it up again. Michelle Malloy was about the rudest crudest person I knew, with a megaphone potty mouth. She was a riot. A buzz. Even in her dark moment of all puke and smelliness on her doggy knees she was my dream girl. This girl needed the help of the D-Boy Dylan Mint.

'What about some water?' I said.

'Do you have any?'

'Not on me but I could go back in and get some,' I offered.

'OK, but if you dare say anything to that spunk bucket Flynn, you're a fucking dead man. Got it?'

'I won't say a word, Michelle. Cross my heart promise.'

'Bring me two bottles.'

I ran as fast as anyone at Drumhill had ever run. I'd have won the school's Senior Boys Sprint 60 Metres at a canter; it was in June though, so another blinking thing up the swanny. What she didn't know was that I'd swiped her Converse bag as well, in order to clean it. Not to rifle through her stuff. I soooooooooooooooooooooooooooooooooooooooooooooooooooo wanted to, but one thing you could say about Dylan Mint was that he was no Snoop Doggy Dogg.

'Two bottles of water, sir,' I said to Mr Grant at the bar.

'We only sell vodka at this bar, young man,' he said, but this was no time for dafty role playing.

I didn't want to be all RudeTube and scream 'Hurry up, Grant, you shirt-lifter. This is a matter of life and death, man', so I went along with it. 'OK, two big bottles of your finest vodka and hurry it up, barkeep.'

He smiled and produced two bottles.

I swiped them, handed over the dosh, bolted to the bogs to scrub Michelle Malloy's Converse bag and back out with the water. I saw Amir dancing along to some boy-band song about, I presumed, one of their members who wanted his girl to return to him; he kept singing that he didn't mean what he had done to the girl and if she returned it would be forever this time. Likely bloody story, boy-band guy. The bold Amir was getting his spice on with the bold Priya, who was getting her own spice on. They were a spicy couple. He clocked me and gave me our sign that everything was A-OK. Two thumbs up. I returned only one thumb as I had to hold the water, but he got the message. Amir was happy, which made me happy . . . and also a wee bit sad. But this was no time to eye-spy Amir and his chick getting their groove on – I had to split rapido style.

'Here! I ran as fast as I could, Michelle.' I handed her the bottle.

'Ta,' she said, putting her hand out.

I saw her face for the first time. Jiminy Cricket, it was like looking at the saddest clown in the circus: green eyeliner sprinting down the side of her face, red lippy smudged as if she'd been snogging a camel, black stuff all over her cheeks. Sweaty and bogging. Wowzers! Michelle Malloy in front of me on her knees, sweaty and bogging. Gulp-a-lulp. She still looked cute though. She sank the first bottle of water down in two gulps. Impressive. She would definitely make it on to mine and Amir's Fastest Drinker Challenger Team.

'STINKING FUCKING BAG.'

'Where's my fucking bag, Mint?'

'Sorry, Michelle. I took it to the bogs and cleaned it up for you, in case it got all crusty and minging.' I handed her the bag. She grabbed it off me.

'Did you look inside it?'

'No.'

'Did you fucking look inside it, Mint?'

'No, I didn't. FUCK YOUR BAG. SLUT.'

'You better not have.'

'I didn't. Major promise.'

She reached out for the second bottle and started drinking. Out of nowhere the eureka moment hit me like a ping-pong ball on the temple.

Boom!

Michelle Malloy was wellied, steam boats, pished as a fart, trollied, blotto, bloottered, sozzled, wrecked, drunk.

'Have you been drinking, Michelle?' I asked her.

'What do you think, Einstein?'

'I'd say so.'

'It's like being here with Jimmy McFuckingNulty.' Aw, I got it. Doughnut had filled Michelle Malloy up with the booze he'd blagged from his dad.

'Did you drink some of Doughnut's crapper?'

'What?'

'Did Doughnut give you the drink?'

'Why the fuck would Doughnut be giving me drink?'

'He had some earlier.'

'I wouldn't even talk to that fat mong.'

'So did you buy it yourself?'

'What is this, Mint, the Spanish Inquisition?'

That stopped me in my tracks. What the Spanish had to do with Michelle Malloy being blitzed in Drumhill School's playground in Glasgow had my head frazzled. I said nothing. I sat down beside her.

'If you really want to know, I was in the park,' she said.

'What park?'

'What the fuck does it matter, what park?'

'Just asking.'

'It had trees.' Her head wobbled and her speech slurred, but that could have been the effects of the medication she was on.

'I'd say you must have had a lobotomy, Michelle,' I said, trying to cheer her up.

'You don't half talk shite, Mint. What are you on about now?'

'You said that you would only come to the Halloween disco if you'd had a lobotomy.' I smiled at her in my I've-got-your-card-marked-sister way.

'Am I in there?' she said, pointing to the gym hall.

'No.'

'Did you ever see me in there tonight?'

'No.' She hadn't been in there tonight; I'd have fixed my peepers on her earlier if she had.

'Am I dressed up as anything?' She could have been for all I knew. A lady of the night, for example.

'No. WHORE.'

'So then, I haven't been to your fucking loser Halloween disco.'

'So why are you here then?'

'I'm looking for someone.'

'Who?'

'You won't know them.'

'How do you know I won't?'

'Because they don't go to this school.' Now, I'm not a forensic expert or a DI or a DCI or even CID, but Michelle Malloy's reason for being at the Halloween disco so she could search for her friend, who wouldn't have been at the Halloween disco in the first place, sounded like a big giant juicy pork pie.

'That seems a bit Billy Bonkers.'

'Talk normal, Mint. You're not a fucking baby.'

'It sounds weird that your friend, who doesn't go to this school, would be at the Drumhill Halloween disco.'

'Did I say they were at the disco?'

'No.'

'Well then.'

Then we did silence for a bit. I thought of going back in and finding Amir. Michelle Malloy put her head in her hands. 'I'm fucked. I'm really fucked.'

'What do you mean? Are you OK?'

'I can't go home in this state. My mum will go PURE ape-shit.'

'You could sneak in through a window.'

'With these fucking legs?' She had a point. 'I was supposed to be staying at my pal's tonight but she decided to fuck off with these two wankers we met at the park. I can't find her and now I'm fucked.'

'Was it these two wankers who gave you the drink?'

'Yeah.'

'Do you think your pal will be OK with these two wankers?'

'She's going out with one of them, sort of.'

'That's heavy-duty stuff,' I said.

Michelle Malloy still had her head in her hands.

'What did these two wankers give you to drink?'

'Buckfast and a toke of hash.' Then came my second eureka moment. A golfball on the head this time.

'Were any of these wankers called Gaz or Fritz?'

Michelle Malloy lifted her napper. 'Do you know them, Mint?'

'Not really, but I've bumped into them and I can confirm that they are a couple of wankers.'

'Too right they are.'

'Why is your pal going out with one of them?'

'Because she's mental.'

'But you said she doesn't go here?'

'She doesn't.'

'Is she at the normal school then?'

'Yeah.'

'I hope she'll be OK with the two wankers.'

'She'll be fine. It's me who's fucked. I haven't a clue what I'm going to do.'

'There must be something,' I said.

'There's no fucking way I'm going home in this state.'

'What else are you going to do, Michelle?'

'Fuck knows, Mint. I suppose I'll have to do an all-nighter.'

'What, stay out all night?'

'What else can I do?'

'But it's freezing.'

'It's a bit chilly.'

'You'll freeze to death.'

'No I won't.'

'You only have a short skirt on and a pair of tights. You'll die.'

'I'll break into the school.'

'How?'

'I was going to sneak into the losers' disco and just stay inside when everyone left.'

'You can't do that.'

'Yes I can.'

'You don't even have a costume.'

'I'll say I'm a drunk tramp.'

Then she puked again yet nothing came out this time except a big worm of bile that hung from her mouth. I made a face to myself because this was a rank yuck moment. I liked spending time with Michelle Malloy apart from the vomit bit, snot, sweat and swearing. She was my kind of woman. She stopped puking.

'I'll just tell that minge-face Flynn I'm dressed as a fucking spazzie student, then she'll let me in.'

'Not in that state she won't.'

'Thanks for the encouragement, Mint,' she said.

That was when I had my *third* eureka moment. A bowling-ball-full-force-in-the-face eureka moment.

'Why don't you crash at mine?' I tried to whisper this question because sixteen-year-old fellas don't usually ask sixteen-year-old lassies to crash at theirs overnight. I wanted Michelle Malloy to think that I was dead sensitive and vulnerable and cute, that I was a Prince Charming trying to help a beautiful damsel in distress. But it wasn't a whisper; it came out more like a 'WHY DON'T YOU CRASH AT MINE?' scream, all aggressive and pervy.

Ohhhhhh, sugar shit, Mint!

What have you done, son?

Silence.

Stupid question.

Stupid idea.

Stupid me.

Michelle Malloy put her head between her legs and didn't say anything for yonks. My head flicked from side to side; thankfully she couldn't see me. Her head eventually came up from her lady area.

'What?' she said.

'What, what?'

'What did you ask me, Mint?'

'Well ... I ... erm ... said ... SHITBAG DYLAN ...'

'Come on, stop hiding behind your condition. What did you just say there, Mint?' she asked again.

I heaved my chest and sucked in as much air as possible.

'I said, why don't you just crash at mine?'

'Your gaff?'

'Yes.' Gaff was such a brilliant word; I was raging I hadn't used it. It seemed that Michelle Malloy liked cool words. I'd try much harder to use them too. 'Yeah, my gaff,' I said.

She sniggered.

'I'm not joking, Michelle, honestly I'm not.'

'Yeah, that's why I'm laughing.'

'Really, you can roll in my crib tonight if you want,' I said.

She laughed harder, which confused the bejesus out of me because here I was offering to be a damn good bud to her, and it's not polite to laugh when someone is offering to be a bud or help you out when you're in a tricky sticky situation.

'What shite are you talking about?'

We looked at each other. Not in a fantastic romantic way. More like two beasts ready for battle.

'You're a fucking head-wrecker, Mint, you know that?' she said.

That was the straw that broke the donkey's back. I came back all knives blazing. Dylan Mint turned from being a weak-arsed boy into a brave-arsed beast. Dad would have been boom boom booming with pride.

'Look, Michelle Malloy, I only offered to help you because you're in a Hell of a state. I mean, look at you. You're so wrecked that you're just like a burst couch and your breath smells like an alkie's carpet. If you dare try to go home in that nick, your old dear will blow her gasket and maybe chuck you out for good and you'll have to live on the streets and sleep in a cardboard box and sell *The Big Issue* outside Tesco in order to buy your drugs and cider. And all because you refused my offer to crash at my crib. If you want to look a gift horse in the teeth, then it's your loss. But don't say that I didn't try.' At that point I was just getting ready to go back into the Halloween disco and strut some stuff.

'Don't think this means you'll get a shag out of me,' she said.

'What?' I said.

'I'm not going to shag you, Mint,' she said.

I thought my heart was going to need those two heavy irons placed on it to restart it, it was pounding so much. Mad CPR style. I couldn't believe Michelle Malloy had actually used the word *shag* in my company. In real conversation. Twice. A-mayonnaise-ing or what? The fact that she said she *wouldn't* shag me could mean that she really *did* want to shag me. Dad says that if a woman says she wants to do one thing usually what she means is that she wants to do the opposite of that thing. Maybe this was one of these times? Oh, I didn't know. Women are bloody confusing people.

'If I crash at your gaff, that's all it'll be,' she said.

'I know, that's why I said it to you.'

'This isn't anything, Mint,' she said, waving her finger between the two of us.

'I know it's not.'

'No handjob either.'

'I know, Michelle, absolutely no jobs.' It was a puzzle why when people spoke of sexy stuff the word *job* was often in there somewhere.

'And definitely not a shag.' Three times. I couldn't wait to tell Amir. Maybe he would be getting his own job tonight.

'Of course.'

'Not so much as a kiss.'

'It's just a crash, Michelle.'

'OK, then I'll crash,' she said.

Wow! Times eighty.

Michelle Malloy would be sleeping in my bed tonight, with her head on my pillow. Bonkerinos! Maybe our feet would stroke each other as well, which would be a supersonic weird machine feeling with her big foot and wee foot beside my normal feet. Touching. Oh! Jiminy Cricket!

'But if you try any funny business, Mint, I'll cut your fucking balls off. Got it?'

'Got it,' I said, and there defo would be No Way, José funny business cause I really wanted to keep my balls. I liked my balls.

'OK, let's go,' Michelle Malloy said, getting on her feet. 'Fuck me, my head feels like a rocket has hit it.'

'I just need to tell Amir that I won't be around after the disco. I'll get you at the main gate, OK?'

'OK.'

I rushed back into the Halloween disco and looked for Amir. He was still dancing with that girl, Priya. I went up to him right there on the boogie floor, pulled him to one side and had a bff word in his shell.

'Amir, I have to go.'

'What's happened?' he said.

'Michelle Malloy is crashing at mine cause she's blotto and she's waiting for me at the gate and we're going to go back to my room, but we defo won't be shagging each other.'

Amir's eyes lit up and his teeth became whiter than Daz. 'You're sh-sh-shitting me.'

'I'm not, it's so true.'

'Are you going to poke her?'

'No, she'll cut my balls off if I do. It's just a crash, bud. I'll explain all later.'

'OK, captain.'

'You two seem like a packet of cheese and onion,' I said.

'Dylan, Priya's the DBs.' This means the dog's bollocks. 'I think we've hit it off big time.'

'Do you think you'll need any Johnny-bags?'

'No, she's a n-n-nice girl.'

292

'What's wrong with her?' I only asked because there was always something wrong with Drumhill students – why else would they be at the school?

'Not sure yet, but she's a cracker.'

'OK, bud, I have to dash. Michelle Malloy will be waiting for me,' I said.

I opened my gob and eyes super wide as if to say, *Blinking, bloody Helen of bloody Troy*. Amir did the same. It was a happy time for both of us. There was no danger now that we were Reservoir Dicks. I flew out of the Halloween disco, speeding past Miss Flynn at the door and heading towards Michelle Malloy, who would be sleeping in my bed.

MY BED!

25
Crying

Tony the taxi driver drove us to the hospital in his burgundy car. Mum was still a bit Mad-agascar about the whole Michelle Malloy crib-crashing night, but at least we were talking again.

Hong Kong Phooey!

I'd read that some men put this insane psycho drug into girls' booze or grub so that they conk out and, when they do, these maniac men try to dip their wick into the conked chick. When we were walking home to mine on the night of the Halloween disco, I was thinking that if I lobbed a drug into the tomato soup I was going to give Michelle Malloy when we got home I could have ticked *have real sexual intercourse with a girl* off my *Cool Things To Do Before I Cack It* list. But I had NO sex drugs on me and I was NOT a maniac psycho

AND it probably wouldn't have counted, as only one of us (me) would be doing the heavy breathing and mucky talk.

If I'd known Michelle Malloy was going to yank all over my room, piss the bed and squeal at the top of her lungs cause she thought she was going to snuff it then I would never have asked her to crash in the first place. No, that's not true – I still would have.

Even though I didn't get a poke or any kind of job or as much as a kiss I did get a good old-fashioned huggy hug. When it all got too much for her and she was roaring like a banshee in a fire, I had to cuddle Michelle Malloy, soothe her head and wipe her tears away. I liked that part. She snotted on my shoulder, but I didn't mind – after all they were Michelle Malloy's snotters. Watery snotters at that. When she went back to her own house to puke in peace, have a bath and sip some tomato soup (that was my idea) I found a wee note she'd written for me on my computer.

Thanks, Mint, you are a mad ☆.
Sorry for being such a F?*%ing B@?ch to you.
Give me a call sometime.
M ❤

Mum went gorilla-shit *and* -piss with anger when she found out. After Michelle Malloy's old dear came to pick her up from our house in the morning Mum and me did some screaming, grunting and barking at each other. She went, 'DYLAN, YOU ARE A BLAH-RDY BLAH BLAH', and I went, 'I FUCKING HATE YOU, THIS HOUSE AND ALL THE BLAH-RDY BLAH BLAH'. She said that it wasn't that I had a girl vomiting in my room all night that 'incensed' and 'hurt' her so; it was the fact that I told her a 'horrible and heinous' lie about Amir's uncle's funeral and that I had actually *lied* about 'some poor man's death'. Tony the taxi driver put another hole in our water-shite plan when he told Mum that Muslim people bury their dead after only twenty-four hours. It seemed that Tony the taxi driver wasn't as thicko as all the other taxi drivers. I didn't come out of my room for donkey's days, which was tough because it still ponged of Michelle Malloy's vomit and the stains on the walls wouldn't come off. I did some serious brain gym in there and nearly twiddled Green out of existence. Tony the taxi driver told me that Mum put tea bags and cucumbers on her eyes for two solid days after our scrap. We had a wee snigger to ourselves and he said, 'So don't offer a cucumber sandwich to anyone if they come in for a blether', which Tony the taxi driver found hilarious-issimo. I pretended to laugh as I didn't want him to feel super embarrassed cause he'd made such a rubbish joke. Why on Hell's bells would you offer someone a cucumber sandwich if there were Pot Noodles and tomato soup in the cupboard? ADULTS!!!

It wasn't all bad spending time in my puke room. I wrote a letter to Dad and sealed it with Pritt Stick, extra strong Sellotape and two staples. Just to be sure Mum wouldn't sneak a peak. She had previous and that counted for something around here.

77 Blair Road

ML5 1QE

2nd November

Hi big dude

How's it hanging? That's American movie language. Yes, you've probably guessed it: I have been watching trillions of Yank films. My favourites are *Reservoir Dogs*, *Clerks*, *Weird Science*, *The Breakfast Club* and *Buffalo 66*. Have you seen any of them? Actually, I'm not really sure if you and the boys get to watch films where you are based. It's probably in case the airwaves are intercepted by the terrorists and they could quickly detect your whereabouts. Thinking about it, it's not a good idea to put your lives at risk because of *Reservoir Dogs* or *Clerks*. If you want, I can write you a detailed synopsis of them??? That's what we're doing in Mrs Seed's class except the films she picks are soooooooooooooooooooooooooo Utterly Butterly mince. *Titanic* and *The English Patient*. OMG YUCK!!!!!!

Things are probably A-OK here. Mum is still the same. We've been having lots of fights (not fisticuffs) recently. I think it's maybe because I am going through that phase – you know, the one boys go through when all they can think about is nudie women and doing the things that mums don't like? Well, I think I'm going through that period. It would be good to have you here so we could talk about all that stuff and you could give me some man-to-man advice. I suppose I could ask Tony. He's Mum's new pal. He's a taxi driver, but he's got a brain in his head. I'm not sure but I think he reads books when he's waiting long hours on a fare; in a way it's good brain gym. He comes round sometimes to chat and have a cuppa, but it would be too weird to ask him for some man-on-man chat cause Tony the taxi driver isn't my main man. By that I mean he's not my dad. I used to think he was a right whalloper but he's not a bad big chap. He's a mega fan of Pink Floyd and the Kinks. Do you know them?

I can't take all the blame for the fights because I think that Mum is going through the mental change in her life. She is at that stage where women change their brain thoughts from one day to the next and they don't feel like they're a woman any longer. It's Billy Bonkers. Who would be a woman, eh? We have been doing exactly that topic in the 'adult section' in our biology class, but to tell you the truth I'm not fully grasping it. It's number 77 in the textbook, but I haven't read it all yet. I'm more into English, drama and PE.

One of my buds from school stayed over for the night and Mum went barmy army because this bud was a girl. Nothing happened though. She slept in my bed and I crashed on the floor. She snored loads and kept me up most of the night. That's a good one to use to take the pure p*** out of her in the future. My best bud, Amir, the one I told you about, he has a new bird. She's like him, if you know what I mean. Her name is Priya. She's in the year below us at school. I keep calling him a paedo cradle-snatcher, which he hates. But even though she's his new girl best bud I will always be his real best bud cause I won't ever say things like 'I don't want you to kiss me any more, Amir' or 'Amir, I don't want you to hold my hand'. He met her at the school's Halloween disco (that's another story). I haven't asked Amir yet if *I* will always be *his* best bud (I will). Girls come and go, but best buds are like brothers from another mother for life, no?

I saw on the news that some of the troops are being sent home because our side has almost won the war and the people don't really need their help any longer and if they stayed they'd become a nuisance in the eyes of the people, who would then start to hate and resent them. Is that where you are? Have you been given a date to return? I have asked Mum loads of times when you'll be back but she just says that you'll 'be home when you're home'. I even asked Tony the taxi driver, but he said it was 'out of his hands'. Tony the taxi driver used to park in your space, but after I gave him an old-fashioned tongue wagging he wouldn't Dan Dare. I told you about it in my last letter, but there was a problem with the delivery of that one which is ultra-boring to go into now. I'll bend your ear when you get home. I'm not really going to 'bend' your ear – it's just a saying.

Now it's November, March is just around the corner so it would be the DBs (that means dog's bollocks by the by) if you could be here for that. It would be mega cool to have you here before Christmas though. If not, maybe you could write me another letter and give it to one of your secret ninja spy mates to smuggle out for you. I wouldn't tell a soul. No worries if you can't. In fact I could say the whole letter you wrote to me in my sleep because I've read it that much. Insanity or what?

Right Ye Are.

I have to get some serious shut-eye as tomorrow is a BIG day ... All will be revealed. All I will say is that I'm off to see a big brain doc.

I will try to send another letter asap. Hang in there, dude!!!!

Dylan Mint xxx

On the way to the hospital my hands were Sweaty Betty soaking wetty and my legs were shaking like a puppy in a microwave. My mind was playing Good-News-Bad-News-Good-News-Bad-News tennis, which was driving me round the bend. To try to stop the tennis I thought about Michelle Malloy and added her name to my phone's contacts list, giving her the *Rehab* song ringtone so I could identify her as soon as she phoned. That was my little joke to myself.

'Just give me a buzz when you're on your way out and I'll pick you up,' Tony the taxi driver said to us when he pulled his burgundy car up near the hospital's entrance.

'You don't have to do that,' Mum said. What? A free lift!

Of course we'll take it. I hated getting on public buses. People laughing and staring. Glaring. Not caring how I felt.

'I want to,' Tony the taxi driver said.

Nice one, Tony the taxi driver, I said to myself.

'OK, I'll give you a tinkle,' Mum said.

I noticed not one but TWO Crazy with a capital C things. Firstly, Mum used the word *tinkle*, which means *piss* or *pee-pee* for little boys and girls. Or it can mean a wee boy's wee willy. She could have said bags of words instead, like *buzz*, *bell* or *ring*. These are called *synonyms*. Using *tinkle* was like Mum being a wee girl again. Crazy. Secondly, she touched Tony the taxi driver's arm when she said, 'I'll give you a tinkle'. He was doing what all taxi drivers do, leaning their arm out of their rolled-down window as if to say, 'All right, love, where are you off to then?', when Mum placed three fingertips on Tony the taxi driver's BARE leaning arm. Crazy.

'Right, let's go, Dylan,' she said to me.

'Go get 'em, kiddo,' Tony the taxi driver said to me.

I waved at him as he drove off.

I have to breathe through my mouth whenever I go into hospitals. The smell reminds me of those special rooms in Drumhill where students are taken to wipe their mouths or bumbums clean. I've never been there, nor has Amir.

'Do you want a drink?' Mum asked as we passed the shop that sells flowers for dying people. I don't want flowers on my deathbed. I want sexy nurses touching my willy.

'I won't be able to drink,' I said.

'Why not?'

'Because it's a hospital. I can't drink in hospitals.'

'What about a snack then?' I love snacks; I'd definitely have had a snack if we were at home. One of Mum's Ryvitas or some nuts.

'No.'

'Not hungry?'

'I can't eat in hospitals either.'

'This is all news to me, Dylan,' Mum said. I looked at her and gave her a Jesus-no-one-understands-me look. Parents just don't understand teenagers these days.

'Their food would give you the dry boak.'

'Well, you'd better hope they don't keep you in or you'll starve.' That made me panic and the cartwheels spun around inside.

'They're not going to keep me in, are they?' I said. 'Mum, they're not, are they?'

'Don't panic, Dylan, of course they're not going to keep you in. This is just a check-up.'

Mum put her hand through my hair and softly rubbed my head. She does this when she knows the panic is coming, or when the shit will rattle the fan. The people who were buying flowers or magazines for the brain-dead tried not to stare at us, at me, but they did. See, I was doing this mix between groaning and growling which sounded a bit like a car trying to start itself on a cold winter's morning. Dad's car did this sometimes. Mum held me tight. That's when I knew we were Mum and Son Buds again.

'You'll be OK, sweetheart, you'll be OK.'

'A-OK?'

'A-OK.'

'Promise?'

'Promise.'

'I love you, Mum,' I said, because teenagers don't say that too much to their mums yet mums are the only thing teenagers need when the fear comes.

'I love you too, Dylan.' Mum stroked my hair, like I had a horse's mane.

The doc who came in the room was NOT the doc from before. This was a different doc from the one who spoke gobbledegook the last time we were here – the doc who dropped the bombshell and made Mum's eyes look like she'd been swimming in a pool full of salt. This new doc was younger, had funky hair all gelled and spiked and didn't wear a tie. A doc without a tie! That was Ice Cream Cool. With the other doc I had to be seen and not heard, but this doc made me feel like I could be seen *and* heard and he smiled at me, but not in any way that made me think he wanted to do pervy things to me. This doc was a dude. This doc wanted *me*, and not Mum, to answer some of his questions. And, when you think about it, this made super-sensible sense because all the stuff was happening to me and it was in *my* napper and I was the only one who knew what the bloody Hell's fire was going on in there and no one else, not even Mum. Bless her cotton tights. She knew tons of stuff about me, but not the

    deep

    deep

    deep

    stuff.

Not even the bold Amir knew that.

'You must be Dylan?' the doc said. He put out his hand for me to shake.

I shook it, but didn't say 'Hi' or 'Hello' or 'Yes, my name is Dylan'. The doc then shook Mum's hand.

'Morning,' he said to Mum.

'Morning,' she said back.

'How are you, Dylan?' the doc said.

I looked at Mum.

'Answer the doctor, Dylan,' Mum said.

'Erm . . . I'm fine.' I was only like this because I still thought I had to be seen and not heard.

'My name's Doctor Cunningham. Colm Cunningham.'

'My name's Dylan. Dylan Mint.'

The doc laughed, but I wasn't making a joke. He told me his name, I told him my name – that's what people do.

'Is he always like this?' the doc said to Mum.

'Always,' Mum said.

'You can call me Doctor Cunningham, Doctor Colm, or just Colm if you'd prefer.'

'I think I'll call you Doc Colm, if that's OK?'

'Sure thing, Dylan.'

I nodded my head.

'OK, let's see. I've had a look at the case files.'

'Am I going to have to stay in hospital, Doc Colm?'

He laughed again and looked at Mum, who shook her head.

'No, Dylan, you're not going to have to stay in hospital. Whatever gave you that idea?'

'Just because.'

'No, this is just an initial meeting for us to discuss the course of action,' Doc Colm said.

'Just listen, Dylan,' Mum said.

'So, I'm simply going to ask you a few questions, Dylan. Is that OK?'

'Sure. Shoot, Doc Colm.'

'He's some fellow, isn't he?' Doc Colm said to Mum. She giggled.

'You better believe it,' Mum said, giggling again. I think if I hadn't been in the room Doc Colm and Mum would have been doing flirting with each other. Thank God I was though in case it got out of hand and Doc Colm lost his job. Then where would I be?

'OK, Dylan, we're going to talk about your Tourette's now. Is that OK?' Doc Colm said.

'A-OK,' I said.

'Would you say that your Tourette's is getting worse, better or is just the same?' Doc Colm asked.

'Just the same.'

'Apart from vocal and facial tics, what other symptoms do you have?'

I looked at Mum, who gave me the all-clear.

'I swear sometimes and say strange things.'

'By strange things do you mean inappropriate things?'

'Yes.'

Doc Colm wrote down the things I said. 'Offensive things?'

'Sometimes.'

'Do you get anxious a lot?'

'Yes, but it depends on the situation.'

'Do you sweat profusely?'

'What does *profuse* mean?'

'Do you sweat a lot?'

'Yes.'

'Where on your body?' This was a strange question. Maybe I'd tell Miss Flynn this one.

'My back.'

'Anywhere else?'

I didn't want to tell Doc Colm that I sometimes sweat on

my willy and ball-sack; that would have been too embarrassing so I kept that one to myself.

'My head and under my arms.' After saying this I ticked like a maddie for five seconds or so. Doc Colm paused to let me finish and Mum put her hand on my thigh.

'Relax, Dylan, it's OK.'

I was trying so much not to swear at Doc Colm that I was doing that profuse sweating thing. I could feel it running down under the back of my boxers.

'OK. You're doing well, Dylan.' Doc Colm then turned to Mum, which I thought was my cue to be seen and not heard. 'Does Dylan demonstrate any signs of obsessive or compulsive behaviour?'

'Like OCD?' Mum said.

'Exactly,' said Doc Colm.

'He does, yes.'

I watched them talking about me as if they were two tennis players thudding an invisible ball back and forth.

'Can you elaborate for me, Mrs Mint?'

'Well, let's see. He tucks his ears into his head, especially when they're cold.'

Doc Colm's eyes squinted, which meant he didn't know what Mum was talking about. She picked up on this, like, ESP woman style.

'He just holds them into his head. I think it provides comfort or something.'

They both looked at the dummy. Doc Colm scribbled more stuff.

'Does it give you comfort when you tuck your ears in, Dylan?' the doc asked.

'A little.'

'Only a little?'

'A lot.'

'Good man.' Scribble. Scribble. 'Anything else?' Doc Colm said to Mum.

'Well, he can't go to sleep unless his socks are at the bottom of his bed.'

Confused Doc Look. 'What do you mean?'

'He takes his clothes off and puts everything into the dirty washing basket – everything, that is, except for his socks, which have to be placed at the bottom of the bed.'

'I see,' Doc Colm said. He gave me a little look that said, *Awwwwwww, poor wee soul*. My tic control was all shot to shit. *Shot to shit*: American AND alliteration. 'And this is every night or just occasionally?'

'No, it's every night,' Mum said.

I put my head to the floor dead embarrassed because I did all these stupid things. I didn't want to do them. I really didn't. Miss Flynn told me that I had to accept the fact that I did these things that other people simply didn't do. So I accepted it. But what she didn't know was that other people do things that spazzie people don't. We don't fight on the street and vomit all over the place (Michelle Malloy doesn't count as it was a one-off), we don't steal from shops or mug people, we don't blag from the social welfare, we don't get teenage girls pregnant, we don't drink as much as we possibly can and we don't wander the streets wearing cheap sports gear (sports gear should only be worn when playing sport). It's not rocket engineering, duh! Teachers didn't know everything about the word on the street.

'And do you ever get depressed, Dylan?' Doc Colm asked me.

Again I looked at Mum for her nod. 'Sometimes.'

'Do you just feel down sometimes? Do you ever just sit in your room and not want to see anyone?'

'Both.' Scribble. Scribble.

'Do you have any friends?'

'Yes. I have Amir, who's my best bud, and I have a new friend called Michelle Malloy.'

'Is she your girlfriend?' Doc Colm asked with a wee smirk on his face like he wanted us to have mega boy talk and have me tell him about all the brilliant bonking we had been doing. Bad luck, Doc Colm.

'No. Mum doesn't like her.'

'Dylan!' Mum said. 'That's not true at all,' she said to the doc.

'And you're still taking all your medication?'

'Yes.' I had to take all these mad tablets, about a gazillion of them every day. It was a major pain in the bahookie. I couldn't even pronounce their names. Mum and the school nurse made sure I took them.

'Well, I think we're going to wean you off most of them, Dylan.'

'What?' I said.

'We're going to reduce how much you take,' Doc Colm said.

'Why?' Mum asked.

'Mainly because they're not functioning as a preventative agent for the type of Tourette's Dylan has; they're merely suppressing the symptoms. There's a school of thought, which I subscribe to, that suggests a prescription of such magnitude does very little for the allowance of cognitive development and thus a move towards prevention.'

My head hurt with Doc Colm's mental adult words.

'So are you saying you can prevent Dylan's Tourette's by taking him off his drugs?' Mum said.

Sorry, what? I was confused.

'Not exactly. We just want to take a different tack, try a different approach.'

'Which will stop his Tourette's?' Mum asked.

'Well, which will calm it down at least, but you have to remember that Tourette's, as it stands now, is non-curable, but that doesn't mean we can't try other means and techniques in order to radically reduce its symptoms.'

This was mind-blowing. The last doc said that I had until March. That doc's chat with Mum had bamboozled my brain. Now Doc Colm was talking about prevention and reducing the swearing, Mr Dog, the ticking, grunting, groaning and shuffling.

'And that can be done?' Mum said.

'Let's not get ahead of ourselves here. We wish to place Dylan on a new trajectory.'

'Which is?' Mum said.

'Well, we want to allow his brain to learn new habits.'

Mum looked at both of us.

'We believe that Dylan's brain function has become so used to the tics, shouting, swearing et cetera that it has learnt the patterns and practices of these and so produces them involuntarily. What we aim to achieve is for Dylan's brain to reboot itself and learn a new pattern and practice.'

'How are you going to do that?' Mum said.

I was super excited to have my brain rebooted just like a computer.

'We've developed a new technique that we're pioneering with a few patients. We think Dylan would be the perfect candidate – if permitted, that is.'

Mum looked confused.

'I have to tell you, Mrs Mint, that the early results in the trials with other patients have been nothing short of astonishing.'

The two of them looked at me. Did they need me to approve this, whatever it was?

'What do you think, Dylan?' Mum said.

'Erm . . . I'm not too sure I understand,' I said.

'Let me explain,' Doc Colm said.

My heart was pumping. Did Doc Colm not have any idea what was going to happen to me in March? Did he miss that page out when reading my case notes?

'We're going to take a mould of your mouth and teeth,' Doc Colm said.

'Why?' I said, and I could tell that Mum wanted to ask the same question. 'My teeth are A-OK. I don't need to go to the dentist.'

'Of course not, Dylan. We believe that a lot can be understood from the teeth and mouth in controlling the tics and physical movements you make.'

'So what will happen exactly?' Mum asked.

'We'll make Dylan a bespoke mouthpiece that he'll have to wear at all times except for at night.'

'And this will help him?' Mum said.

'We think so, yes,' Doc Colm said. 'Let's be clear, Mrs Mint: this won't magically cure Dylan's Tourette's, but we believe that it will dramatically reduce his symptoms, especially the tics.'

'Well, that's good, Dylan. Don't you think?' Mum said to me.

My head was about to explode with the confusion. The sweat was worse than ever. My bum was soaking. I just had to get it out.

'LYING BASTARD DICK.'

'Dylan!'

'But the other doc said that I was going to die in March.' There. I said it. I blurted it out. No going back. This was my time. My hour.

'What?' Mum said. But the look on her face was more like, *What the fuck are you saying, Dylan, you fucking headcase?*

Doc Colm smiled and chuckled like he was thinking, *Wow! This eejit is even madder than I thought. This clown will need more than a bloody mouthpiece to save him.*

'What are you saying, Dylan?' Mum said.

'The other doc said that in March the Tourette's would make me cack it.'

'When was this, Dylan?' Mum asked.

'The time we went to see about the scan,' I said.

'That wasn't *your* scan . . . I was with you, Dylan,' Mum said. 'I was with him, doctor, and I can assure you that wasn't what was said.'

'It was. He said something about it being so incontrovertible and you were crying. I didn't know what that meant so I looked it up in the school dictionary and then it all made sense to me.'

'No, it's not what you think, Dylan,' Mum said.

'He also said that you had to prepare me for what's going to happen. But he gulped before he said the words "what's going to happen".'

'You've got this all wrong, Dylan,' Mum said.

'But you were crying,' I said.

Mum didn't say anything. I looked at Doc Colm.

'The other doc said that life as I know it will come to an abrupt end. I remember, Doc Colm, I remember,' I said.

Doc Colm leant back in his chair. 'Dylan, I can't comment on these things – they're for you and your mum to talk about – but I can assure you that Tourette's is a non-degenerative condition, which means that it won't progressively deterio-rate over time, which means that it won't get worse, which means it *won't* kill you.'

'Why was Mum crying then?'

'I think when my colleague spoke you just picked up something incorrectly and got the wrong end of the stick.'

'But why were you crying, Mum?' I asked.

'You've got this so wrong, Dylan,' Mum said. She looked at Doc Colm for support, but I think the big man was wondering why Mum cried that day too. 'And I can't remem-ber if I cried.'

'You did, and you cried on the way home and you cried when we got home and you became a bear with a dead sore head in the days after and I thought I'd done something mega wrong and I was really scared because I was going to cack it

314

in March and you didn't care,' I said. 'How could you not remember?' My head flew from side to side and back and forth. My eyes blinked and I was doing what the docs call physical grimacing. No sign of Mr Dog though. We stared at Mum.

'I cried because . . . I cried . . . I was crying because . . .'

'Mrs Mint, if this is a personal matter . . .' Doc Colm said, just before we got to the Juicy Lucy bit. Nice one, Doc Colm.

'No, it'll have to come out sooner or later,' Mum said.

'Would you prefer if I left you two alone?'

'That won't be necessary,' Mum said.

And I could see her breathing in and out. The atmosphere was so thick that you would have needed a good sharp set of garden sheers to cut through it. I was concentrating so much that all my tics and noises disappeared in one big whoosh. We waited and waited. Mum took one gigantic deep breath like the breath you take when you want to try to swim a full length underwater (I'd never managed it. Amir said he had, but I wasn't there to witness it so it didn't technically count). Mum came up for some air and then unloaded the big guns.

'What's happening in March is . . .'

'Yes . . . ?'

'What's happening is that I'm going to have a baby, Dylan.'

'A baby?'

'Two, in fact.'

'Two?'

'Twins.'

WELL, FUCK ME SIDEWAYS, as Doughnut sometimes said.

'I'm pregnant, son. You're going to have two wee brothers or sisters, or maybe one of each,' Mum said.

I looked at Doc Colm, who looked at the wall behind Mum's left shoulder. Mum looked at the ground because she knew that I knew that she knew that I knew that Doc Colm didn't know.

FUCK ME UP, DOWN AND SIDEWAYS. That's what I say.

'So I'm not going to cack it then?' I asked Mum, just to be one hundred and twenty-five per cent sure.

'No, you're not. The doctor was saying all those things about the babies, not your Tourette's, love,' Mum said. 'That's why I was there that day in the hospital. It was my scan we were discussing, not yours.'

'And that's why you were crying?'

'Yes.'

'So my life as I know it will *not* come to an abrupt end in March then?'

'No. Absolutely not.'

'So the reason you were crying was because you're having a baby?'

'Two.'

'Two babies . . . Nick Nack Noo!'

'Yes.'

I looked at Doc Colm. 'Women are strange,' I said. He laughed. 'So why did I think I was dying then?'

'I think you just misinterpreted what the doctor said, Dylan, that's all,' Doc Colm said.

'So he was a baby doctor?'

'Sort of,' Mum said.

'But why did you take me with you that day if it was just for lady talk?' I asked Mum.

'I needed you with me for support and to remind me that having a baby is a beautiful thing.'

'Is that why you gave me *499 Footie Facts To Amaze Your Mates!*?'

'I gave it to you because you wanted it.'

'Thanks, Mum.'

*

When Doc Colm was putting this yucky plaster in my mouth he didn't need to say 'Open wide' because my gob was as wide as a hippo's yawn. I think they call it flabbergasted. I was chuffed to bits that I wasn't going to cack it also.

What a day!

26
Truth

I'm not really into biology; all that stuff goes over my head. Section 6.6 in our biology course confused me. My face and neck went all rosy red when the teacher spoke about willies, women's parts, eggs and swimming sperm. Apparently you could even count the sperm cells swimming around. Some job that would be! The class was super silent when our biology teacher spoke about all that stuff. Amir was embarrassed even though you couldn't see it in his face; he just made these mad best bud eyes and I knew what he was thinking.

I may be rank rotten at biology, but I knew what was needed in order to make a baby. A man and a woman. I knew that mums needed dads to make babies. And I knew that *my* dad wasn't in the country to make my mum's two babies. It did go through my nut that he could have made a covert visit home, quickly made the babies and then hightailed it back to the war zone. But the more I thought about that idea the more it seemed major mind-boggling. There was no danger the army would let any of their men bolt home for that reason, especially someone as important as Dad. I did some detective work in my head – a bit like brain gym, though this one was more like brain-melt gym – and I came to the conclusion that Mum's new babies were not Dad's new babies and Dad probably didn't have the foggiest idea that Mum was going to have two babies. It was a wowee zowee moment. As soon as it was crystal clear I stroked Green, rough as anything. I groaned, barked, swore, ticked and shook. I cried my peepers out into my pillow, which became a wee bit salty soggy. I blubbed because I was going to have new wee brothers or sisters or both who didn't belong to Dad. I felt heart sorry for Dad because I knew he would be

rage

rage

raging

that he wasn't going to be the daddy and his voice would really get

loud

loud

louder

and he could quite easily

scud

scud

scud

something or someone

and it would be so terrible because he wouldn't be able to do any of the fun dad stuff like nappy changing, babysitting, feeding and reading bedtime stories. I also cried because if the babies didn't come from Dad it meant they only *half* belonged to me. I'd be like some of the insane people who go on *The Jerry Springer Show*. I didn't know what to do: write to tell Dad the bombshell news or wait until Mum told him straight to his face? It was like when contestants have to make a word out of jumbled letters on *Countdown*. Problemo grande.

Dylan Mint's major dilemma.

BUT I wasn't going to cack it after all and that made me cry happy tears. Doc Colm told me that I would have 'a long, wonderful and fruitful life'. Even though it was a huge PHEW off my shoulders it meant that my *Cool Things To Do Before I Cack It* list was as useful as an ashtray on a motorbike. It was a crying shame I didn't get to have proper sex play with Michelle Malloy, but she did sleep (and puke) in my bed so that was almost like the real thing. But I really did fight Heaven and earth, tooth and nail, dungeons and dragons to stop Amir getting called names about the colour of his skin. I did stop people at school slagging him off all the time

320

because he smelled like a big pot of curry. And I did help him find a new best bud. Yes I did.

Who?

ME.

The new long-wonderful-and-fruitful-life ME.

His new best bud couldn't be that girl he was dancing with all night at the Halloween disco because girls just can't be best buds with guys.

Period.

The biggie now was number three: *Get Dad back from the war before . . . you-know-what . . . happens.* But the *you-know-what* part had changed from *before I cack it* to *before Mum pops it.* That would have made Einstein's head hurt.

To stop the shaking and everything I put my spanking new tongue blade that Doc Colm gave me in my mouth. It looked like a big file that ladies use on their long nails. It was easy. All I had to do was bite on to it when the stress and tics came. Whenever I bit on to the tongue blade my head stopped shaking from side to side, I stopped grunting and generally felt less sweaty and stressed. It worked. It was a capital M Miracle. A Miracle of Miracles. Doc Colm told me to use the tongue blade until he had made me an actual proper mouth brace. I could only use the tongue blade at home because I would look like I was straitjacket material if seen wandering the streets with a big ladies' nail file in my gub, but with the mouth brace I could wear it all the time and the bonkers thing was that nobody would be able to see it or have a clue I was a grunter, ticker, swearer or barker. Doc Colm was eighty-five per cent confident that it would be a rip-roaring success. Doc Colm should have been nominated for the Nobel Peace Prize, an Oscar, a Blue Peter badge and a Great Scot Award rolled into one. He was just like Jesus, if you believe in all that stuff. I was thinking that maybe Doc Colm could do something for the bold Amir's mental madness and I should mention Amir's problems to him the next time I saw him. I wondered if he could fix Michelle Malloy's gammy legs and do something about her potty tongue. I couldn't wait to have my mouth brace; it would be like having a new life.

Me and Mum weren't not speaking; it just seemed like the whole house was made of this gigantic eggshell and we were afraid that if we spoke or shouted or ran up and down the stairs like a herd of goats the eggshell would crack and all this yucky yoke would seep out and drown us. We did a lot of smiling and comfortable silence stuff and Mum sometimes asked how I was getting on with my new tongue blade.

'How are you getting on with your new tongue blade?'
'Fine.'
'It seems to be working.'
'Yes.'
'That's good, isn't it?'

'Suppose.'

'It's made a huge difference, don't you think?'

'Suppose.'

'Well, I think it has.'

'Good.'

'Doctor Cunningham will be delighted when he sees you again.'

'Suppose.'

I wanted to say loads more to Mum and ask her all the questions that were rattling around in my napper, but I was a bit scared in case she told me things that I didn't want to hear. When I was lying with my tongue blade in bed, I thought of ten questions I wanted to ask Mum:

1. Who is your new babies' daddy?
2. Why isn't it the same daddy as mine?
3. When did you make the babies?
4. Did you make the babies in this house or did you go to a special place?
5. Are you sad because you're having two new babies?
6. Are you not far too old to have two new babies?
7. What are you going to call the new babies?
8. Do you think Dad will go Billy Bonkers when he finds out that he is not the new babies' daddy?
9. Do you think Dad will fly off the handle and lash out again?

10. Will you love the new babies more than you love
    me?

Numbers one, two, eight and nine were the questions that kept swingballing around in my brain night after night after night after night. For number seven I had two names in my head: if they're boys they could be Mustafa and Samir, and if they're girls they could be called Maleeha and Dhivya. These are the names of Amir's cousins who still live in Pakistan so they'd never know that we stole them, and I really like the idea of the alliteration with my second name Mint. But that idea was blown out of the river because the answer to question number one meant that they would have a different surname from me.

I was going to tell Amir, cause that's what you do when you have a weight on your shoulder – you blurt it out to your best bud. I nearly did as well.

awright d boy?

rap it, were u been amir ma man?

hangin with priya, u?

shit has hit the fan at home

tell ur bud the crack?

2 complicated

shit that does sound bad

its a face to face explanation

I hear u bro, I hear u

wots the deal with the burd?

who priya?

yes

shes dead on

r u in luv?

shut it ya dick

ur a dick

UR a dick

UR DICK van dyke

who?

Never mind … lol.

need to go d boy

rap it, c u soon

4 sure

wot u up 2 2day?

I'm goin out with priya

give her 1 for me

shes not like that

sorry … lol

laters

c u soon bud

I was glad I didn't blurt it out to Amir as this was a family thing and not a best bud thing. In fact this was a bit of a rosy redneck.

*

325

After another day of trying not to crack the eggshells that were holding up the house and another night of tossing, twisting, turning and kicking the bedclothes off me I thought, *Right, Dylan, you have a few questions you need answering, my old son. Get to it.*

I heard Mum pottering about downstairs, making loads of noise. She wasn't out at her boot camp, even though she'd been there three times in one week alone, which I thought was devil dangerous. I'm not a fully qualified doctor, and being at Drumhill I don't think I'll ever be able to become a fully qualified doctor, but I do know that doing squat thrusts, star jumps, burpees and sit-ups in some smelly park somewhere can't be any good for two babies inside a woman's belly. If babies in bellies could talk, they'd probably shout, 'Would you stop bloody bouncing me around your belly like a wee Smartie, Mum, and sit down and watch some telly or something instead?' when their mums decided to run about in public places with a load of other fat women. It wasn't on. I didn't think Mum should be doing the boot camp with a belly full of babies. Then forked lightning hit me: maybe that was why I had to go to Drumhill for all these years, cause Mum ran about like a maddie on crack with her boot-camp crowd when I was just a tiny tot floating about in her belly – maybe she did one star jump too many. Maybe I landed full force on my head on to some tough part of her belly and I ended up like this. It could have happened. It could have.

Mum was doing a lot of huffing and puffing and slamming cupboard doors in the kitchen as I walked in. When she saw me, she stopped slamming. There were two used tea bags on the table but no cups. She looked unhappy. I loved my mum and wanted her to feel A-OK like I did when I left Doc Colm's hospital that day.

'You A-OK, Mum?' I said.

'Yes, Dylan, I'm fine.'

'Have you been crying?'

'No.'

'Are you sure?'

'Yes I'm sure.'

'Are you sad?'

'Why are you asking?'

'Cause the tea bags are out and you only put them on your eyes when you're sad or crying.' I sat down next to the tea bags and squeezed them between my fingers until the cold tea juice came out.

'They help with the puffiness and bags.'

I thought this was funny snigger, not funny ha ha.

'What's so funny?' Mum said.

'Using these wee bags to help your other wee bags,' I said, pointing to her eyes.

'Very funny, Dylan.'

'Are you sad because of the babies in your belly?'

She folded her arms across her tummy. Then there was a

tough silence. 'No . . . yes . . . no . . . Well, yes and no, but mostly no.' Mum sat down across from me and this was the first time since we came back from seeing Doc Colm that we had sat at the table together for some chat time. 'Look, Dylan . . .'

'Can I ask you a question, Mum?'

'What?'

'Promise you won't get mad?'

'I won't get mad.'

'Promise?'

'Promise.'

'Mega promise?'

'Mega promise.'

'Is my dad the dad of those babies in your belly?'

Mum looked at me then looked away like she was thinking so super hard that her brain was about to explode. Then she looked back at me.

'No, Dylan, your dad is not the father of the twins,' Mum said, and rubbed her tummy like you would a wee bald man's head. A part of me felt chuffed because I detected this all along and it meant that I knew the score. My power of deduction was spot on.

'I knew it,' I said. I wasn't angry or annoyed.

'Knew what?'

'That Dad wasn't the dad.'

Mum flicked her eyes up to the ceiling as if to say, *No shit,*

Sherlock, but I could tell that she was being sarcastic, which is one of the main things adults do to make them different from children or teenagers at Drumhill.

'Well, he's not,' I said. 'Who is?' This was the biggie.

Apart from Dad I only knew four grown-up men who could make a baby:

1. Mr Comeford. But he was married and his wife was a cracker. (We saw her at the Drumhill fundraiser for wee Mark Gilmour's new liver and lung.)
2. Mr Grant. He was a straight no-no because he was a double adaptor.
3. Mr McGrain. A definite no-no because he was about 905, had a huge nose and bad skin – Mum would never find him nude attractive.
4. Mr Manzoor, Amir's old man. But Dad would have been mega mega mega mad if he found *that* out.

Actually, there was one more, but I tried to block him out.

'Who is it?' I said again.

'You've met him,' Mum said.

'Where?'

'Right here, sitting where you are now.'

I shook my head. 'Who?'

'Tony,' Mum said, and let the name explode from her mouth and into my brain. 'It's Tony, Dylan.'

'The taxi driver?' I said, trying to sound flabber flabber flabbergasted, but deep down I sort of knew.

'Yes.'

'How?'

'What do you mean *how*?'

'How is Tony the taxi driver the dad?'

Mum looked at me as if she thought my how question was all about the birds and the bees. It wasn't. My how was a *how could you take a taxi, have a chat with the taxi driver, offer him a cup of tea in our house and then have a baby together?* That part didn't make sense.

'We met a while ago.'

'In a taxi?'

'No, not in a taxi, Dylan. I told you we were old school friends.'

'Like me and Amir?'

'Well, we were probably a bit closer than you and Amir when we were at school.'

'Like bf and gf?'

'Speak English please.'

'Boyfriend and girlfriend.'

'Exactly, we were boyfriend and girlfriend when we were at school.'

'So why did you leave each other then?'

'We were kids then.'

'So? Amir is my best bud and we're kids now, but I bet

we'll still be best buds when we're dead old like you and the taxi driver.' Mum gave me one of her stop-talking-shite looks. 'Does the taxi driver know that you have babies in there?'

'Can you do me a favour, Dylan?'

'What?'

'Can you stop calling him the taxi driver please. His name's Tony and I'd appreciate it if you could start using it.'

'Does Tony know that there are babies in there?' I said, and pointed to Mum's belly.

'Of course he knows.'

'So what's going to happen then?'

'What do you mean, what's going to happen? You know what's going to happen – the babies will be here in March.'

'We only have two bedrooms so where will the babies sleep?'

Mum became silent and puffed out her cheeks. A sure sign that something was on her mind. I put my tongue blade in because I could feel the pressure ball rising.

'That's something we need to discuss, Dylan, but not now.'

'So when?' I said, but with the tongue blade in it sounded like a long *eeeennnnnn*.

'Not now. I have enough on my plate without discussing all the nitty-gritty stuff right now.'

I took my tongue blade out. 'What about Dad?'

'Oh, for the love of God, Dylan,' Mum said, and stood up like people who are in an I'm-up-to-high-dough state do. Or who have an invisible jumbo-size railway sleeper on their chest. Mum took deep breaths in and out, in and out.

'Well, what about him? It's not fair to Dad.'

'Sure it's not,' she said in a soft voice that she didn't want me to hear, but I heard good enough.

'I was going to write him a letter and tell him everything,' I said, but I was only kidding cause news like that could have affected his judgement and an affected judgement in a war zone is a bit like being covered in raw-meat jelly and thrown in a kennel full of pit-bull dogs.

Mum looked at me and blew her top. 'WHAT HAVE I TOLD YOU ABOUT WRITING A LOAD OF RUBBISH TO YOUR DAD?'

'But he'll want to know why you did it with Tony the taxi driver while he was away at the war.'

'TONY! TONY! JUST TONY,' she screamed. I think Mum had a problem with Tony's chosen profession.

'But Dad will want some big questions answered, Mum.'

Mum stared at me and then out of the window.

'Like, if you love Dad why would you make two babies with someone else?'

Major annoyed sigh. Breaths in and out. Deep raging breaths. In. Out. I joined in. We sounded like we were wearing *Starship Troopers* costumes.

'I don't love your dad any more, Dylan,' Mum said, in her low voice. All calm and soft. This was her scary voice.

'What?' Shock-a-roony bombshell.

'I am not in love with your dad, Dylan.'

'Why?'

'Too many whys.'

'But you slept in the same bed.'

'I wasn't in love with him.'

'What, ever?'

'Not for the last few years.'

'Really?'

'Yes, really.' Wow!

'Do you love the taxi . . . I mean Tony?'

'Yes.'

'Really?'

'Yes, Dylan. I'm in love with Tony.'

'Does he love you back?'

'Yes.'

'Really?'

'Yes, really.'

So Mum loved Tony the taxi driver and he loved her back? Heaven help us! This was one of those moments in your life where you never ever forget where you were when something big happened, like when that president of the USA got shot donkey's years ago. I would always remember that I was sitting at our kitchen table rubbing a used tea bag between the fingers of my left hand and Green with the fingers on my right when Mum told me she didn't love Dad any more and that she loved Tony the taxi driver now. Jings!

'Mum?'

'What?'

'Can I ask you another question?'

'Why not, it's open season,' she said. I didn't really know what this meant. Adults = crazies at times. 'What is it?'

'Does Tony love me?'

'Well, you haven't been very nice to him, have you?'

'I have. I listened to Pink Floyd.' It was Strange with a capital S talking about love and stuff with Mum. It felt like an adult conversation without all the big massive words. 'So Tony doesn't love me then?'

'He loves me, Dylan, and I love you, so in a roundabout way I suppose he does love you, but you probably have to spend more time with each other for any love to develop between you.'

I could see what Mum was going on about. Important alert! Tony the taxi driver would love the babies because they were his very own babies and I would love the babies because they would be my very own brothers or sisters or both even though they were only half wee brothers or sisters or both. I couldn't have cared less; I'd still love the wee monkeys. I'd be the best big half-brother in the world and show them the ropes, the word on the street and all of life's nooks and crannies. That meant that me and Tony the taxi driver would love the same three things: Mum and the wee monkeys. He'd have to love me after that. How could he not?

'Does Dad love *you*?' I asked. If Mum's head was see-through you'd have been able to see her brain spinning around inside.

'I'm not sure he does.' She said this with a smile on her face.

'Why, what did you do?'

Mum sniggered. It was good to see her happy and laughing a bit. 'What did I do?' She said this to the ceiling. 'What did I do?' She was still laughing. Strange behaviour.

'Yes, what did you do?' I really did want to know.

'I'll tell you what I did, shall I?'

'OK.' I couldn't wait to find out what Mum did. I sat up in my chair.

'I was the one who looked after you when *he* couldn't be bothered, or was too drunk to even notice you were there. I was the one who took you to school when you were little because *he* was too embarrassed to be seen outside the gates of Drumhill. I was the one who didn't question him when *he* stayed out for days on end hanging out of whatever floozy was flavour of the week. I was the one who acted as his human punchbag when *he* was feeling tied down or imprisoned here with you and me. I was the one who had to lie to everyone and say *he* was somewhere with the army when he wasn't. That's what I did, Dylan. There. Happy now?'

A mammoth, epic
KERPOW
CLANG .
BANG
SCUD MISSILE
moment to beat all others.

Jesus H. Jones, as the Americans say.

I thought about what Mum had said and I really wanted to give her a hug and tell her that I loved her and that I'd never in a month of Mondays use her as a human punchbag. Never ever ever. No Way, José.

'Does Dad love me?' I asked Mum.

'In his own way I suppose he does.'

'Why didn't you tell me he was using you as a human punchbag?'

'You were a kid, Dylan. It was something you should have been protected from. I tried to shield you from all that crap.' Mum turned her back and pretended to be doing busy stuff in the kitchen. I knew she was doing pretend cleaning though I didn't say anything. 'And, anyway, you had your own problems to contend with, like your Tourette's. You didn't need to know about the problems that your mum and dad were having.'

'I could have told Miss Flynn – she's good with things like that.'

Mum stopped pretending and turned around. 'Well, that's exactly why I didn't say anything.' She ruffled my hair, which

I really really liked. It made me tingle inside when Mum ruffled my hair.

'But what did you do for him to treat you like a human punchbag?' I said.

Mum started laughing loudly, but this certainly wasn't a hee-hee-hee-oh-that's-so-blinking-funny laugh.

'You're definitely your father's son.' Which was a strange thing to say because *this* piece of information I already knew. 'I didn't do anything, Dylan. It was his way of having some recreational fun when he wasn't out with his cronies or with one of his little hussies or in some pub.' Then she sort of changed the look on her face and pointed her finger at me. Her finger was dead angry. 'No man has the right to lift his hand to any woman. No man. Do you understand?'

'Yes,' I said. I agreed with her. But then if a woman attacked a man with a hatchet or hammer then surely that man could defend himself. I didn't say this to Mum though in case she thought I was being a male chauvinist runt pig. 'But why did Dad do that?'

'You'll have to ask him that, Dylan.'

'Did he punch you for real, like, full force?'

'Slapped, punched, kicked, headbutted, shoved . . . You name it, he did it.'

My head rattled and a few WHOOPs came flying out. I put the tongue blade in again and bit as hard as I could, almost all the way through it. It was a Mr Angry bite. I wanted to cry for Mum and for her to give me one of her hug specials, or for me to give her one of my hug specials. I was like earth-quake lava with rage flowing inside me because I had this picture in my head of Mum being flung around the living room when Dad used her as a human punchbag. That was not on your nelly. The picture made me want to bubble or scream. I breathed hard through my nose and then took my tongue blade out.

'But I don't understand, Mum. Why did he do that? That's not nice, not nice at all. Why would he do that?'

'You're telling me. I really don't know why he did it.'

'He's a big man bully.'

'He is.'

'I don't like people who bully other people.'

'Me neither, son.'

'It's just not right.'

'I know it's not.'

'Does Tony use you as a human punchbag?'

'No. No, Tony is gentle and caring.' I was hoping Mum was going to say something like this because I didn't know what I'd have done if Tony the taxi driver liked his women to be punchbags. I would've had to have a word in Amir's shell so we could've come up with a proper plan of action. No need thankfully.

'That's what I want to be when I grow up – caring and gentle,' I said, because that's what all good men should be like. Even if you don't have money to buy swanky dinners in flashy restaurants like Nando's or T.G.I. Friday's or wear trendy clothes or have a shit-hot hot-rod car, you can still be gentle and caring. All those other things don't really matter that much. 'If I'd known what Dad was up to maybe I could have stopped him. I could have done something.'

'He was an animal, Dylan. No one could have stopped him.'

'Not even the army?'

Mum sat down next to me and took my hand in hers. My hand was Sweaty Betty and hers was Clammy Sammy. She looked at me directly in the eyes, really serious, like, the same as when me and Amir were having one of our major blinking competitions, which I always won. Amir said it was because Pakistani eyelids are more sensitive than Scottish ones and he needs to blink more, which I never realised before. People's bodies are bonker machines! Mum stared at me.

'Look, love, your dad left the army a long time ago.'

'Yes, I know.'

Mum seemed surprised that I knew serious stuff, as if she thought I was the smallest birdbrain in Britain or something. 'You do?'

'Yes, he's in some special forces now. It's a bit like a higher-up version of the SAS. Major Intelligence Unit, I think.'

Mum shook her head and her eyes had a Feeling Sorry look about them.

'No, he's not, son.'

'He's not?' Now I was confused dot com like in algebra class.

'He left the army last year.'

'2013 last year?'

'June 2013 to be exact.'

'He left last June? Why?'

'When I say left, he didn't exactly *leave*.'

'So he didn't leave?' Now it was like double algebra class with algebra detention after school followed by algebra homework and a crossword at bedtime.

'He was asked to leave.'

'Asked to leave the army?'

'Yes.'

'Why?'

'Because of his poor discipline.'

'What does that mean?'

'He was drunk on duty, fighting with fellow soldiers . . . Lots and lots of things . . . He was a loose cannon.'

'So they asked him to leave for being a loose cannon?' There were a few loose cannons at Drumhill; they were the ones who were proper straitjacket material.

'They did, yes.'

'That's, like, getting the sack from a job, isn't it?'

'Exactly.'

'So Dad got the sack from the army?'

'Yes.' Just how the Devil's daughter can anyone get the

sack from the army? The army! Even people at Drumhill know that the army is full of all the knobs, thickos and bullies from schools up and down the country. How can anyone get the sack from a place that is already full of psychos? That's what I didn't understand.

'But that's bonkers. Nobody gets the sack from the army, do they?'

'He was a bad man, Dylan. They had to sack him.'

'But what about all my letters?'

'He got them, I made sure of that.'

'But I wrote Iraq on some of the envelopes.'

'They didn't get sent to Iraq.'

'He wasn't even in Iraq?'

'No, he wasn't in Iraq.'

'So how did he get them?'

'I still sent them to him, I just changed the address on the envelopes you had put them in.'

'So he got them?'

'Yes, I presume so.'

'Why hasn't he ever written back then?'

'Only he can answer that.'

'Where did you send them to if you didn't send them to Iraq?'

Mum took one of the tea bags that were sitting on the table and squeezed so hard that all the tea juice came running on to the table and made a wee tea puddle, which was stupid because she would just have to wipe it clean later; I didn't make the mess so I wasn't cleaning it up.

'Where did you send my letters to?'

'I sent them to your dad in Barlinnie.'

'Where?'

'Barlinnie,' she said again, which didn't make any sense at all as I didn't know where or what it was. She could have said the word all day long and it wouldn't have made a dent in my noggin.

'You can keep saying that but I still don't know where it is.'

'Barlinnie is a prison, son. Your dad's in prison.'

MASSIVE CAPITAL LETTER PAUSE.

I felt like my brain was going down a huge escalator towards a deep black hole. It took me a

long

       long

            long

                long

                    time

to get the correct answer but with the agony of thinking so hard I eventually got it. Dylan Mint, a true brain-gym master. A gold star for Dylan Mint.

27

Robber

Mum said she had to leave me with my head on the kitchen table for about half an hour before she plucked up the courage to come and give me one of her hug specials and explain to me what really happened with Dad, and why he had to go to prison and all that. When she kissed me full force on the cheek and told me she 'loved me sooooooooooooooooooooooooooo much' and that me, her, Tony the taxi driver and the little monkeys were going to be one happy family, my tears connected with her tears and flowed down both our cheeks together, like best bud tears holding hands all the way down to the chins. But when she dropped that bombshell bolt from the blue, that knockout punch, that sledgehammer to the balls, I badly needed some nasty-ass brain-gym questions to get me through the initial blast. My tongue blade wasn't enough on its own.

THIS IS THE STUFF MUM TOLD ME:

When Dad was booted out of the army for being a major embarrassing pain in the arse to them, he couldn't get a job anywhere for love nor money. The eejit spent all his time at the pub getting sloshed or at the bookies spending all his little savings and dole money on mad things like betting on speedway and skiing. Anyway he lost all his dosh super-rapido style because what he knew about speedway or skiing you could write on your eyelid. He was left with only his dole money to keep his head above the grass. Dole money's crap and the papers say that it's only tramps, thickos and lazy people who are on the dole and it's a pure redneck to be on the dole and that's when I thought Dad had some nerve on him to say it was a redneck for me to go to Drumhill when *he* was on the bloody rock and roll. Anyway, he still managed to get mangled at the pub all the time and did some odd jobs for some guys he knew, putting bricks and other rubbish people didn't want into a skip. He started hanging about with these pure badass hoodlums and that's when he got into doing some real dodgy stuff. Mum didn't know what because she was afraid to ask in case she became a human punchbag again, but her detective head told her that Dad was up to no damn good. Around that time she and Tony were graffitiing each other's Facebook walls. All of a sudden Dad had new hip clobber, did his car up to the nines and bought a top-of-the-tree mobile phone and drank tons of super-alcoholic booze, champagne, Martini and Lambrusco wine. He was going about the place thinking he was some kind of big-shot playboy James Bond type. Or the dog's bollocks. Mum said I hadn't a clue what was going on because Dad couldn't be arsed with me, and, anyway, he wasn't at home for days on end, so it was easier to tell me he was away on army duty so I wouldn't ask too many Dylan Mint Questions.

Then one day when I was at school, police with motorbike helmets came to the door with a big red battering ram and dragged Dad out of his bed while he was sleeping off a massive booze binge and huckled him downtown to read him his rights, throw the damn book at him and charge him for 'aggravated armed robbery'. When Mum told me what *aggravated* meant I wondered if there was any other form of armed robbery. The police do have funny names for crimes. The funny-ha-ha-belly-laugh thing was that Dad only had his pants on when they huckled him downtown. Mum laughed because she said that she hoped he had clean pants on that day. When she got to the station, Dad was wearing a bright orange railway worker's suit (Tango Man) and had a hangover that would have knocked a camel out. Dad didn't want to see her and she didn't really want to see Dad either, but the police had some serious questions for Mum and put her through the ringer for five hours and forty-two minutes.

And I remembered that day so well because that was the day I had to remain in school for what seemed like ages and ages and ages for no reason at all and I listened to Sigur Rós and Mogwai in Miss Flynn's office.

Dad the dafty head case had only gone and robbed a wee post office in a tiny borders village, tied up the man and lady who ran the wee post office and smashed a baseball bat into the poor man's legs until he gave up the information about where all the dosh was stored. He hooked the poor man four times on the face and gubbed the poor soul of a lady twice on the jaw AFTER they told him where the loot was. He got away with 763 quid (not very wow!) and hightailed it back to Glasgow *in his own car*. What a tool! The police huckled him the very next day because they saw him on the wee post office's CCTV camera with his face uncovered. What a total tool! He put his hands up, said it was a fair cop and pled guilty to the dastardly deed.

Because Dad was the world's worst armed robber and the world's biggest tool he received a fifteen-year stretch in the notorious Barlinnie Prison. Fifteen years for £763. What a total bloody tool you are, Mr Mint!

Out of the ninety-two teams in the English leagues, which teams have the shortest and the longest one-word team name?

A teasing
tease

of a

teaser,

especially as English leagues weren't on any of my 'specialist subject' lists.

Long hard think.

Lots of staring and not talking.

Bury

and

Middlesbrough.

Brain Gym Champ Extraordinaire!

Game over!

28
Shopping

When I told the bold Amir that I wasn't going to cack it after all because the docs at the hospital had made one almighty dick-up, I think he wanted to give me a bone-crushing bear hug. (I was too embarrassed to tell him that it was in fact my own almighty dick-up. I didn't want my best bud to think I was a mad dumb dumb yoke. So I kept schtum.) In the end he didn't give me a bone-crushing bear hug partly because we were out in the open and partly because that's what sausage jockey men do with each other before they get down to the real nitty gritty, and we weren't in the slightest bit sausage. There was no nitty gritty to be had.

'It's bl-bl-blooming annoying as well though, isn't it?' Amir said. He did some severe blinking, which he only did when he was upset or shocked or didn't know the answers to easy questions in class, like when Mr McGrain asked him what the capital of the USA was. Amir took a tortoise's lifetime to answer New York. The class chuckled and Amir blinked like the start of the movie in the cinema. 'Do you not think it's a wee bit bl-bl-blooming annoying?'

'How?'

'Because you won't get to do all those cool things on your to-do list now.'

'I can still do them, Amir.'

'How?'

'It just means I'll have more time to do them in, and when you think about it I can add more top-notch things to my to-do list and do them over a longer period of time. See? That's what makes living ace.'

'You think of everything, don't you?'

'It's up here for the thinking, down here for the drinking,' I said, pointing to my head and then to my willy.

Amir sniggered. 'You're men-men-mental, Dylan.'

'Want to know another thing?'

'What?'

'I can still have my *Cool Things To Do Before I Cack It* list because the way I see it we are all going to cack it anyway. That's one hundred and eighty-five per cent fact.'

'Suppose.'

'I can add you to the list if you want.'

'Can you do that?'

'Special rules for best buds.'

Then Amir put his thinking hat on . . . Danger Alert!

'So,' he said, still wearing his thinking hat. Abort! Abort! 'You want to do *me* before you cack it?'

'Not on your nelly, Amir.' Sometimes Amir's mind worked differently from other people's. This was one of those times.

'So how could I be on your list then?'

'I mean I could just change it to a *Cool Things For Dylan And Amir To Do Before They Cack It* list.'

Amir blinked and hit himself four times on the thigh. It was a pity that there was no mouth brace for him to wear. Mine was working wonders. Not so much as a tic session for a week or so. I sort of missed Mr Dog. Not too much, but enough. Sometimes I made a few wee head shuffles on purpose so Amir wouldn't feel all alone with the stuff he did. I could tell he liked my idea of the new list.

'I like that idea.'

'Excellente, capitano.'

'Can we change it a wee b-b-bit though?'

'That's what we just did.'

'No, I mean, can we change it again?'

'To what?'

'To *Cool Things For Dylan, Amir And Priya To Do Before They Cack It?*' he said like a wee lost laddie.

Since they met at the Halloween disco Amir and Priya had become bf and gf. For a lassie she was as sound as a pound.

And because she was from India and Amir was from Pakistan they did a lot of

> *you're a pure fanny,*
> *no, you're a pure fanny.*
> *You're a stupid arsehole,*
> *no, you're a stupid arsehole*

type banter to each other. Their parents didn't know they were Velcro knickers though. If they had known, a river of shit would have been unleashed. I promised never to open my gub about the bf–gf thing. They were a fantabulous pair and I liked having Priya cut around with us; it was good to have another person's mind and a woman's opinion about stuff. One thing I didn't like though was when they spoke to each other in their own dub-a-dub-a-dub language because I thought that they were taking the micky out of me. Amir told me they weren't and I believed him. He was my best bud, after all, and trust is everything. The worst thing was when Amir and Priya said goodnight, and I had to wait around the corner of a shop, at the back of a bus shelter, at the front of the community centre or behind a tree while they snogged each other's faces. The bold Amir always returned as if he had just come straight from Santa's grotto. I wondered how poor Priya put up with his breath, but she smelt a wee bit like curry too so I suppose everyone was as happy as Harry.

It was so much better when Michelle Malloy started to

hang out with us because I had someone to talk to and didn't feel like the big green hairy-suited monster. Me and Michelle Malloy didn't kiss in front of people. We hadn't done real kissing yet, though sometimes our hands would touch and we held them there for a while. We did some damn good talking about super-crazy stuff like parents being annoying, school being shit, normal people being idiots, walking like a wonky donkey, reality telly shows being utter crap and music that old people listen to.

Michelle Malloy liked the fact that I didn't call her SLUT BITCH any longer. Sometimes I'd text nite nite slut bitch to her as a joke and she'd text back something like: ur a prick mint! lol. nite hun. It made my tummy tingle when Michelle Malloy said *hun* or *babe* or *hey, you* in her texts. She and Priya got on like a garage on fire so everything was cushty jubbly.

Recently me and Michelle Malloy had begun to do little mini hugs with each other. She hadn't experienced one of my hug specials yet. I didn't think it would be too long though. Fingers crossed. I even showed her Green and let her have her own wee rub of it. I began snogging my forearm as practice for the main event. I couldn't wait! Fingers, toes, arms and legs crossed. I told her she could be on our list if she wanted and she was majorly down with that idea. So *Cool Things For Dylan, Amir, Priya And Michelle Malloy To Do Before They Cack It* was definitely the way forward and was taking shape. We just needed some cool things to put in it.

*

Mum and Tony were going to the flicks to see some duff Christmas romcom; Mum said that she needed some chewing-gum brain crap to take her mind off getting fat. That meant I had the house all to myself FOR THE FIRST TIME EVER! Tony told Mum that I was still the man of the house and that I could be trusted not to burn it down.

Way to go, Tone-Meister!

So, here's what I did: I invited Michelle Malloy over to spend some quality time with her new bf. ME. And when we made plans on the phone I did a mega un-Dylan-Mint thing.

Just before we said the 'Goodnight, babes' part, I said, 'Wear the red Adidas high-tops, babe.'

Nutzzzzz.

She said, 'No probs, hun.'

Double dunter nutzzzz.

Then my heart began to beat even faster than it did the day I thought I was going to cack it. Michelle Malloy, my new gf, was coming over to my house.

My gaff.

My empty gaff.

To chew the cud.

'Chew the cud' was a *euphemism* (my new word) and we both knew it.

Good Golly, Miss Molly!

I had to tell someone, so I told Tony, who was like my second best bud now, and it's OK to tell your second best bud things as long as you tell your first best bud too. I didn't say anything about chewing the cud though. Wink! Wink! I only asked him what I should wear (jeans and a nice crisp shirt, he said), what we should eat for snacks (anything but soup, he said) and what music I should put on. Tony suggested some fella called Marvin Gaye and gave me this CD called *Let's Get It On*, which is a euphemism for 'let's pump each other silly'. And Gaye made me giggle because it was a super-ironic name given that it was a dude and a chick who were going to be chewing the cud. Wink! Wink!

But then I had to tell the bold Amir as my nerves were shattered just thinking about my empty gaff, Michelle Malloy, red Adidas high-tops and chewing the cud. My original *Cool Things To Do Before I Cack It: Number One: have real sexual intercourse with a girl. (Preferably Michelle Malloy)* was actually going to happen and I was shitting big bazoongas.

'The first thing you'll need to do is get J-J-Johnny-bags, Dylan,' Amir said.

'Suppose.'

'Suppose nothing. You don't want any of her eggs to be fer-fer-fertilised by your seed.' Amir was really into the reproduction section in biology.

'I ditto that.'

So Amir wingmanned me to Boots on my Johnny-bags buying mission.

'There's shitloads of them, Dylan.'

'Shut up, Amir,' I said, because we were like a couple of semen demons hovering about the Johnny-bag section. 'Someone will hear us and lob us out.'

'But how do you know which ones to get?'

'How should I know? I've never bought Johnny-bags before, have I?' I tried to pretend I was looking at the deodorant and shaving-cream section but really my eyes squinted towards the stacks and stacks of Johnny-bags. It hurt my eyes doing this.

'There's, like . . .' And Amir started counting the different kinds of Johnny-bags you could buy. '. . . four, five . . .' All different coloured boxes. '. . . eight, nine . . .' All for different things. Promising different pleasures. This was a stress headwrecker. Green was soaked in my damp hands. '. . . eleven, twelve . . . TWELVE different kinds. Fuck me sideways.'

'Come on, let's go, Amir. This is bonkerinos.'

'Bonkerinos exactly, Dylan. Look at these!' Amir was holding a yellow box up to my face. 'These taste like ba-ba-bananas.'

'I'm not going to eat them, Amir.'

'I know, but . . .' He did the nudge nudge game we sometimes play.

'But nothing,' I said. 'Come on, this place is making me feel nervous.'

Amir picked more packs off the shelf. 'These ones are called Tingle.'

'Shut your fucking cave. Come on.'

'Does that mean your dingle tingles, or the girl's flower?'

'How the fuck . . .' I could feel wet on my spine by this stage.

'Ultra-confusing, Dylan. Ultra-confusing.'

'You can look at Johnny-bags all day if you want, Amir, but I need to get out of here quick styley.'

I did. I needed to make a rapido exit because I could feel him coming, like he was sitting on a wall ready to

pounce

swoop

or

leap

on the next person who walked past.

I could see him there with saliva hanging from his teeth, tongue dripping wet.

GGGGGRRRRROOOOOWWWWWLLLLLIIIIINNN-NNGGGGG.

I hadn't seen him for a while, which tickled my happiness because When Mr Dog Bites it's an unpleasant present to the peepers and lugs.

Please don't let Mr Dog get out, not in Boots.

Please don't let Mr Dog get out, not while I'm browsing the Johnny-bag section.

Please don't.

Please.

And guess what happened?

Mr Dog came out.

*

'It's OK, Dylan, I'm here.' Amir was sitting next to me on the pavement with his arm around my shoulder. Not in a doolally batty-boy way, more in an I'll-take-care-of-you-bud way. 'D-d-do you want some water?' he said, handing me a bottle.

'Thanks, Amir.'

'That's what best buds are for, isn't it?'

'You bet.'

'You OK now?'

'A-OK. What am I going to do, Amir?'

'Have some water.'

'No, with Michelle Malloy.'

'Tell her some j-j-jokes. That'll put her at ease.'

'Telling her rubbish jokes won't woo the knick-knacks off her.'

'Well, maybe these will,' Amir said, and handed me a small white Boots poke. 'Here.'

'What is it?'

'Look inside.'

I looked.

'Aw, Amir, you bought me Johnny-bags.' It was, like, the nicest thing anyone has done for me. What a top-notch bloke. And what a lucky dude I was to have such a top-notch bloke as my best bud.

'I did. *Extra safe with extra lubrication,*' he said, pointing to the writing on the box. 'Now you can pump Michelle Malloy all night long and your willy will be super safe.'

I wanted to say thanks but the gobstopper in my gub stopped me from doing it.

So I hugged him instead.

29
Empty

The extra safe Johnny-bags are in my top drawer. Marvin Gaye's *Let's Get It On* is on pause ready to spring into action. I'd put a twenty-watt light bulb in my bedside lamp – Twenty's Plenty and all that. The sheets and pillowcases have been given a chick makeover: they now smell of aloe vera and lavender. All my socks have been removed for safety reasons. All the internet sites I used for doing some last-minute-dot-com research have been cleared from my browsing history. And I have two boxes of Pringles (Hot & Spicy Wonton and Salsa De Chile Habanero), a box of Maltesers and a bottle of Irn-Bru on the sideboard for mega munchies and a debrief afterwards. But no matter how much I prep the gaff, leaving no brick unturned, I still need some momentous brain gym to calm the old tense nervous-energy jets. So I try to think of my top six big-belly-belter jokes that I can tell Michelle Malloy in case the conversation becomes weird or she has one of her ODD moments.

When the doorbell rings, I swear to Jesus, Allah, Buddha, Samson and Doc Colm I almost shite a bazoonga.

'Hi, Michelle. Glad you could make it.'

'Make what? Oh, God, you're not having a weird night, are you?'

My tongue twists, I can feel the gobbledegook coming on.

'Did you hear about the dyslexic man who walked into a bra?'

Michelle Malloy squints her face and shakes her head.

'Get it?'

Joke number one is a disaster.

Michelle Malloy's get-up is anything but. Black tights (hard to remove, skill required) under a wee red tartan skirt (no clue as to what clan) and a T-shirt with a banana on it and the words *The Velvet Underground* (I know it isn't a comfortable mode of transport she's promoting) AND the red Adidas high-tops. Absolute class! My teen dream queen.

'Marvin Gaye's in my room if you want to go up? PUMP. RIDE. DRILL,' I say. (But I sooooooooooooooooooo want to say, 'You look like the first thing I've seen since twenty years of blindness, Michelle.') 'Oh, shit, sorry, Michelle. I didn't mean . . .'

'Calm the fuck down, Mint. I'm not even in your room yet. Come here, hun.'

She puts out her arms and we come together for a hug special. Her hair is in my face. I close my eyes, take an inhale of her astounding scent and think, *This moment is a gamillion times better than sitting in Heaven munching on an ice cream with a big cherry on top any day.*

Michelle Malloy isn't too good with stairs – she lives in a bungalow – so I help her up. That's what any decent bf would do for his gf who has stair-walking difficulties. If I had my way I'd fling that dame over my shoulder and carry her up the blinkin' stairs.

In my room the twenty watt is doing its thing. Michelle Malloy sits on my bed. I wonder if the chick makeover is doing it for her.

'Want a glass of Irn-Bru and a couple of Pringles?' This is what's called playing it cool before the main event.

'Rank! No.'

'Malteser?'

'No.'

'Maybe for after.'

'After what, Mint?'

'Nothing. BONKING. Fuck!'

'Got any water?'

'Water? FUCK WATER'S DICK. Sorry, Michelle.'

'It's OK. Relax.'

'I didn't plan for water.'

'So what have you been planning for?'

'I'll run down and get some.' I make my way to the door.

'Take a chill pill, will you?'

'OK, chill pill. Got it.'

'Come and sit here, Mint.'

'Where?'

Oh Sweet Billy Pilgrim! She only wants me to sit next to her on MY bed.

'Here,' she says, and pats the bed next to her.

'What, there?' I point.

'Yes.'

I sit. Thank God I do because I think my arse is going to collapse.

'Are you sure your mum and her boyfriend aren't coming back until late?'

'The romcom runs for one hour and thirty-eight minutes and then there's seventeen minutes of crap ads before it comes on and then there's chat time afterwards then time in the car home so I think that makes well over two hours and thirty-three minutes until they're back.'

'Good,' she says.

'Good?'

'Very fucking good, Mint.'

Crash! Bang! Wallop!

It happens.

SMACK-A-ROONY full force on the lips.

Michelle Malloy grabs my crisp shirt and pulls me towards her. SOMEBODY CALL THE HEART TRANSPLANT DOCTOR – NOW! I'm not joking – I think someone has planted an IED in my chest.

We do little kisses at first, like longer *Goodnight, Mum* pecks but on the lips. I don't really know what to do so I follow Michelle Malloy's lead as she is clearly the experienced one. Then our lips kind of stick to each other's and go around in a wee circle for a while, fast, slow, fast, slow. I enjoy it. So does my heart as it goes back to just beating-fast pace. So does my willy as it starts to wake up like an alligator in the Florida Everglades. Then Michelle Malloy's tongue enters my mouth and jabs in and out as if she's playing a game of tongue sword fighting. If that's the game she wants then I'm her man, I think, so I jab my tongue in her mouth and we play tongue sword fighting together. When the tongue sword fighting stops we do some mouth-to-tongue sucking. And boy, oh boy, oh boy, oh boy, does my willy like this game! When our mouths separate, I don't want to clean my face of the slobbers in case Michelle Malloy thinks I'm being RudeTube to her saliva.

'Wow, Michelle.'

'Enjoy that, Mint?'

'A-mayonnaise-ing.'

She laughs. YEEEESSSS. I make Michelle Malloy laugh.

'You are fucking mad as a bottle of crisps, aren't you, Mint?'

I want to make her laugh again. I want to make her laugh all night. 'A sandwich walks into a bar. The barman says, "Sorry, we don't serve food in here." '

She doesn't laugh.

I jump off the bed. 'Want to listen to some Marvin Gaye?'

But it's too late – Michelle Malloy clocks it. Her eyes aren't on my eyes. No, siree. She's staring at my Matalan jeans, which are a crap fit. I've forgotten all about my willy.

'Wow, Mint. I am impressed.'

'No . . . Shit . . . Sorry . . . I didn't mean . . . It's not mine . . . COCK . . . Shit!'

'Relax, Mint. I'm paying you a compliment.'

'You are?'

'A fucking big one.'

Her fucking big compliment matches her big smile.

'So will I put Marvin Gaye on then?'

'You'd better do it quick.'

*

I'm not going to talk about the nitty gritty or any Dirty Biz, but know this: it was capital letters

RUDETUBE

A-MAYONNAISE-ING

BONKERINOS
SHIZENHOWZEN
JEEZE LOUISE
and
NO WAY, JOSÉ
all rolled into one.

Afterwards we did some hugging and holding of each other while looking at the stains on my ceiling. Not even the twenty-watt could hide them. Under the covers I rubbed my foot up and down Michelle Malloy's misshapen foot. Her foot felt as though it had been made out of a big piece of clay, her toes like little courgettes poking out from the bottom of it. I soooooooooooo badly wanted my foot to transmit to her foot that I'd always be there for it, that I'd always take care of it and that I'd try and protect it from any badasses out there. I wanted to kiss Michelle Malloy's misshapen foot all over, play tongue sword fighting with her wee toes and tell all five of them that I'd love them forever. Maybe even tell Michelle Malloy, MY gf, that I loved her forever as well.

'Babe?' I said.

'Yes, hun.'

'Did I tell you that I met a Dutch girl with these mega inflatable shoes last week?'

'No.'

'I phoned her up for a date but she'd already popped her clogs.'

My gf lay beside me laughing.

Heart rate: normal.

Actual heart: swollen.

*

Once it was just me and Amir. A best bud twosome. But now we're a foursome, like *Friends* except without Phoebe and Ross. And we know that what doesn't kill *us* will make us stronger.

Now that's what I do call Billy Blazing Bonkers.

Eh?

What?

Life!

30
Goodbye

77 Blair Road

ML5 1QE

15th December

Mr Mint

Mum told me everything, so don't try to deny it. I'm not writing this to tell you about the pure brilliant things I have been getting up to, all I will say is that there have been millions. But you'll never know what they are, ever. I'm not going to talk about football, school stuff, girls or my future plans either. I just wanted to write so I could get something off my chest. I want to tell you that you are the baddest man I have ever known, possibly even badder than that mad doc in England who killed all his patients because they were too old and therefore a pain in his arse. But the thing about that psycho doc is that he didn't use his wife as a human punchbag every other week and leave her black and blue lying in her own blood and tears on the living-room rug. Did he? No he didn't because I checked it out on Google and it said, *he was a loyal and loving husband*, which is something you definitely were not and I feel heart sorry for Mum for having to put up with you for all those years. If it was me instead of Mum you were punching for fun, I'd have had your arse for garters and dragged it down to the nearest cop shop quick style. No man has the right to lift his hand to any woman. No man. Even if he is a frustrated dad on the dole with no job prospects. OK? Mum agrees with this.

I also think that you must be one of the stupidest robbers, if not *the* stupidest, that Scotland has ever known. I mean, who goes to do a post office job using their own car *and* without a mask? What a wally! If we had been born in Ohio, Utah or North or South Dakota I would have entered you in that programme, *America's Dumbest Criminals*, so you're lucky we weren't. But what you did to that poor man and woman who ran the wee post office makes you much more evil than Evel Knievel ever was. I was ashamed to be associated with the name Mint when I heard that story.

Amir said you were a gutless wonder because you didn't have the balls to write back and tell me the truth about where you are now living. Living, that's a laugh! I felt worse than a gutless wonder because I thought you were an actual war hero fighting the Axis of Evil but all along you were in Barlinnie doing a fifteen-year stretch for aggravated robbery because YOU were Evil. You made me feel like a pure zoomer. Amir was right about you. I also told Amir that you are a nasty racist pig because you called the guy who has the corner shop down the road from us horrible names all the time and whenever people with different colour skin came on the telly you called them *apes* and *jungle bunnies*. Amir agreed with me and he should know because he has to face up to nasty racist pigs every day of his life. So you better watch it when you get out of that place because me and Amir hate nasty racist pigs and aim to hunt them down and run them out of town. Miss Flynn said that society has no place for racists and I agree with her, but that's all I'm going to tell you about school. For the record I also think that society has no place for racists and robbers and men who use women as human punchbags and dads who can't be arsed to play with their children. I think you are in the best place for people like you.

If you really weren't arsed with having a son, then you should have said so when I was in Mum's belly. I'm sorry that me being a Tourette's sufferer was such a mega embarrassment for you. I didn't ask to have it. It wasn't my fault. You can't just catch it like the sneezes. You don't get it because you have been bad or are ugly or something – you're just born with it. It's just your Donald Duck! I was innocent, unlike you, you guilty man. I was the one who everyone stared at and laughed at and took the piss out of, not you. Anyway, things have changed now: my Tourette's goalposts have been well and truly shifted. I shouldn't really be telling you this but I will: I went to see this amazing new doc who has developed this super-duper mouth brace that stops all the tics and twitches and grunts and barks. It's utterly mind-blowing. I bet if you were here and loved your son you would be dead proud because no one can tell the difference between a normal guy walking down the street and me, but you will never get to see the new me, ever, not after what you've done.

I've got, like, a new dad now. Well, I know he's not my blood dad, but we do things that other dads and sons do, which means we are just the same as a dad and son. No one can tell the difference. He's got a job as well. A cool proper job. See, when the football is on the telly I'm now allowed to shout at it and have an opinion about formations and tactics and we play a brilliant new game called If I Were The Coach during the match. We also listen to all this new music like Pink Floyd, Bob Dylan, Creedence Clearwater Revival, Button Up and the Jam. It's twenty-five times better than that doof-doof music you used to listen to all the time. We read cool books about cool stuff, like Friedrich Nietzsche – you've probably never heard of him. He's this brilliant philosopher. I think I might even do something like that myself when I finish school. We also go for long drives in his groovy car up the Trossachs or the Campsies, which I never even knew existed before now. Wonder why? He also takes me to the industrial estate, where he teaches me to reverse-drive, do three-point turns and parallel-park. His car is in your parking space, which is now his parking space; it looks really good from the living-room window. We don't miss your car any longer. Our new house is going to have driveway space for TWO cars – his and mine – when I pass my test. I'll probably get an old banger like yours to start off with. Best of all though is that he DOESN'T use Mum as a human punchbag.

I'm going to go now because I've a million and one things I need to be doing and I can't be spending all my precious time writing letters to someone who never thought of writing back. Not even once. The bold Amir says that maybe you can't actually write. And when I re-read that letter you wrote me last December I thought, *Mmmmmm, maybe Amir is right about that.* I ripped it up by the way. I don't want letters from you now. This will be my last one to you. Last night I typed *100 things to do before you die* into Google and it came up with tons of really cool stuff for me to be cracking on with so me, Amir, this girl called Priya (you wouldn't like her because she's Indian) and Michelle Malloy (my new angel gf) are going to try to do as many as we can. But the belter thing is that none of us is actually going to die. Well, we will one day, but not for a

    long

    long

    long

    time.

Goodbye and Good Luck.

Dylan Mint

(No xxx this time)

Acknowledgements

You wouldn't be reading this book right now without the following people. My wonderful and inimitable agent, Ben Illis at The BIA, for his savvy eye, support and continued guidance. The whole crew at Bloomsbury, who have worked diligently on the novel, especially my editor, Rebecca McNally, who took my hand and walked me through the murky waters of Mr Dog; her suggestions throughout were brilliant. Helen Garnons-Williams and Madeleine Stevens, whose kind words, graft and guile made Dylan and his cohorts shine even brighter.

I'd like to thank Sinéad Boyce for casting her beady eye over early drafts of the book; her work continues to be invaluable to me. And Yvonne Kinsella at Prizeman & Kinsella for recommending *When Mr Dog Bites* as a possible title . . . I wish I could take the credit for this, but I can't. So thanks for allowing me to use it.

I would like to thank my friends and family.

Finally, I'd like to thank my great friend Norrie Malloy, who I knew was deeply proud of his mate's writing career, even though he took to calling me Jessica Fletcher from *Murder, She Wrote*. Just sorry you couldn't have held a copy in your hands. This book is dedicated to you.

Brian Conaghan

Brian Conaghan was born in 1971. He was raised in the Scottish town of Coatbridge but now lives and works as a teacher in Dublin. He is the author of *The Boy Who Made It Rain* and has a Master of Letters in Creative Writing from the University of Glasgow. Over the years Brian has made his dosh as a painter and decorator, a barman, a DJ, an actor, a teacher and now a writer. He currently lives in Dublin with two beauties who hinder his writing: his wife, Orla, and daughter, Rosie.